CATWMAN

By Elizabeth Hand

Screenplay by John Rogers, Mike Ferris, and John Brancato

BALLANTINE BOOKS • NEW YORK

Catwoman is a work of fiction. Names, places, and incidents either are products of the author's imagination or are used fictitiously.

A Del Rey® Book
Published by The Random House Publishing Group

www.delreydigital.com
www.dccomics.com
Keyword: DC Comics on AOL

ISBN 0-345-47652-2

Text design by Caron Harris

Manufactured in the United States of America

First Edition: June 2004

OPM   10   9   8   7   6   5   4   3   2   1

CATWOMAN

Cats . . . have succeeded one another through the Tertiary epoch, therefore, for many thousands, or more probably millions, of years; and in their capacity of butchering machines, have undergone a steady though slow and gradual improvement . . .
—T. H. HUXLEY,
Natural Rights and Political Rights, 1890

PROLOGUE

Midnight is alive.

Her eyes glow green-gold as emeralds, brilliant as the chips of malachite winking from the eye sockets of the statues in the temple around her. Each one sits as Midnight sits, small pointed ears erect, tail curled. But the statues' tails do not twitch with expectation, as Midnight's tail does, and the statues' eyes do not follow the movements of the young woman in the temple, the priestess who serves Bast; the priestess who serves Midnight.

The young woman's hair and skin are dark as ebony, her motions as graceful as the cat's. She kneels carefully before each statue, lighting braziers filled with fragrant resins—balsam, cypress, chunks of amber the size of a child's fist. Tendrils of smoke rise from the copper bowls, mingling with other scents: the warm smell of sandalwood, the sweetness of beeswax candles; the heavier odor of the orange-and-civet oil the priestess anointed herself with before coming here to make her offering to the cat-goddess Bast. There is another scent as well, one which the woman does not smell but Midnight does—the scent of fear, of death, a raw cold reek that is not disguised by the woman's perfumes, and is not hidden by the supple linen folds of her ritual garment, more a shroud than a robe.

"O Bast, O Akh, O Luminous One," the woman chants softly. "O grant me refuge when leaving this world I enter yours. O grant me refuge, and safety, and peace, O Bast."

Midnight watches, and waits.

The priestess knows the cat is there. It is a Mau, the feline most sacred to Bast. Its ancestors are the delicate-featured, sinewy desert cats that stalk the wild places surrounding the ancient river delta.

But generations of careful breeding have made the Mau bigger, stronger, more beautiful than its ancestors. Its fur is smoke colored, dark spotted, like a cheetah's; its skull is sleek, and in the center of its smooth forehead the image of a scarab has been tattooed in black kohl and red henna, symbolizing eternity. Silver salvers holding milk and fresh-caught fish have been set out for the Mau, in front of the rows of mummified cats that line the walls. The priestess does not call the cat "Midnight," of course. The name she speaks is softer, more a purr than a word; but Midnight hears it all the same. Midnight hears the edge of terror in the woman's voice, and she sees the blood drain from the woman's face as the sound of footsteps echo from outside the temple's arches.

"It is time," a low male voice calls.

The priestess stands, shivering. Her small cold hands move up and down her bare arms, vainly trying to warm herself. At her feet something moves, something dark and smooth as black silk.

"Midnight," the woman whispers. She bends and strokes the cat; then picks it up and holds it to her breast. "Oh Midnight—I am so afraid. . . ."

Midnight stares at her, emerald eyes unblinking. She meows softly, and for an instant bares teeth sharp and white as the ivory needles used to sew shut the eyes of the dead.

Do *not fear*, the goddess says, though the priestess hears only a cat's low, urgent growl. Do *not fear, daughter*. . . .

The embroidered hangings at the entrance to the temple are pulled aside, slowly, respectfully. The acolytes are there; they bow their heads as the priestess passes between them, her head held high, the cat gazing with glittering green eyes from the woman's arms.

Do *not fear, daughter*, the goddess says again, as the ebony black cat purrs throatily, its fur warming the priestess's icy hands. *Fear no man, fear no death, not while I am within your grasp*. . . .

Outside, the full moon hangs suspended above the gleaming white expanse of the altar where the high priest awaits. It is midnight now. As the priestess approaches the altar, the avatar of the goddess purring softly in her arms, she is suddenly no longer afraid.

Because Midnight is immortal, as is Bast. And the cat-goddess shares her gifts with those who trust her.

Smiling, her face aglow beneath the moon, the priestess lies down upon the altar, the cat at her side; and waits to be reborn.

ONE

"Oh, *please* . . ."

Patience Phillips groaned and yanked the pillow from her head—not for the first time that night, either. She blinked, bleary eyed, and reached for the clock radio at her bedside.

Four A.M.

"It can't be," she moaned softly, and sat up. "It was four A.M. the *last* time I looked. . . ."

Outside, night was giving way to the faintest gray-blue glimmer of dawn, glinting at Patience's window.

Inside, though, it might as well have been midday, certainly by the sound of things. From the apartment next door, the throb of electronic music rose and fell, barely muffled by the brick walls that separated Patience from her neighbor's duplex. Raucous laughter echoed through Patience's spartan studio, followed by the sound of breaking glass and a gleeful whoop.

"That's it," Patience muttered. She swung her feet over the edge of the bed, freeing her nightgown from the mound of blankets, then stood. "Ouch!"

Her foot caught in the sheets and she stumbled,

catching herself on the nightstand, then crossed to the window. She drew aside the gauzy curtain and gazed out at her neighbor's window. Garish light streamed from it, so that she could clearly see the writhing figures of people dancing, heads thrown back as they shrieked in time with the throbbing music. Patience watched them for a moment, her expression annoyed, mostly; but also slightly wistful, even envious.

Finally, she sighed and turned. She made her way past her drafting table, where portfolios holding her most recent work were stacked neatly alongside brushes, Rapidograph pens, carefully aligned bottles of ink. Beside the drafting table, an easel held sketches for Hedare Beauty's most recent advertising campaign. Patience ignored all of these and made a beeline for her closet, its contents as neat and spare as the rest of her apartment. She pulled on her coat, opened the front door, and stepped into the hall.

Here the music was even louder. Patience winced. Clutching her coat tightly, she stepped across the hall to her neighbor's door, hand raised, then knocked gently. The music blared on.

The door swung open to reveal a hulking young man her own age, thirty or so. Long hair hung lank to his shoulders, and his sleeveless shirt exposed heavily muscled arms covered with elaborate tattoos: a serpent devouring its own tail, a grinning skull. He looked at her blankly, squinting as though trying to see through heavy mist.

"Um, hi." Patience smiled timidly. "I'm sorry to bother you. Patience . . ."

The young man blinked at the figure in front of him. A shy, slender young woman, long dark curls mussed from her sleepless night. Her almond-shaped eyes gazed at him imploringly from a piquant face: high cheekbones, full-lipped mouth, small pointed chin. "Excuse me?"

"I mean I'm Patience," she went on, and shifted uneasily beneath his stare. "Patience Phillips?"

He continued to stare at her, his gaze cold and empty. Behind him, music roiled and drunken laughter echoed loudly through his apartment. Patience swallowed. She hated imposing on people, especially people she didn't know; especially people like this guy. . . .

"Um," she said. She smiled ingratiatingly, as her words came out in a rush. "See, I live across the way and I have a *really* big day at work tomorrow, so I was already having trouble sleeping since I'm turning in an important project and, well, I'm kinda nervous about it, you know?"

Her voice trailed off. In front of her, the tattooed young man was looking her up and down. His blank gaze grew openly lascivious.

"Patience, huh?" His mouth widened in a leer. "Hey, I'm pretty *impatient* myself. . . ."

Patience froze. For a moment her eyes locked with his. Then she quickly looked away, pulling her coat more tightly about her.

"I just . . . it's just that it's kind of late, and I do have to get up early. I mean, I always do," she went on, her voice cracking. "But tomorrow especially, because of the, the . . ."

She hesitated, then looked up at him desperately.

"I was just hoping, um, that you could—well, maybe you could just turn the music down a little?"

The young man stared down at her. Abruptly his expression grew sympathetic. "Yeah? Oh, man—that's all you're hoping? For real?"

"Yes!"

He smiled, then held up a finger, signaling her to wait. He turned and ducked back into the apartment. Patience let her breath out in a grateful sigh, just as the music suddenly roared out, twice as loud as before.

Her neighbor's head loomed above her as he shouted, "Hey—how's THAT?"

Hoarse laughter rang out counterpoint to the deafening music. Patience stood, motionless and defeated, as the door slammed in her face. She shoved her hands into her pockets and turned toward her own apartment. A small movement caught her eye, and she looked sadly at the leopard-spotted cat watching her from the hallway.

"Guess I told him, huh, kitty?" she said, chagrined, and went back inside.

And found comfort where she always did: in her painting. A few yards away, the music from the adjoining apartment continued to pound and throb.

But Patience no longer heard it. She'd dressed, for the most part, thrown an oversized, paint-spattered shirt atop her work clothes, then settled in front of her easel. The canvas in front of her was like a psychic reflection, all violent slashes of purple and black and crimson, sparked here and there with jots of gold or brilliant white. Patience lost herself in her art, so intent upon her paints that it was a full minute before she registered that the music, at last, had stopped.

"Thank God," she murmured, sighing with relief. She wiped a blob of deep violet from her brush, turned to dip it into a paler lavender when a sound halted her.

"Mrrrooooorroowwww. . . ."

Patience frowned. The sound grew into a louder, mournful yowl. She set down her brush and hurried to the window, yanked it open, and stuck her head outside.

Cool morning air washed across her face and she blinked gratefully, then turned as another *meow* sounded—quieter, sad even, but insistent.

"What? Where did you come from?"

Patience craned her neck and saw a cat with a dark-spotted coat and luminous green-gold eyes staring beseechingly at her from atop a cornice where it stood, frozen, afraid to move.

"Are you stuck?" Patience shook her head, marveling. "How'd you get there, anyway? Come on down, cat."

She stretched her hand out tentatively, mindful of keeping her own balance, but the cat only yowled piteously and retreated farther on its precarious perch.

"Hey, it's okay, don't be scared."

Patience drew a breath and tried again, but it was no good. She couldn't reach it. As if sensing the danger it was in, the cat gave a single, faint, pitiful mew, gazing at Patience with wide frightened eyes. The young woman sighed, then glanced several stories down to the street. She took a deeper breath, then scrambled out onto the window sill on her knees, clutching at the sill.

VRAAAARRGGGGGHHHHH!

"Oh!" Patience cried out, startled. She looked down to see a late-model Harley roaring out into the street. A long-haired, leather-clad figure crouched over the controls as it zoomed out of sight—her neighbor.

"I thought 'party all night' was a figure of speech," Patience said, exasperated; then shouted after the bike, "Have a nice day!"

She turned her attention back to the cat. "Come on," she said soothingly, reaching for it. "I'm sleep-deprived. Work with me . . ."

It didn't budge.

Patience's exasperation grew. She stuck her head out farther, until she could peer at the window next to hers. It held an air conditioner—a very *big* air conditioner. For a moment, Patience sat there, brooding. The cat gave another pathetic cry.

"Oh, all right, I'm coming. Keep your shirt—er, your fur—on."

Very carefully, she crawled out onto the ledge. It was wide enough for her to stand on, but just barely. Gingerly she sidestepped toward the adjoining window, then, bracing herself against the wall, stepped onto the air conditioner.

From here she could reach the cat—she hoped. Tentatively, she began to extend her hand, when suddenly beneath her the air conditioner wobbled. Patience screamed, grabbing the cornice and trying desperately to steady herself. The air conditioner straightened, seeming to catch more firmly in the window; Patience let her breath out in a gasp, eyeing the cat just inches away.

"Okay, you," she muttered as she reached for it. "On the count of three—one, two—"

"HEY! Hold on! Don't you move!"

Patience started, nearly falling as the voice shouted up at her. She grabbed the cornice and looked down to see a tall figure in the street below, shading his eyes as he stared up at her.

"Whatever you're thinking, whatever you're feeling— it's not worth it," he called, his voice at once calm and commanding. He took a step forward; Patience saw his car parked haphazardly on the sidewalk be- hind him. "Understand? I'm a cop. Maybe I can help."

Patience looked at him in puzzled disbelief. She shook her head. "No, thank you. I'm fine. It's just—"

"What's your name?"

"*What*?"

The man's kindly voice wafted up to her. "Your name."

"Patience. Patience Phillips."

The man nodded. He took another step closer to her building, his gaze still fixed on her. "We're going to get through this together, Patience. You and me."

Patience's bewilderment grew more pronounced. She looked at him, then turned back to the cornice.

The cat had vanished.

"He—he's gone!" she gasped. "The cat . . ."

She looked down, a little desperately, and saw the tall man looking back at her. He smiled and gave her a reassuring nod.

"Sure, lady," he said in the patient tone one would use with a feverish child. "It's a beauty, real cute—"

"No." Patience shook her head. "The cat's not here anymore."

"I know." The man nodded again, his smile replaced by a look of solemn sympathy. "And I know that makes you very sad."

Patience glared at him. "Right," she muttered through gritted teeth. "Enough of this . . ."

She turned back to her open window, once more hugging the wall as she carefully stepped from the air conditioner to the ledge below. Her hand grasped at the window frame as she stepped toward it; then abruptly, she stumbled.

"O*h*!"

The cuff of her loose trousers had snagged on a corner of the air conditioner. With a sickening lurch, Patience fell, crying out in terror. She flailed and grabbed at the wall, righting herself just in time to keep from plummeting to the street.

From below, the man's urgent voice shouted, "What's your apartment number?"

"Twenty-three!"

Panting, she leaned against the wall, trying in vain to yank her leg free. There was a harsh grating sound as the air conditioner shifted again, its bolts pulling loose from the wall. Desperately, Patience strained against it, but it was no use—the air conditioner's weight was too much. It was starting to fall, and with her leg pinned to it, it would pull her down too.

"Oh God, please . . ." she whispered.

From inside her apartment echoed a crash. Seconds later a man's head was thrust out of the window at her side.

"Give me your hand!"

He leaned out the window, reaching for her. Her hand reached back, fingers barely touching. Suddenly, with the ear-splitting shriek of metal against metal, the air conditioner came loose. Patience screamed as it plummeted to the street, landing with a crash. The torn cuff of her pants flapped in its wake; then she, too, began to fall.

"*Help* . . ."

Her voice was almost inaudible. She could scarcely feel the grasp of the man's hand around her own as she stared up at him, her body hanging limply in midair.

"I got you," he cried, straining to pull her back toward the sill. "I got you . . ."

Her bare feet kicked at the wall, trying to find purchase. The man's hold on her hand grew tighter, firmer. Slowly, he began to pull her back up toward the sill. With one last heave, he dragged her onto the ledge, then through the open window and into her apartment.

With a cry, Patience tumbled onto the floor, the man landing with a thud on top of her. She gasped, struggling to catch her breath; then looked up to see him gazing at her, his face creased with concern.

"Close call," he said.

She nodded, still too shaken to speak. At last she said, "Thank you."

For a moment the two of them lay there, silent and relieved. Then Patience blinked, taking in the whole picture: herself in her dishevelled clothes with a strange man lying atop her. She sat up, brusquely pushing him aside, and hurried to her feet. The man continued to gaze at her, concern now tinged with a faint regret.

"You okay?"

"Fine!" Patience replied, too quickly. "Never better! You?"

The man stood, rubbing a hand across his dark hair. He was tall and broad shouldered, with a gymnast's wiry frame and a thin, ascetic face saved from prettiness by chiseled features and deep-set, hazel eyes. "I'm fine," he said at last. "But . . ."

He hesitated, looking first at Patience and then, awkwardly, at the floor.

That was when the Mau chose to return. It stood on the sill, regarding the two humans coolly, then gave a casual leap through the open window onto the floor. It stretched, yawning; looked up at Patience and meowed loudly before darting out the open door into the corridor.

Patience waited until it was out of sight. Then she turned to the man and deadpanned, "That was the cat."

His hazel eyes widened. "You weren't kidding."

"No."

"You went out there"—he gestured at the window, shaking his head—"to get your *cat*?"

"No. I mean, yes, I did—but it's not my cat."

"You climbed out there to rescue somebody else's problem?" The man stared at her, then shook his head, impressed. "Huh. That's . . . something else."

"Why? *You* came out to rescue *me*."

"Thing is, I thought—"

"I know what you thought," Patience broke in, gently

teasing. "You thought, 'We're going to get through this together. You and me.'"

The man shrugged. "They train us to do that."

"Well, it worked. You saved me."

For a long moment they stared at each other. The man's lips parted, as though he were trying to frame a question—*Who are you? Can I get to know you better?*—but the woman before him wasn't used to this kind of attention. Flustered, she looked down; her gaze caught her watch and she let out a small cry.

"Oh, my God. I'm going to be late! I've got to go."

"But—"

Patience began to run about the room, frantically gathering her things. Portfolio, briefcase, a cylinder holding more artwork, her purse.

"I've got this big presentation," she gasped, grabbing a stack of memos on her desk. "I'm sorry."

"Oh." The man watched her, intrigued, then added, "Well. Good luck with that."

"Thank you!" Patience shot him a smile, then headed for the door.

And stopped, staring in dismay. The door hung slightly askew on its hinges. The man's gaze followed hers.

"Don't worry about the door," he said reassuringly. "I think it will hold."

"Really?" Patience gave him a grateful smile. "Thanks again—"

"*Go.*"

Patience nodded. She turned and ran out into the hallway, stumbling and dropping her purse. She grabbed it, then raced off.

The man stared after her, then tugged the door

again to make sure it stayed locked. He was turning to go, when he saw something on the floor. . . .

Patience's wallet.

"Huh," he said. "Must've fallen from her purse. . . ."

He picked it up and shook his head, smiling, then went on his way.

TWO

A beautiful face is of all spectacles the most beautiful.
—JEAN DE LA BRUYÈRE, *Les Caractères*, 1688

The gleaming monolith of the Hedare Building looked as it always did: slightly ominous, sleek and self-contained in its immensity, and utterly without warmth. Patience raced through the lobby, portfolio clutched in her arms, her heels echoing on marble floors so slick it was like walking on black ice. Brushed steel and bronze signs covered the walls and ceiling of the vast, high-tech lobby.

HEDARE BEAUTY

Above the company name loomed Hedare's logo: a classically perfect woman's profile, gazing serenely into the distance. Just in case the casual visitor didn't get the point, plasma screens were placed strategically throughout the lobby; each displayed the smiling image of an almost supernaturally beautiful woman with cropped ice blond hair, green-blue eyes, a complexion clear and flawless as rock crystal— Laurel Hedare, the company's CEO. Patience passed the image again and again on her way to the door leading to the elevators.

"Excuse me, excuse me, excuse me," she gasped like a mantra, as she weaved in and out of the crowds of rushing people. Finally, she reached the large glass door and, hands full, pushed it open with her hip.

"Mmmphh," a man mumbled. He waltzed through the open door without a glance at Patience. She shifted the portfolio awkwardly to her other arm, bracing the door with her elbow. Another man walked past, bumping her roughly without a word of apology.

"Excuse me," Patience said in a low voice.

By now a steady stream of people was going in and out. No one thanked Patience. No one even looked at her. Patience tried to inch inside, but every time she moved someone else would breeze by, jostling her back to her starting position.

"Um, if you're still here at lunch, should I bring you a protein bar?"

With a sigh of relief, Patience craned her neck to see her best friend, Sally, standing in the lobby.

"Sally!" Patience cried as her friend strode toward her. "Hi. . . ."

Sally shook her head and took hold of the door. "We talked about pathological good manners, right? It's an unnecessary accessory."

She ushered her friend toward the elevators.

"I bet Mrs. Hedare didn't waste time holding doors," Sally said, wrinkling her nose at one of the huge smiling images of Laurel.

"You don't know that," protested Patience as they stepped into the elevator. "I think she's nice."

"And after good manners?" Sally rolled her eyes. "We're gonna start working on 'naïve.'"

Patience laughed. Sally was her age, a chic, compact woman with sleek dark hair falling to her chin, and the kind of trendy wardrobe Patience wished she had the nerve to wear. "Are they already in the meeting?"

Sally nodded. "Yup. But I think you're okay—they won't be ready for you for at least fifteen minutes."

Patience nodded. They were the only two people in the elevator, but she still couldn't bring herself to put down her portfolio. She shifted it to her other hand, her fingers slick with sweat, and murmured something under her breath.

"What was that?" Sally asked.

Patience blinked. "Oh, nothing. Sorry. Just going over what I'm going to say." She smiled wanly at her friend. "I wish I had your nerve."

Sally looked at her sympathetically. "Don't worry. You'll be great. Your stuff is gorgeous." She nodded toward the portfolio. "I'll stick around with you until it's time. Moral support."

Relief flooded Patience's face. "Thanks, Sally! That would be great."

The elevator came to a stop. The sleek metal doors slid open, and they stepped out to make their way down the long corridor to George Hedare's office.

Meanwhile, several floors above Patience and Sally, a meeting was in full swing in the Hedare board-room. At the head of the room-length conference table sat the flesh-and-blood face of Hedare Beauty,

Laurel Hedare herself. Two bodyguards, Armando and Wesley, leaned against the wall in silence. Board members sat around the table; in front of each of them was a thick informational folder bearing the Hedare logo, but no image of Laurel. In the front of the room a man paced: in his late forties, fair-haired, with proud, rather chilly features and a restless glint to his blue eyes. He stepped from one board member to the next, making fleeting eye contact with each one before moving on. In her seat, Laurel Hedare watched her husband impassively, though a careful observer might have noticed a certain cool amusement in her eyes.

"Botox, collagen, dermabrasion, plastic surgery," George Hedare intoned. On the wall behind him a plasma screen showed a dramatic series of before-and-after pictures, showing a woman transformed from haggard to beautiful. "We all know women will suffer for beauty. More important to us, they'll also *pay* for it."

A ripple of laughter from everyone—everyone but Laurel, whose expression hardened as she continued to watch her husband.

"We've been selling cold cream and face paint," George went on, "watching our market share decline. But that's about to change. In one week we will launch the most exciting product to hit the beauty industry since *soap*—Beau-line. It doesn't just hide the effects of aging. It *reverses* them. Just as it is going to reverse the fortunes of this company."

He turned and gestured grandly at the plasma screen. The executives burst into applause. Only

Laurel's expression was inscrutable as she watched her husband's performance.

"However," said George. His tone grew softer, more serious. "With change comes sacrifice. As we move into the future, we must set aside the past."

The board members glanced at one another, eyebrows raised. They turned back to George, who remained silent for a moment. Then, with measured grace, Laurel Hedare stood. The board members stared at her in astonishment as she began to speak.

"My husband—and I—have decided it's time for me to step aside as the face of Hedare. It has been a magnificent fifteen years, but after a great deal of thought and research, we have chosen a new face to represent Beau-line—a younger face."

A murmur of disbelief as Laurel sank back into her seat. In the front of the room, the image on the plasma monitor began to ripple and shift. Slowly a new face began to fill the screen: that of a dark, exotically beautiful woman, her sloe eyes and full, crimson mouth signaling that the New Face of Hedare was light-years away from Laurel's ice-goddess features.

"Meet Drina," announced George. As though she heard him, the dark-haired woman on the plasma screen smiled, lips parting to show arctic white teeth. Beneath her smoldering image, the words TO BE MORE scrolled across the screen. "The future of Hedare Beauty."

The board members applauded. "I look forward to seeing you all at the gala," George went on, "where you can toast our success in person."

"Careful, George," said Laurel dryly. "She's not old enough to drink."

The board members laughed. The mood of the room had changed suddenly, from apprehension to celebration. Only Laurel appeared unmoved. She gave her husband a hard look. George returned her gaze calmly. A current of anger ran between them; anger and something else.

Something worse . . .

"I think we can safely consider this meeting to be over," George said at last. He looked at those assembled around the conference table. "I'll give you all a chance to review the information you've received. We can discuss this at greater length tomorrow."

With a curt nod to his bodyguards, he turned and left the room.

THREE

Patience walked nervously down the long hallway on the executive level of the Hedare Building. For the hundredth time, her hands compulsively smoothed her skirt. Beside her, Sally walked more calmly, shaking her head in amusement as she watched her friend's anxiety level rise.

"Don't be intimidated. Sure, he's a brutal corporate pirate who would rip the beating heart out of your chest if it served his interest," Sally said. "But that's no reason to hide your light under a bushel. Whatever *that* means."

Patience continued walking, too nervous to laugh. "It's just—well, this is my first lead campaign. I want everything to be perfect, you know?"

Sally made a face. "Yeah, yeah. Rule Number Two—and I only have two, so pay attention: You've got more talent than anybody in this building. I believe in you, *you* believe in you, we *all* believe in you! Got it?"

This time Patience did manage a small smile. She stopped in front of the door to George Hedare's office. From the other side came the muffled sound of voices—*angry* muffled voices. Patience and Sally stared at each other. A moment later the sound of breaking glass rang out from Hedare's office.

"I was just kidding about the beating heart," Sally said in a low voice. "No I wasn't. Yes I was. No. Yes . . ."

Patience ignored her friend. She got a firm grip on her portfolio, then knocked on the door.

Silence. The two women exchanged a look. Patience raised her hand to knock once more, when George Hedare's impatient voice commanded, "Come in!"

Patience took a deep breath.

"Good luck," whispered Sally.

Patience nodded glumly. She pushed the door open and entered.

Inside, George Hedare sat ramrod-straight behind a console desk roughly the same size as Patience's living room. A few feet away Laurel stood, staring out the window. The only evidence of the harsh words Patience had heard moments before was the shards of a broken lamp scattered across the floor.

"You didn't need to make quite such a scene out of it, Laurel," said George calmly.

Laurel didn't look at him. "What's the matter, George? Did I steal your moment?"

Patience resisted the urge to clean up the mess on the floor. Instead she approached George's desk, clearing her throat before she greeted him.

"Mr. Hedare. Hi . . ."

Hedare didn't seem to know she was there. Laurel did not turn from the window. Patience looked around uneasily, then said, "Um, did you still want me to—"

"Sit," snapped George.

Patience sat, portfolio balanced precariously across her knees. At his desk, George began to examine an artist's proof—the new Hedare logo that Patience had designed. After a minute he shook his head.

"Phillips, I'm not pleased," he began. "You're not entirely untalented. But—"

Patience nearly stopped breathing, as he went on.

"But that's not even close to what I wanted. This is banal in the extreme! Trite where it should be evocative, and worst of all? It's not even *close* to what I wanted. I can't imagine what you were thinking."

Patience stared at him, stunned. "I . . . I'm so sorry. I—"

"Look at this red!" George disdainfully held up the proof. "It's all wrong. I wanted something darker—"

"But I remember," Patience broke in. Her voice was barely a whisper. "You specifically said—"

"I *know what* I *said*," George continued as though she hadn't spoken. "And I hate cross-hatching."

"We talked about the cross-hatching."

"*What*?" George's face darkened.

Patience swallowed. "Maybe I misunderstood," she said in a tiny voice.

"Clearly, you did."

"Mr. Hedare, I'm so sorry. I can fix it." Patience's voice rose desperately. "If you'll just give me another chance. . . ."

He shook his head, staring disdainfully at her. "I don't reward incompetence. I have no idea why I expected your art to show more taste than your wardrobe."

Patience lowered her head, defeated.

"And try a manicure," George added.

"Please, Mr. Hedare—"

"Oh, for God's sake, George. Let her fix it!"

Patience started as Laurel abruptly turned from the window to stare at her husband. "You change your mind every hour! It's good and you know it."

George glared at her. His mouth opened to speak, but then he clearly thought better of it. Instead he stared at the proof on the desk before him. After a long moment, he spoke.

"Whatever. By midnight—tonight."

"No problem!" Patience's words came out in a gasp. "I won't let you down, Mr. Hedare! I promise. Thank you!"

She grabbed her portfolio, rising to leave. As she crossed the room, she looked back at Laurel and mouthed the words "Thank you." Laurel gazed back at her, then, with the smallest of smiles, walked out of the office.

Patience made a quick stop at her cubicle. She was hurrying toward the ladies' room when she almost ran into someone coming down the corridor.

Laurel Hedare.

Patience stopped, torn between embarrassment and gratitude. Laurel looked at her and smiled. She tipped her head at Patience's outfit. "If you ask me, I think you look fabulous."

Patience stood, tongue-tied, and smiled wanly. "Maybe he's right," she said at last. "I am a little—"

"Making other people feel small is his game. You can't win. You have to refuse to play."

"I really thought I knew what he wanted."

Laurel shook her head. "Don't feel bad, honey. I thought I did too." She smiled, touching Patience lightly on the arm. "Hang in there."

Patience smiled back, then hurried on.

She found Sally waiting for her in the ladies' room. Her friend's eyebrows arched as Patience dumped her portfolio on the floor and began to check her makeup in the mirror.

"So?" Sally asked.

"I did everything he asked. And he—he just *lied* about it. I worked *so* hard. . . ."

"Oh, please." Sally rolled her eyes, but put a consoling hand on Patience's shoulder. "It's never enough. Hedare gets his kicks out of making people squirm. The squirmier the better. Ignore him."

Patience sighed. Her face brightened. "Well, you won't believe this, but *Laurel* gave me a second chance."

"You're right. I don't believe it."

Sally looked at her reflection in the mirror. She grimaced, and began to dig into her purse until she found an aspirin bottle.

"Headaches again." She popped three aspirin. "My brain's all cranky. . . ."

She replaced the aspirin bottle and began searching for something else. She held it up: a small, unmarked jar half-filled with a creamy salve. Patience looked at it, then shook her head.

"You know, you're addicted to that stuff."

"Happily," retorted Sally. "Beau-line is magic in a bottle."

"How do you keep getting it? Production doesn't even start until tomorrow."

Sally shot her friend a complicit grin. "Mike in R&D. Steady supply."

"Still?"

Sally dabbed the salve on her face and winked at her reflection. "Want some?"

She held out the jar, but Patience waved it away. Sally shrugged and dropped it back into her purse.

"Well, some of us need more help than others. I'm not going to be the only woman in the world who looks over twenty-five."

Patience smiled. "I better get back. Especially if I'm going to get this done by midnight."

The rest of the morning passed quickly. Patience loved drafting. Even if it wasn't her own work, the detailed process of combining line and color and shape into something that eventually had meaning always seemed a sort of magic to her. Her cubicle in the art department was no larger than anyone else's, but it had everything she needed: paints and inks and pens, heavy watercolor paper and onionskin, a laptop loaded with design software, even samples of various Hedare products, few of which Patience herself had ever tried. Her desk also had lunch—Sally's lunch, anyway. She leaned against the wall, watching as her friend transformed the rejected proof into something new and—she hoped—better.

"These bagels are good," Sally remarked, holding up what remained of one. "Patience, you should eat something. You'll get a headache if you don't."

Another artist, Lance, came strolling past Patience's cubicle. He hooked a bagel from her desk, then said sotto voce, "Man sandwich, twelve o'clock."

Sally looked up sharply. "Oh, my God. . . ." She glanced at Patience, her head still bent over her work, then murmured, "Please, God, let it be me, let it be me . . ."

A shadow suddenly fell across Patience's desk. She frowned, then looked up to see a tall figure standing above her. Sally gave him a slow, sexy grin, but he gave her just a passing glance: His own smile was for Patience alone.

"Hello," he said.

"Oh! Uh, hi . . ." Patience looked around awkwardly. "Sally, this is, um, the detective I told you about. From this morning . . ."

She hesitated. I *never got his name*! she realized, embarrassed.

The man's smile broadened. He held out his hand. "Tom Lone."

"God!" groaned Sally. "That is *such* a good name. Tom Lone! Rhymes with phone, bone, cone—not that rhyming's *all* that important. . . ."

She gave Patience an exasperated look. Patience stared back at her. So did Tom. Sally shook her head.

"O-*kay*. I'll be right over here. In my cubicle—*alone*."

She flounced off, leaving Patience to look up at Tom, flustered.

"So," she said. "Well."

Tom just stared down at her. Finally he said, "You know what I like about you?"

"No. Not really."

"You were born on the first day of spring. My favorite time of year."

"Wait." Patience's mouth dropped open. "How did you . . ."

He held out a wallet—*her* wallet. "You dropped it on your way out. You can really cover ground when you're in a hurry."

"Oh." She took it, then looked at him. "You didn't have to . . . I mean, you could've just left it in the apartment. . . ."

Tom held her gaze, then smiled and changed the subject. He pointed to one of the drawings in Patience's open sketchbook—not her designs and drafts for Hedare, but one of her own sketches. "This is nice."

"You think?"

Tom nodded eagerly. "Absolutely. It reminds me of early Chagall. Elegant but whimsical. The way the light and dark do that thing together—very much in the old Dutch masters tradition." He stopped, taking in Patience's quizzical look. "The old masters? Who were Dutch?"

He trailed off, as Patience began to laugh.

"Okay." Tom grinned sheepishly. "I don't know the first thing about serious art. But I googled it at the office, and just between you and me? I thought Dutch masters was a cigar my lieutenant used to smoke. Anyway, I was just trying to impress you." His gaze grew earnest, and he gestured at her sketchbook. "I don't really know anything about it. But I like it. A lot."

Patience glowed shyly. "Thank you."

Tom hesitated, then said, "They say that people who meet under extraordinary circumstances have a special bond, and considering that cat and everything . . ."

From Sally's adjoining cubicle came a muffled *thump*. Patience glanced at the cubicle wall and suppressed a smile: Sally must be *dying* over there, trying to hear what was going on!

But Tom mistook her silence for disinterest. "I was hoping that could lead to a cup of coffee," he went on quickly. "There's this Italian place right around the corner. Grecio's. On Sixth."

Patience stared at him, not daring to reply. Tom added, "How about tomorrow? One o'clock?"

Patience took a deep breath. "That . . . that sounds great," she said at last.

"O*kay*!" Tom's relief was palpable. "Tomorrow, then."

He waited for Patience to say more, but she only smiled. His eyes flickered past her, to the cubicle wall she shared with Sally. Right on cue, Sally's head popped up. Tom regarded her with mock seriousness.

"You'll make sure she gets there, right? I'm counting on you."

Sally gave him a crisp salute. "Yes, Officer. Captain. Generalissimo. Sir."

Tom laughed, then gave Patience one last look. "Tomorrow," he said.

Patience and Sally watched as his lanky form made its way through the maze of art department desks. Sally sighed noisily. Then she turned to Patience, all business.

"Okay: pre-game drill. Don't eat today, only water. And wear that leather outfit I got you for your birthday—"

"Hel-*looo*?" chimed in Lance's voice from his cubicle.

Sally went on without missing a beat. "Lance would like me to remind you that he pitched in for the leather, too."

Patience looked at her two friends in amusement, but her tone remained unconvinced. "Hello? A, it's just coffee. And B? That leather 'outfit' is not leaving my closet in anybody's lifetime, including mine. Now if you'll excuse me, I have a deadline to meet."

Sally and Lance exchanged looks. Patience already had her head bent over the drafting table, back at work on the new logo design for George Hedare.

FOUR

The hours passed swiftly, as they always did when she lost herself in her work. She vaguely registered when first Lance, and then Sally, said goodbye, and the long parade of her coworkers in the art department as they departed. Then there was only the cleaning crew, and eventually even they were gone. Patience had the entire art department to herself—a somewhat gloomy prospect this late at night, with the cubicles veiled in shadow and only the pool of light cast by her halogen lamp illuminating the empty room.

Her design was completed. She sat staring at it idly, tapping a pencil against her lips. She was pleased with the way it had turned out: less innovative than her own instincts would have made it, but, she was dead certain, exactly what George Hedare had in mind.

Unless, of course, he had changed his mind. Again.

Shaking her head, she started to stretch her tired back. And stopped.

"Oh, my God!"

In front of her, the clock read 11:45.

She rushed to her cubicle, slid the boards into her portfolio, and began frantically punching numbers into her phone.

"Hi. This is Patience in the art department. I'm expecting a courier to take— But he was supposed to be here by midnight! No, of course you're right, I'm sure it's not his fault, but—"

She caught herself on the verge of apologizing for someone else's screwup, and stopped. She looked at the clock again, sighed, and said, "Okay, look. Why don't I just bring it over there myself?"

She resisted the urge to slam the phone down— what difference would it make?—grabbed her portfolio and purse, and hurried down to the lobby.

The Hedare factory complex was on the far side of the city, on a bluff overlooking the river. It was a bleak place, its air of desolation heightened by dark clouds of smoke roiling from grimy smokestacks above a half dozen or so low-slung buildings. This is where the *real* miracles of the Hedare Corporation took place; Patience always thought it remarkable that things that supposedly made people more beautiful could emerge from such an ugly, dispiriting setting. She hurried past a large sign bearing the old Hedare logo, making her way toward one of the nondescript warehouse-style buildings. She walked up to the door labeled PRINTING and tried the knob.

It was locked.

She looked at her watch.

Midnight.

"Oh, please, no," she groaned. She knocked on the heavy metal door, then pounded. Nothing. She craned her neck to peer through a filthy window. There were lights on, but no sign of anyone on duty. She pounded on the door again.

"Oh please, *please*! Someone is here! Please, let me in!"

Still nothing. She stepped back from the building, stared at the upper story. "Hello?" she shouted. "Anyone?"

Silence. Patience stomped in frustration, then ran alongside the building, searching for another door. On the far side of the factory she saw more lights, all on the upper floor. She stumbled on heaps of broken brick and other industrial detritus—coils of rusted wire, broken windows, discarded bits of computer circuitry. Other things, too: broken glass vials, a pile of unlabeled plastic bottles similar to the one Sally carried around in her purse. Patience ignored all of these, pressing her face against gritty windows and trying door after door.

Until, finally, she found one that was open.

"Thank God," she gasped in relief. She yanked the door open and stepped inside.

"Hello?"

Her voice echoed eerily through the vast black space. Ventilation pipes formed an elaborate cross-hatch near the ceiling, high overhead. Larger pipes ran along the floor. Threads of steam rose from some of them, and a faint acrid smell. Near the door, a small metal sign proclaimed HEDARE CORPORATION: R&D DIVISION.

Patience walked carefully, trying to keep her over-sized portfolio from coming into contact with the heated pipes. The silence was oppressive, and the darkness. She turned a corner warily and was relieved to see a pale glimmer of light in the distance—an office of some sort.

"Looks like someone else is working late," said Patience to herself, trying to boost her courage. She headed toward the light, her footsteps quickening.

Her relief would have been short-lived, had she been able to hear the conversation going on behind that door.

"You're not listening to me!"

A heavyset man stood beside a video screen, gesticulating angrily—Dr. Ivan Slavicky, the head of Hedare's research and development division. The room around him was not an office, but Hedare's primary research lab. Slavicky's domain, his kingdom; one that he shared reluctantly, under the best of circumstances.

And this was certainly not the best of circumstances.

"The FDA didn't find anything in the trials." Slavicky leaned forward, so that the light from the video monitor cast a greenish pall across his features. Myriad forms darted across the screens, red and black and turquoise—digital images of living bacteria as viewed under an electron microscope.

"And I don't care that they never saw the head-aches, the nausea, the fainting spells. Those are symptoms I can live with. And with what we stand to make from consumers demanding their fix, I can even live with it being addictive. Because once you start treatment, *you cannot stop*. Twenty-five percent of all users will manifest symptoms within two years.

"But these side-effects from the long-term studies . . . I can't live with turning people into monsters."

He gestured at the monitor. The screen filled with horrifying images of women whose skin slid from their faces as though melting. "But these side effects from the long-term studies—I can't live with turning people into monsters."

From the shadows across the lab came a sudden intake of breath. Dr. Slavicky stared at the figure standing there, and nodded. "I thought I could live with it," Slavicky said in a low voice. "I was certain I could. But I'm not . . . I'm not sure anymore. . . ."

Outside the laboratory, a slighter figure moved— Patience. She looked around with increasing unease as she approached the lab door. It was cracked open, and as she drew nearer she could hear a man's voice intoning, as though to himself.

". . . *not sure anymore.*"

Patience stopped. She raised her hand to knock gently, then hesitated. Instead she very tentatively pushed the door open, glancing at the metal sign on it as she stepped inside. DR. IVAN SLAVICKY.

"It launches next week," Patience heard a second voice pronounce. "There will be no turning back."

From where she stood, Patience could see only the man's silhouette, backlit by the glowing monitor. As she stared, trying to make sense of the wriggling blobs and darting shapes, the screen abruptly changed. Gone were the enlarged and enhanced bacteria. Instead, an elderly woman's face filled the screen. Her skin was heavily lined, and pouched beneath the eyes, her jawline soft.

As Patience watched, the woman's face began to shift. The lines smoothed out, the soft edges of her jaw blurred, then grew sleek and firm. The grayish complexion brightened to pink, the skin became smooth and unblemished. Patience caught her breath, as for an instant the beautiful young woman seemed to gaze directly into her eyes, her skin dewy and glowing, her lips parted as though she were about to share a secret.

And then, as quickly as she had grown youthful, the woman changed once more. Her features grew taut, her expression severe, increasingly gaunt. The skin pulled back from her mouth, revealing grayish teeth and gums; as though fire licked across her face, the flesh began to shrivel and blacken. The beautiful young woman was gone. In her place was a skeletal visage with gaping, empty eyes and a tight, thin-lipped grin, a stony carapace as dry and lifeless as a cicada's husk.

"Oh!"

Instinctively Patience recoiled; as she did, she struck a table. It clattered noisily against the wall.

"Who's there?" Dr. Slavicky's voice echoed menacingly through the lab. "Who is it?"

Patience opened her mouth to speak. But then she caught a glimpse of Slavicky's enraged face, half-lit by the glowing screen. With a stifled cry she turned and fled. At the sound of her retreat, Slavicky grabbed a telephone, punched in a code, and barked a command.

"On my way," a gruff voice replied, as the scientist slammed the phone back down.

Heart pounding, Patience raced down the corridor. *If I can just make it back outside!*

But as she rounded the corner, she saw the outside door opening. She froze, then ducked back around the corner, but not before she saw a hulking figure brandishing a handgun come through the door. He started quickly toward the lab—and Patience. She looked over her shoulder and saw a second figure rushing from the lab. Blindly, she turned and bolted down another corridor.

"That way," whispered Armando, the man who'd come from outside.

Wesley, his partner, nodded silently. The two hurried after the sound of Patience's footsteps.

Patience ran, terrified, down the dark hallway. She looked around desperately for a way out, finally saw a larger, darker room opening off to the right. Behind her, the sounds of pursuit grew louder, closer. She darted into the open area—a storeroom, filled with packing crates loaded with Hedare Beauty products. She ran past skids piled with wooden cartons, her feet echoing hollowly through the high-ceilinged room; finally she ran, breathless, behind a stack of boxes and crouched there, panting.

In the doorway, two shadowy figures loomed.

"Come on out," called Wesley in a low, soothing voice. "It's okay. We'd just like to ask you a few questions."

Patience held her breath, still crouched in shadow.

"Really, it's fine. Just come on out," Wesley said again, his voice pleading. "Don't worry . . ."

Patience waited, then stood. "I'm sorry," she said, smiling wanly. "I think I'm in the wrong place. I was just looking for—"

Bang!

Patience cringed, deafened, as a bullet shattered the crate just behind her. Glass and liquid makeup flew everywhere. Panicked, she turned and ran.

"Idiot!" Wesley grabbed his partner by the arm, careful to keep the gun well away from him. "What are you doing?"

"You don't boss me!" shouted Armando, and took off after the fleeing woman. Wesley hung back. He pulled out his cell phone, following the others.

"Oh, my God," gasped Patience. She glanced back over her shoulder in disbelief, but continued running. Another door yawned open before her. She raced inside, found herself in yet another immense room, this one filled with pipes and vats and shining industrial equipment, all eerily still. A second bullet ricocheted across the factory floor as she ran. Patience dove behind a vat, listening for the sounds of pursuit. She could see the shadowy figure of her pursuer, just a few yards off.

Now what? she thought desperately.

A metal first-aid kit had been set beside the vat. Soundlessly, Patience grabbed the kit. She silently counted to five, then hurled it as hard as she could across the factory floor. It smashed against another vat. More gunfire echoed through the room, but Patience was already gone, darting out another door.

From behind her, she heard intermittent gunshots and angry shouts from Armando. Before her, the corridor abruptly ended in a spiral stairway leading down. She began to descend, and in a few minutes found herself in the midst of a labyrinth of metal catwalks. Below was a series of open cement tanks filled with dark liquid: the factory's waste treatment area. The sound of dripping or rushing water was everywhere. Huge pipes ran between the tanks; all led to the same exterior wall, crosshatched with more pipes and iron grillwork. Here a number of tunnels began, man-high or larger, all leading outside, all filled with black runnels of wastewater.

Patience worked her way cautiously along the catwalk, but soon found herself unable to go farther—the metal walkway ended at the far wall. A metal ladder hung beside the catwalk. She had no choice but to go down. Carefully, she lowered herself onto the ladder and began to descend.

Above her, the metal walkway shuddered. Patience glanced back and saw two men standing at the bottom of the spiral stairway she had just clambered down. She could just make out the words of the taller one, Wesley, as he spoke into his cell phone.

"She ran down to waste treatment. Armando got a little trigger happy. . . . I know, I know. She could be in any one of these pipes. . . ."

He gazed down at the maze of tanks and pipes below him. "But we don't even know who she is, or what she heard. . . ."

He listened for another moment, then hung up with a sigh and turned to Armando.

"Your way," Wesley said in a resigned voice. "Seal the door."

By now Patience had reached the floor. Silently, she ran from the metal ladder, and headed for the largest tunnel. It was large enough for her to stand in, and she began to race down it, heedless of the foul-smelling water spattering her legs. The air reeked of chemicals and decay. Black strands of rotting fungus or worse covered the tunnel's walls. She ran, terrified, trying not to slip on the slick floor.

She had only been in the pipe for a few minutes when she heard a distant *clang* behind her. The clang was followed by other, more ominous sounds: the creak of gigantic valves closing. Patience began to run even faster, her breath coming so rapidly she thought she might pass out. The grinding sound became a rumble from somewhere deep within the factory. A sudden rush of cold air overtook Patience, as though a gigantic creature had exhaled. The rush of air grew more powerful, and Patience stumbled to the tunnel's sides, pressing against the slippery curved surface to keep from falling.

But still she ran, until suddenly, with a horrified cry, she stopped.

She had reached the end of the tunnel. Before her there was only empty air, black night; hundreds of feet below, the fury of a raging river. Patience gasped. She turned and ran into the passage again, but she took only a few steps when a deafening roar sent her staggering back toward the opening.

A tidal wave of water erupted from the tunnel, smashing into Patience. She had no chance to flee—where could she have gone?—no chance even to take a breath. The water struck her with the force of an avalanche, implacable and terrifying, swept her into a black waterfall plunging to the river below.

Patience screamed, but her voice was swallowed by the river. Around her, frigid water roiled and thundered. She fought to reach the surface but was struck down by the force of the water plummeting from the pipe's mouth far above. Her arms flailed helplessly as she was carried downstream, struggling vainly to grab onto the rock-strewn shore. Water filled her nostrils, her throat; she gagged, retching and gasping for air; then, slowly, her form grew still. Her arms trailed limply at her sides as the rapids carried her on and the water gradually grew calmer, darker, white foam giving way to the broad unruffled surface of a shallow pool. Grayish moonlight filtered down from a sky scumbled with pale clouds. Patience's body floated lifelessly beneath rock outcroppings. At last it came to rest at the edge of a wide uninhabited wetland.

Nothing thrived here; nothing human, anyway. Stunted cattails and sedges grew along the water's edge and rattled dryly in the night wind. Livid green scum clung to the surface of the shallow water, nourished by the effluence from the Hedare plant. There was a faint chemical tang to the air, and wisps of white vapor rising from black pools and hollows. It was by one of these that Patience's corpse had finally come to rest, one bruised and lacerated arm tangled in a clump of rotting weeds.

Yet desolate as the marshland was, it was not silent. Slowly, slowly, another sound began to rise in counterpoint to the dry rustle of cattails and sawgrass. A howl, inhuman yet still fraught with grief. It rose to a shriek, then began again, a low, heartrending sound that became louder and more despairing.

And then a second cry joined the first, and another, and another, until the wasteland echoed with the shrill, relentless keening of myriad unseen mourners. The stalks of cattails and sumac began to shudder as shadows passed between them; only a few shadows at first, but then more and more, until the entire swamp was filled with small seething forms.

Cats. Dozens and dozens of cats.

No—scores of them, perhaps hundreds. Like a living carpet of soft fur, black and gray and tawny orange, tortoise shell stripes, calico-pied; Persian and Siamese, Himalayan and Burmese and Russian Blue; tabbies and strays, kittens and grizzled toms: all heard a summons they could not ignore, and all came now to answer it.

Soft as wind in the reeds they made their way to the motionless figure floating at the water's edge. But they did not touch it; dead things are not as appealing to cats as living creatures that can still be toyed with.

Instead they sat, ears erect, their eerily glowing eyes—yellow and green, ice blue and gold—fixed upon the body of Patience Phillips, and waited.

They had been commanded to come here. Now they awaited the one who summoned them.

A minute in which the moonlight grew steadily, subtly, brighter. It touched the dead woman's face with silver, cast a faint blue sheen upon her knotted hair and torn remnants of clothing. Then, as though a sudden breeze carried some warning sound or scent to the assembled creatures, the cats turned as one; turned and saw their mistress approach.

It was the Mau. She walked tail erect, head low, as though stalking prey. In the moonlight the dappled play of dark and light upon her pelt made it seem as though fast-moving shadows streamed across her. As she drew closer to the woman's body the other cats parted to let her pass, then watched, silent, their elliptical pupils black gaps in a galaxy of shining eyes.

The Mau stepped delicately to where the sedges ended and the rank black water lapped at trailing weeds. She crouched, then leaped soundlessly to land upon the dead woman's chest. Patience's corpse bobbed slightly. Her eyes were open but unseeing, dull as small gray stones. Her matted hair mingled with black weeds; blood seeped from countless gashes, dark as the water was dark, and midges lit upon her swollen lips to feed. The Mau hissed at the insects, lifting a graceful paw to disperse them.

Then, gentle as a mother kissing her child goodnight, the cat bowed her head and nuzzled Patience's lips. The Mau's small pink tongue flicked across the woman's mouth. As though she were grooming her kitten, the cat began to lick the woman's cheek. The mud and blood disappeared; a patch of skin shone through, no longer the leaden hue of a corpse but flushed with warmth. The cat rubbed her muzzle against the woman's neck, then drew back, staring down into Patience's eyes.

A cloud raced across the moon. For an instant, the cat's eyes candled and seemed to hold a flickering green flame. Then the moonlight shone down once more, cold and white. It flashed across the eyes of the dead woman; eyes that were no longer sightless.

Eyes that were no longer dead.

Their pupils abruptly dilated, seeming to flood the irises with black; immediately contracted to pinpoints, tiny as poppy seeds. The black seeds flattened, grew elongated: for a fraction of a second, the emerald eyes that gazed up at the glowing moon each held a cat's elliptical pupil. The Mau watched, gaze fixed upon the woman's face; to some it might almost seem as though the cat smiled.

"*Bastet, protect me . . . watch over me as the Great Mother does, as you who give life to your children watch over all of us who turn to you for comfort and help. . . .*"

The words fell like stones into a deep pool. The voice that intoned them rippled through Patience's thoughts, soothing, easeful.

Where have I heard that voice? Patience thought, dreaming. Other voices came to her then, voices she did recall, girls singing—*let's pretend that we're dead, we'll pretend that we're dead*—then a man's harsh voice, shouting.

"*There will be no turning back. . . .*"

She flinched, moaning. An image flashed before her, a gold-and-emerald scarab beetle; sand-colored buildings, white smoke, a woman turning gracefully to stare at Patience, a woman tall as she was, and dark; but the face that met Patience's shocked gaze was not her own face, nor even a woman's, but a cat's, gold muzzled, emerald eyed, its teeth white and sharp as thorns.

With a cry, Patience sat up. Her hands sank into soft mud. Her wet clothes clung to her like dank seaweed. She looked down, puzzled, at the ragged remains of her shirt, then at her mud-streaked hand. Tentatively, stumbling a bit, she got to her feet and stepped from the fetid water to what passed for dry land here at the marsh's edge. The late-night breeze stirred cattails and dry stalks. From somewhere far away came a low, feline *mrrrowwlll*.

But of the cats there was no sign; and of course Patience did not know to look for them. She had no memory of those hundreds of watchful eyes; no memory of her flight through the Hedare plant or of her fall from the waste tunnel to the deadly river below.

And she had no memory of her own death; nor of what—or who—had brought her back to a place she had never seen before, this wasteland at the edge of a sleeping city. She shook her head, disoriented. Her mouth opened to form a question.

All that came out was a strangled animal sound. Patience bared her teeth, frightened; whirled to see what had made that miserable feline cry.

But there was no cat there. What she *did* see was another pair of eyes staring back at hers from the grass at her feet—tiny glowing red eyes, haloed by a dull crimson, mouse-shaped haze. Patience hissed. With a flick of its minute tail, the mouse disappeared into the underbrush, though its musky scent lingered. Patience licked her lips, tilted her head to stare out across the wetland.

There were other eyes out there, thousands of them—glints of red in the grass and overgrown brush—voles and sleeping sparrows, frogs, water snakes, crickets, centipedes, shrews and squirrels and field mice. Patience felt her mouth flood with sweet liquid at the thought of all of those hidden creatures, but before she could move toward them a sound distracted her. Whip-fast her head turned, to spy a katydid perched upon the tip of a blade of grass. The insect moved forward, the grass bowed. Patience heard the scrape of six minute feet upon the serrated stalk, and another noise. She sucked her breath in sharply, looked up to see a dark shape float in front of the moon. The rush of wind through its wings was so loud she frowned, tilting her head so that the noise diminished. In one fluid motion she was down on all fours, racing through the tall sedges; so carefully and swiftly did she move that the grass scarcely stirred at her passing.

It was almost a mile until she reached the end of the marshland, though Patience did not measure the distance that way. She knew only that the rank smell of bad water and rotting vegetation and millions of small warm lives had given way to other scents, the cold reek of rusted metal and spilled engine oil, the stink of garbage. Her nose wrinkled as she approached a chain-link fence. She was still on all fours, heedless of the bite of gravel and broken glass against her raw flesh. There was a gap in the metal fence and she slipped through, slinking on all fours.

Immediately a volley of fierce barking broke out. Patience looked up, frightened. She hissed in fear and rage as two huge, menacing dogs leaped down from atop a heap of junked cars. The dogs raced toward her, mouths open to show yellow teeth. Patience turned and fled, running on two legs now. She sprinted across the junkyard, hurdling over a pile of broken bottles. Barbed wire snagged her torn clothes. Just a few feet behind her the dogs raced, howling frantically.

Patience ran on, her breath ragged. Her bare feet sent bits of glass and rubble flying back into the dogs' faces. Their barking grew more frenzied. They were close enough now that she could feel the spittle flying from their muzzles, and smell the acrid odor of their mindless rage and hunger.

Just ahead of her loomed another chain-link fence. It was easily ten or twelve feet high. The dogs yelped triumphantly, lunging forward for the kill.

But Patience was gone. With one leap, she had outstripped the dogs, and clung to the fence five feet above their snapping jaws. As they howled and paced below, she clawed her way to the top of the fence. For a moment she perched there and cast a sneering look at her feckless pursuers. Then she began to climb, headfirst, down the other side. When she reached the ground she turned and shot the dogs one last taunting look. Then she darted into the street, to disappear into the waning night.

FIVE

To die and to lose one's life are much the same thing.
—Irish proverb

It was dawn before she arrived back at her apartment building. Afterward she could never remember how she found her way there. Perhaps she traveled as all lost cats do, by a combination of instinct and luck and that odd, near-mystical sense of knowing just where and when to turn, which alleys to take and which to avoid—until, at last, the final alley leads home.

Which was where she was now. Only she was on the wrong side of home—the outside. She stood in the little abandoned-looking courtyard at the back of her apartment house, staring unperturbed at the fire escape high above her. Overhead the sky was brightening. There were the first faint sounds of another morning getting under way: a few cars on nearby streets; grackles and starlings fighting over refuse on the curbside; a solitary rat making its way across the apartment building's ledge. Patience watched it scurry into the shadows, then blinked and turned her attention to getting back into her own apartment.

The fire escape's ladder hung like a broken bit of

scaffolding, perhaps eight feet above the sidewalk. Too far up for Patience, or anyone else, to reach.

But Patience regarded it unfazed. She took a few steps backward, to give herself a running start, then ran toward the building, bounding into the air and grabbing the ladder's bottom rung. She swung herself up, turned, and leaped onto the ledge outside her apartment window.

And here, at last, she paused. The sunlight had not yet reached this window: the glass pane in front of her formed a dark mirror in which a woman's face was reflected. Patience stared at it, frowning, and for a moment, disoriented. The woman in the window frowned back. Patience leaned closer, fascinated but also repelled.

Who is that?

Somewhere beneath this was another, more disturbing, thought.

What is that?

Patience wiped some of the mud from her forehead, ran a finger along the outer edge of her eye, making a long arabesque in the dirt caked there. She did the same to the other eye, gazing at her reflection approvingly, then licked her hands and patted at her matted hair. She glanced at her image once more, nodding, then drew back her hand and with all her strength smashed the window.

Broken glass rained on the courtyard below, but Patience didn't even look. She was already inside, stretching and yawning as she took in her surroundings with fond, drowsy eyes.

It had been a long night; at last she was home.

*   *   *

Hours passed. The sun's rays finally made their way to Patience's window, shone in through the broken pane to brighten the hardwood floors, then moved on. Atop the high bookcase in one corner of the studio, a spot the sunlight always found and warmed, Patience sprawled, sound asleep. Her nightgown had bunched up beneath her, as though she found it uncomfortable, but her face was somewhat cleaner than it had been, and most of the mud had been washed from her arms and legs.

She had slept deeply, so immersed in strange dreams that she didn't hear the first half-dozen insistent rings of her telephone. By the time the sound penetrated her sleep-enshrouded consciousness, the answering machine had already picked up.

She sat up quickly, banged her head on the ceiling, and with a muffled cry tumbled from the bookcase in a heap.

Patience looked up at the bookcase, puzzled.

Just what the hell is happening to me?

She glanced at her telephone and for the first time noticed the answering machine blinking. She turned it on, and Sally's voice filled the room.

"Patience, where are you? Hedare is on the warpath. And Tom called. He said you never showed up for your date. Look, I'm *really* worried. Please call me. What's going on? What happened?"

BEEEEP.

The message cut off. Patience groaned and looked around, panicked. "I don't know," she said aloud. "I don't remember. . . ."

That was when she heard a familiar sound—a low,

plaintive *meow*. She looked over to see the Mau perched atop her dresser, innocently licking one paw.

"*You!*" Patience cried. "Did you—did *you* do all this?"

She stepped over to the cat, carefully but forcefully reaching for the tag on its collar.

IF FOUND PLEASE RETURN TO OPHELIA POWERS, it read, and gave an address in one of the city's recently gentrified high-tech districts. Patience memorized the address, then gently took the cat's head between her hands and gazed forcefully into its calm gold-green eyes.

"You're freaking me out, kitty. I don't know how, and maybe I *am* losing my mind," she said as the cat stared back at her, unperturbed, "but something is definitely happening here—and I have a feeling that it's all *your* fault. You gotta go home. *Now.*"

SIX

It wasn't difficult to find Ophelia Powers's house. It was the only residence in a five-block radius that actually *was* a house—a cozily ramshackle three-story Victorian, tucked like a dried flower between looming glass-and-steel high-rises where the city's young financial wizards lived and worked. Patience approached the house determinedly, holding the Mau at arm's length, as though it were some potentially dangerous piece of hardware. She rang the doorbell, and waited impatiently until the door swung open.

"Hi," Patience began peremptorily. "Are you Ophelia Powers? I think maybe I found your cat—more than once, as a matter of fact. I got her off a ledge, and now she won't leave me alone."

She thrust the cat toward the figure standing in the doorway. A woman in her midfifties, wearing an intricately embroidered tunic over tight jeans and suede boots. Her hair was in myriad tight braids, held back from her forehead with a brightly colored headband. Her features were strong but elegant: deep-set, appraising eyes, high cheekbones, a rather stubborn set to her wide mouth. She stared coolly at the cat Patience continued to hold out toward her, but made no move to take it.

"More likely *it* found *you*," she said at last.

Patience looked taken aback. The woman regarded her with detached interest. Finally she nodded, pulled the door open, and said, "I think you should come in."

"Oh, I can't. . . ." Patience's attempt at firm resolve began to crumble. "Thank you, but I'm late for work and if I—"

But Ophelia Powers had already disappeared inside, leaving the door wide open—and Patience still holding the cat.

She hesitated. "Oh, all right," she muttered under her breath, and followed the older woman.

Inside all was a cheerful bohemian welter of wind chimes, dreamcatchers, and strands of tiny fairy lights looping through potted palms, vividly blooming cactuses, and orchids. There were old woven kilims underfoot and exuberant late-modern paintings on the wall, and an extravagant mix of old and new furniture—Chippendale wing chairs, an Eames chaise, heavily carved oaken sideboards and, in the living room, a very old French provincial settee covered with a pale aqua fabric.

And there were cats. Patience lost count after five of them padded silently down the hall to greet her as she made her way to the living room. They swarmed around her, rubbing against her ankles and purring. She tried to nudge them away, and kept a tighter hold on the Mau.

But it seemed to have no interest in leaving her—

not until she entered the living room. Then, before she could protest, it leaped from her arms and calmly made its way to the couch where Ophelia sat, two other cats on her lap. The Mau ignored them. It climbed to the back of the couch and sat there regally, surveying the room as though it were its private domain.

"Midnight," pronounced Ophelia. She gestured for Patience to sit on the couch beside her.

"I'm sorry? What?" Patience settled uneasily on the sofa. There were more cats circling her feet—there were cats *everywhere*. They sprawled on windowsills, dozing, and perched atop bookshelves and the television and a computer. Ophelia idly stroked the two in her lap. Her eyes seemed as strangely oblique as the cats', at once watchful and distracted; she appeared to take in everything around her, while not actually looking at anything at all.

"Her name," Ophelia explained, handing Patience a steaming mug of tea. She gestured at the cat posed on the top of the couch behind her. "Midnight. She's from a long line of Egyptian Maus, the rarest of all breeds. They were the temple cats of the goddess Bast, or Bastet. Bast is the protector of cats—and the protector of women. Her Maus have special powers. Midnight does, too."

Patience snorted. "Right. Like popping out of nowhere and scaring people half to death? Disappearing for no reason, then coming back again?"

Ophelia smiled. "Among other things. . . ."

Patience shook her head. "This has been a terrible day already. And I can't even remember most of yesterday. And every time I turn around your cat is—

everything's gone wrong since that cat showed up. I met this guy I liked? Scared him off. I got a big opportunity at work? Blew that. And now I'm having a *really* bad day. More than one, actually . . ."

Her voice broke and she looked up at Ophelia. "I . . . I'm sorry. This isn't your problem. I don't even know why I'm telling you, it's just . . ."

The cats continued to nuzzle at her ankles, but Patience no longer pushed them away. She set her tea on the floor, blinking back tears, then looked at the cats at her feet.

The older woman gazed at her, studying her face. After a moment she said, "It's all right. Tell me."

"I don't know . . . I mean, I *really* don't know. I went to the factory, and then . . . I don't know what happened, and no matter how hard I try I can't remember. . . ."

She hesitated, as though trying to recapture a memory.

But it was hopeless. She shook her head in frustration and started to stand. "I've got to get to work. I am *really* late."

Ophelia touched her arm. "Don't go. Tell me about last night."

"I'm sorry. I can't. . . ."

Because I'm late, Patience thought. *And because I'm scared. . . .*

"Then I think you should come back," Ophelia said firmly. "Anytime. I'm always here."

She reached down and lightly smacked the rump of a cat lapping Patience's tea. "Socrates! No caffeine. It makes him irritable," she explained to Patience.

Patience smiled politely and headed for the front door. As she did, Ophelia crossed to a small side table and picked up a small wooden box. She looked at Patience, holding the younger woman's gaze with her own. Then she opened the box, withdrew a small ball formed of molded green herbs, and tossed it at Patience.

Without thinking, Patience caught the ball in midair. She held it to her face and inhaled deeply, blissfully, as her entire body shuddered and her shoulders slumped in relaxation. Then, recalling where she was, she abruptly snatched her hand away and stared questioningly at Ophelia. The older woman stared back, wide-eyed.

"Catnip," she said simply, and snapped the box shut once more.

SEVEN

Patience's morning went from weird to worse. After leaving a hurried message on George Hedare's voice mail, she arrived late—very late—to work, to be greeted by Sally's warning look, augmented by Lance holding up a sheet of paper with the words BE AFRAID. BE VERY AFRAID scrawled on it. Patience slowed her steps as she approached her cubicle. Too late she saw the familiar figure standing there, fuming, in a suit that would have cost Patience a month's salary.

"What the hell is *wrong* with you?" exploded George Hedare. Patience walked past him silently and settled at her desk. "You never delivered the designs. You do not, in fact, even know where they are! And you do not know where they are because, and I quote, you '*can't remember*'? Your incompetence is *staggering*."

Patience listened to him calmly, but without looking up. Absentmindedly, she reached for her sketchbook and a pencil and began to doodle. When George paused in his rant she said, "Hm?" and continued drawing.

"Are you even *listening* to me?" he shouted.

Patience paused in her doodling. She looked up at her boss, thought for a long moment before answering.

"Not as much as you're listening to yourself."

Around them the entire art department grew suddenly silent. In the cubicle behind Patience's, Sally and Lance stared at each other, dumbfounded. George Hedare's face grew dead white, save for two crimson splotches on his cheeks. He stared at Patience, then furiously grabbed the piece of paper she had been sketching on. He held it up, gazing at a vicious caricature of himself, sweat spraying from his face and tendrils of smoke and fire erupting from his head.

Speechless, he looked from the cartoon to Patience Phillips, as though struggling to find some explanation: How could this image possibly have appeared? Here, now—and from *her*? Finally, he crumpled the page in his fist. He turned on his heel and stormed out of the cubicle.

Patience watched him go, then blinked. Like a sleepwalker awakening, she suddenly seemed to realize where she was—and what she had done.

"Mr. Hedare, wait!" she cried, leaping to her feet. "I don't know what got into me. I'm so sorry."

The sincerity of her tone made Hedare hesitate. He turned back to her, glaring.

"Sorry? Is that all? Well, let me tell you something, Phillips: 'Sorry' isn't nearly enough."

In their cubicles, Lance and Sally sucked in their breath. Patience looked at George Hedare. Her eyes narrowed. Her expression hardened into a mask of icy confidence that her friends had never seen before.

" 'Sorry' isn't enough?" she said. "Then let me try the remix. I'm sorry for every minute of my life I've wasted on an untalented, unethical, and unappreciative egomaniac like *you*."

She paused to let this sink in. "And tell me—what *is* enough, George? I really want to know. Should I grovel? Weep and wail? Should I break my heart in two?"

As she spoke, her voice grew huskier; not pleading but playful, almost seductive. Her slender form seemed to grow taller as she stepped slowly forward, one hand idly toying with her pencil as though it were a weapon.

"Let me tell you something, George: Don't hold your breath. I don't have time to take abuse from an ungracious, untalented, unappreciative egomaniac who doesn't know his ass from his elbow.

"Oh, and did I mention that you were dishonest, too?" she added with a sly smile, deliberately raising her voice so that others in the room could hear. "I *really* wanted to make sure I got that in. Because the real question here, George, the one on everyone's mind, is—

" 'What the hell is wrong with *you*?' "

"Holy shit!" whispered Lance. Sally literally fell out of her chair. Around the art department, numerous variations on these two themes played themselves out over the next thirty seconds.

Only George Hedare remained utterly motionless, like a man turned to stone by an incantation. When he finally could speak, he spat his words, as though to curse Patience in return.

"Clean out your cubicle."

He stalked off. Patience stared after him, then glanced down at herself, as though disbelieving that her words had come out of this body. In a panic she began to call after him.

"Wait! Mr. Hedare! I didn't mean—Mr. Hedare! I was kidding. . . ."

Her voice fell to a whisper. She stared at the pencil in her hand, shook her head as she said to herself, "I *was* kidding, right? Wasn't I?"

But George wasn't waiting to hear how the debate between the two Patiences turned out. He was gone, and with his passing the entire room began to buzz with excited, almost exultant, conversation.

Patience alone said nothing. She slumped against the wall of her cubicle, defeated.

This was when Sally stepped into view.

"My hero," she said. She crossed her arms defiantly, looked at her friend, and said, "Hello? I don't know who you are, or where you came from, but . . . if you see Patience Phillips, tell her Sally has *never* been prouder in her entire life."

Laurel Hedare sat at her husband's desk in his office. At the corner of the desk were the proofs of Drina, the "New Face of Hedare." Laurel was doing her best not to look at them. Still, again and again her unfocused gaze returned to the photos. Each time her expression grew disgusted, even repelled, before she'd finally force herself to stare at the copy of the company's annual report before her.

Those projected sales figures should be enough to cheer anyone up, she thought with cold disdain. *Gee, I wonder why they aren't working on me?*

"Ms. Hedare?" She looked up to see Wesley, George's factotum–cum–bodyguard–cum–personal assistant, entering the room. "Mr. Hedare wanted me to inform you that he'll be at the factory for the rest of the afternoon."

Laurel sniffed. "If by 'factory' you mean at the Four Seasons teaching Drina how to open the minibar, consider me informed."

"He just said—"

"Wesley, George hasn't said anything meaningful to me since 'I do.'"

"Would you like me to try his cell phone?"

Laurel gave him a scornful glare. "You really suck the 'assist' right out of 'assistant,' don't you, Wesley?"

Wesley's composure wilted. With a small bow he retreated, shutting the door behind him. Laurel waited until his footsteps died away. She continued to stare at the proofs as though they were cockroaches. Finally she picked them up, stood, and crossed to the window.

The photos all showed closeups of Drina. Very beautiful; very, very young. Laurel gazed at them, her breath catching in her throat. She recalled something she had read long, long ago, back when she was studying ancient philosophy at college; back before she had chosen having a face—being a face—to having a life.

Nature gave horns to bulls, hooves to horses, speed to hares, stealth to cats; the power of swimming to fishes, that

*of flying to birds, and knowledge to men. She had nothing
left to give to women save Beauty. Beauty is proof against
spears and shields. She who is beautiful is more formidable
than fire and iron.*

The quote had enraged her eighteen-year-old self,
caught up in the throes of the still-nascent feminist
movement. But when she'd confronted her professor
with her objection to Anacreon's words, he had only
laughed at her.

"What?" she'd demanded, furious. "What's so god-
dam funny?"

And, saying nothing, he had simply taken her by
the shoulders and gently turned her so that she
faced the mirror in his office; faced the image of herself, young and breathtakingly lovely, her cheeks
flushed with anger and her pale hair unraveling from
its braid.

"*That,*" he'd said at last, inclining his head toward
her reflection. "Brilliant as you are, Laurel, I'm afraid
that is where your greatest strength lies. It's a gift,
Laurel—but it's also a weapon. Don't disdain it. Use
it. Remember: 'Beauty is proof against spears and
shields. . . . '"

Now, nearly thirty years later, the words rang once
more in Laurel's ears.

"She who is beautiful is more formidable than fire
and iron," she whispered. Pained, she tore her gaze
from the proofs and stared out the window, down
into the street. A stretch Humvee idled in the street
in front of the Hedare Corporation's main entrance.

Laurel's nostrils flared. The grotesque vehicle was
typical of her husband's vanity and greed. What was

that old saying? I *pray that people with taste get money, and people with money get taste.* . . .

Once upon a time, George Hedare had possessed neither. His wife's beauty and wit and shrewd business acumen and, yes, taste, had changed all that; but in all their years together, George had never managed to acquire anything but money.

Money, and a few of the accessories that money could buy. . . .

In the street below, two figures were hurrying down the steps toward the open door of the waiting Humvee. Laurel's husband and the new face of Hedare, both dressed in glittering formalwear. George threw his head back, laughing, and let Drina enter the limo first. He gave her ass a proprietary slap, then clambered in after her.

Laurel sucked her breath in sharply, then stepped back from the window. The photos fell from her hand. She turned, too quickly, her hand reaching for and closing around a water glass on her husband's desk. Without looking, she drew it toward her lips.

Empty.

With an explosive curse, Laurel slammed the glass onto the desk. It shattered into fragments. She did not release them; she clutched her hand into a fist, watching numbly as the glass splintered even more, shards falling from between her fingers to cover the desk's surface.

Laurel did not so much as wince; only stared. There was no blood, no pain. She opened her hand slowly, wonderingly. Splinters of glass dropped to the floor. She shook her hand, as casually as though dry-ing it, and more glass fell. Then she drew her hand to her face, her wonder turning to raw amazement.

The flesh was unmarked, uninjured. Not a drop of blood, not a line, not a bruise showed where she had crushed the glass.

Yet the evidence of her fury surrounded her, glinting in the late-morning sun. Laurel turned her hand back and forth, gazing at it; looked down at the floor, then at the mirror beside her husband's desk.

Beauty is proof against spears and shields. She who is beautiful is more formidable than fire and iron. . . .

Very slowly, as though awakening from a long, untroubled sleep, Laurel Hedare began to smile.

Inside George Hedare's stretch Humvee, the New Face of Hedare was not exactly smiling. Drina's face was animated, but she was frowning, an expression she seemed not to have had much experience with. It continually reverted to a sort of simper, as though she had tasted something bad but lacked the will to spit it out, or the proper words to register her complaint.

"So last year I'm up to Number Seven on the Most Beautiful People list? Which you would *think* would be, like, *good*? And out of a hundred, well sure, that's complimentary, sort of. But everybody knows I deserve Number Three? Maybe even Number Two? And with the Beau-line campaign about to start, I don't see why Number One is unnecessarily impossible!"

She turned her beautiful, empty, face toward George's. "You know what I think?"

George lay a finger upon her lips. "Don't."

"What?"

"Think." He pressed his finger harder against her mouth; hard enough that Drina winced. "Not ever. Consider it a condition of our relationship. Comprendez-vous?"

Drina tried to frown again, but this time George was ahead of the game. He leaned forward and kissed her mouth. A moment later she was smiling, too.

EIGHT

It didn't take Patience an entire hour to pack up the meager contents of her cubicle. With Lance and Sally's help, she was finished in about fifteen minutes.

"The two of you are the only things I'm going to miss about this place," she said, giving Lance a quick hug.

"How can you miss us if you won't leave?" Lance countered with a grin, but his eyes were wistful. "You're the lucky one, Patience. I'll call you in a few days. Let's meet for lunch."

"Sure."

She and Sally walked out together, leaving the Hedare Building's chilly cavern behind them.

"That's not exactly true, what I said back there," Patience said after a few minutes. She shifted the weight of the canvas bag holding her few belongings. "About you and Lance being the only things about that place I'll miss? I'll miss the work, too—the design stuff. Being able to do a good job. . . ."

"Yeah?" Sally looked at her friend dubiously. "And

when exactly were you *allowed* to do a good job? Face it, Patience—George is a jerk! Everyone hates him, even Laurel."

"And I suspect she has better reasons than we do," Patience added darkly.

"Suspect? Girl, you better believe it! George is a mean, duplicitous control freak who doesn't know where he isn't needed—like, in the art department? He screws up everything he puts his hands on—"

"Except for making huge amounts of money for Hedare."

"Okay. So that's a minor point in his favor. But believe me, Patience, when you told him off back there, you were speaking for every single one of us. E*veryone* has wanted to say those words to him! I just can't believe it was *you* who finally did it!"

"I know. I mean, I almost don't believe I said it either. I don't know how to describe it. . . ."

Patience shook her head, still feeling slightly dazed from the realization. "It's like . . . it's like I was saying it but at the same time I *wasn't* saying it."

"Well, whoever said it deserves the thanks and eternal gratitude of the entire art department."

"No. You don't understand, Sally." Patience bit her lip nervously. "Back there, when he started in on me like that? I wanted to *hurt* him. *Really* hurt him. And I would have *enjoyed* hurting him. . . ."

They turned a corner onto a side street. A dog walker with a brace of auburn-furred Chows was approaching them on the sidewalk. As Patience came into view, the two dogs suddenly went berserk, barking and lunging at her as they passed.

"Genghis! Kublai!" The dog walker shouted, struggling to yank the dogs back on their leads. "Stop it!"

Sally yelped and jumped back onto the curb, but Patience stood her ground, stiffening as her face contorted and she stared at the Chows. She let out an angry hiss, unconsciously clawing at her bag.

"Sorry! I don't know what's gotten into them!" the dog walker called apologetically as she dragged the dogs around the corner. "They're really very sweet dogs."

"Sweet compared to, like, the Terminator?" Sally yelled after her. "Or sweet compared to Godzilla? Jeez!"

She turned to stare in disbelief at Patience, still standing tensed, with her teeth bared. "And what *was* that?"

"Huh? Oh!" Patience made a great show of sniffling loudly and rubbing her nose. "Umm, nothing . . . allergies?"

"Allergies?" Sally looked at her dubiously, but said nothing more.

They started walking again. Patience took a few deep breaths, trying not to obsess on the question Sally had just posed; the same question that was now racing through Patience's mind.

What the hell was that?

They were almost at the next block when something glinted at the edge of her vision. Patience blinked, shaking her head as though a bit of dust had gotten in her eye. Then abruptly her eyes widened. She paused, turning to stare at a shop window.

It was a high-end jewelry store, one of the most expensive shops in the city; a place she'd passed a thousand times over the years, going to and from work. Sometimes she'd glance at the window, but always with the same sort of mildly detached interest she might show at a museum exhibition, or at photographs taken by the Hubble Telescope. Yes, indeed, these were beautiful things, but they belonged to an entirely different world than the one she inhabited.

Now, however, she was stopped dead in her tracks.

"Pretty . . ."

She wasn't even aware she had spoken the words aloud. Her entire being was flooded with nothing but the image of what was before her in the store window.

A necklace, but not just a necklace: an eidolon, something so mysterious and compelling in its beauty and strangeness that it almost seemed itself to be alive. It was carefully arranged on sinuous folds of heavy black velvet, a cascading array of gold filigree within which myriad claws were set, each bearing a single winking diamond. The claws ranged from minute specimens no larger than a thorn to the necklace's centerpiece: a single large, gold-tipped claw as long as Patience's little finger, set with a diamond so large its facets seemed to reflect Patience's eyes as she stared at it, entranced.

"Sooooo pretty," she murmured. Louder this time, her voice growing throatier, more a purr than a casual remark. "Sooo pretty."

That was when she remembered Sally, standing behind her. Patience coughed, making an effort to make her voice sound more normal.

"Don't you think, Sally? Sal?"

Patience turned. Sally stood on the sidewalk, staring at her friend. Her mouth opened but no words came out. She lifted her hand, as though waving farewell. Her eyes rolled back in their sockets. Without a sound she collapsed unconscious on the sidewalk.

NINE

It seemed to take forever for the ambulance to come. Patience dialed 911 from her cell phone, then knelt beside Sally's limp body, pillowing her friend's head on her own coat until the emergency crew finally arrived.

"We'll take it from here," an EMT said, curtly but not unkindly, as he jumped from the ambulance.

The other emergency medical technicians hurried to check Sally's vital signs, then bundled her onto a gurney and into the waiting vehicle.

"Let me come with you," Patience begged as she watched her friend being strapped down inside.

"Are you related?" The EMT began closing the ambulance doors.

"I'm her sister," Patience said frantically.

"Her sister?" The EMT looked doubtfully from Patience to the unconscious Sally. Then he shrugged. "Sure. Climb aboard. And hang on."

* * *

The EMT's kindness in allowing her to accompany Sally in the ambulance didn't extend to letting her go with her friend into the emergency room.

"You'll have to wait there," he said, gesturing to a crowded waiting room.

"But—"

"One of the ER nurses will let you know when we have news," he shouted grimly over his shoulder. "Just wait."

Patience watched miserably as Sally's gurney was lifted from the ambulance and hurriedly wheeled down a white corridor and out of sight.

Patience spent the next two hours in the ER waiting room, leafing nervously through ancient issues of *Modern Maturity* and *Reader's Digest*, surrounded by people in various stages of anxiety—parents, lovers, street people, druggies, college students. When an orderly finally rolled Sally out of an examining room, Patience jumped up and ran over to greet her.

"Have you noticed," Sally began weakly, as her friend walked alongside, "that when they keep you for observation, nobody ever actually observes you?"

"Sal. Do they know what's wrong?"

Sally shook her head. "Not a clue. They keep running tests, but . . ." Sally took in Patience's anxious expression and quickly added, "Hey, upside—you should see my doctor."

Patience smiled gratefully. "Sounds like you're getting better already."

The orderly rolled the gurney into an empty room, then helped Sally into a hospital bed.

"Check it out," Sally said as the orderly left. "The

real miracle of the American health-care system—a private room! Which reminds me . . . what's up with the handsome yet modest but nobody cares 'cause he's so gorgeous detective?"

Patience shook her head and sighed. "I don't think it's going to work out."

Sally pulled herself up, suddenly all business. "You *never* think it's going to work out, Patience! But you know what? This time I will *not* let you sabotage a good thing."

Patience smiled. "You talk a pretty mean game in that backless hospital gown."

"My shoulder blades are my best feature. Look, Patience—if it's broke, fix it." She looked past Patience into the hall. "Now get outta here. The hottie doctor's coming, I need to look vulnerable."

Patience laughed. She leaned over to pat Sally's hand. "Thanks. I needed that. I'll check in later, okay?"

Sally winked. "Sure, sure. But I want a good report, all right? My blood pressure's low, I need something to raise it. Speaking of which, hello Dr. Johnstone!"

With a last smile, Patience turned and left.

The Rainbow Spectrum Community Center was in one of those parts of the city's downtown that had not been gentrified by the recent tech boom, or by any other boom, for that matter. Still, the adults who ran it did their best. Paint was cheap, and went a long way toward brightening the cinder block interior walls. Artwork by the kids who frequented the center helped too, as did the overstuffed pillows and beanbag chairs scattered across the floor in one of the center's resource rooms.

This was where Tom Lone was sitting, at a battered table covered with crayon scrawls and smudges of tempera paint. On the floor surrounding him, a dozen children between the ages of eight and ten sprawled, a few of them yawning as they pillowed their heads on beanbags and caught a few minutes of much-needed sleep. Tom Lone didn't begrudge their lack of attention. He knew the kind of homes some of these kids came from, places where he might be—had been—called in the line of duty.

He liked the job he was doing right now a lot better.

"Why? Because it's *wrong*," he said, leaning back in his chair as he surveyed the kids looking back at him. He had most of their attention now, even the ones who seemed half-awake. "You can't just take something without paying for it. There's no such thing as a little bit against the law, okay? It is or it isn't wrong. Period. And if you forget that? Well, then you're the bad guy."

"Can I see your gun?" a kid suddenly blurted.

Abruptly *everyone's* attention was on Tom Lone.

"No," he said smoothly, not missing a beat. "And we don't like bad guys, do we? We like—"

"Is it loaded?" another boy interrupted.

Tom fought to keep what he was feeling—equal parts annoyance and amusement—from showing on his face. "Yes. We like good guys. You know what makes somebody—"

"Will you shoot it?" eagerly broke in a third kid.

"No. You know what makes somebody a good guy?"

"Can I shoot it?" demanded the first kid, the one who'd started all this.

Tom sighed and ran a hand across his forehead. That was when he spotted the slender woman in the back of the room, cradling a cup of take-out coffee in her hands. He looked at her, startled; a little wary, too. Then he brought his attention back to the kids at his feet.

"Look, guys. Money doesn't make you good. Living in a big expensive house doesn't make you good, either."

The kids mulled this over for a moment. One of them raised his hand.

"But it would be okay if we did?" he asked. "Right?"

Tom felt his heart contract with compassion. "Yeah, it would," he said, and smiled. "But no matter what, you have to remember something. Being good is something you keep in your heart because you *choose* to put it there. Understand? You learn the difference between right and wrong. And you keep that in your heart, too. I'm not saying it's easy. I'm not saying that some people don't choose to be bad. But I want something different for you. I want you to be the good guys."

He spoke with quiet fervor, and absolute certainty. In the back of the room Patience listened, moved by his words, and by the way the kids all stared at him raptly. After a moment Tom smiled again and leaned forward.

"Okay. Any questions—"

Several hands immediately shot up.

"—that *aren't* about my gun?"

All the hands went back down. Tom laughed, shaking his head. "Then let's go shoot some hoops."

The kids jumped up, cheering, and ran for the exit. Patience waited till they were gone, then shyly approached Tom.

"Hi," she said softly. "I called the station. They said you might be here." She held out the take-out cup. "You never got your coffee."

Tom looked at her, then down at the cardboard cup. It had been decorated with colored pens, a cheerful psychedelic swirl of rainbows and flowers with the word SORRY at the center of the design. He smiled, then accepted the peace offering.

"Thanks."

Patience nodded. "Look . . . I'm sorry I was so . . . weird. It was just one of those crazy days. You ever have days like that?"

Tom sipped his coffee, staring at her over the edge of the steaming cup. "Not exactly," he said. "But *this* day? It just got better."

"Not too crazy?" asked Patience, a little nervously.

Tom grinned. "Not yet."

Patience smiled back at him. She turned toward the exit, cocking a thumb at the door. "So . . . you want to go shoot some hoops?"

They walked outside, into a desolate expanse of concrete surrounded by chain-link fences topped with razor wire. Two rusted basketball hoops stood at either end. In the distance, the worn brick facades of the projects rose defiantly against the cloudless blue sky. The children raced around the playground, shouting gleefully, seemingly oblivious to the bleakness of their surroundings.

"I have to admit—you are a brave man, facing a mob like that." Patience watched the kids, smiling. "And with no backup! I always thought detectives came in twos."

Tom took another sip of his coffee. "I work alone. Most of the time."

"By choice?"

He smiled ruefully. "Yes—theirs."

Patience laughed as he went on. "Oh, I've had partners. But it turns out I take my job a little too seriously."

"Sally always says that about me. She says I'm fun-deficient."

Tom looked at her. His dark eyes grew thoughtful. "I don't believe that—whoa, heads up!"

A basketball came flying toward them. Tom set his coffee down and jumped for it—but Patience jumped higher, snagging the ball in midair.

"Nice!" Tom said in surprise. "That's quite a jump you've got there!"

Patience seemed a bit surprised herself. "I haven't played since I was a kid," she said, and bounced the ball experimentally.

"Go ahead." Tom pointed at the hoop where the kids milled about, watching. "Take a shot."

"I was never any good."

"That sounds like the F-word—Fear—talking," Tom said in mock seriousness. He narrowed his eyes, staring at hers. "Can't say I blame you. I wouldn't want to go up against me either. . . ."

"Hey, c'mon!" one of the kids yelled. Patience

looked over to see them standing beneath one of the hoops, motioning excitedly for her and Tom to join them. "What, you scared?"

Patience shot Tom a look, then darted out onto the court, dribbling the ball. She batted at it with one hand and then the other in an odd, feline fashion, like a cat playing with her prey.

Tom watched, impressed. She didn't move like a pro, that was for sure, but her grace and skill were evident. She drew near where the kids waited; a few of them ran toward her, but she swatted at the ball in midair, sending it flying straight down through the hoop.

"Whoa!" The kids cheered and gave one another high fives, then greeted Patience the same way. "See that?"

Patience was even more startled than her young audience by this little display of her newfound skill. Tom raised his eyebrows.

"Seems like you've been keeping something from me," he said with pretend gravity. He put his coffee aside and took to the court himself. "Only one way to deal with that. . . . One on one!"

Tom and Patience squared off. The kids moved to the sidelines to watch, noisily enthusiastic spectators. The two adults started out tentatively, testing each other's abilities; careful not to push too hard or too fast.

But gradually their game grew more heated as they feinted and dodged, the ball now in Patience's hands, now Tom's.

"Not bad—for a girl," he said, panting, as Patience loped past him.

"Oh, you are *so* asking for it," she retorted, swatting the ball from him even before he registered what she was up to.

"What the . . . ?"

She played in such a strange, freestyle fashion that Tom was completely outmaneuvered. And somewhat unnerved. She pounced on the ball when it was free, jumped unnecessarily, swiped the ball from him whenever he was preparing to shoot. Finally she leaped in front of him, her hand reaching out to dab at the ball, but with enough force that it went flying, up, up, up—then smack down through the hoop once more.

But her effort was enough to send *her* flying as well. With a muffled *oof*, she smacked into Tom, and the two of them tumbled onto the ground, limbs entwined. For an entire minute they lay there, panting as they caught their breath; both with faces sweat streaked, pulses racing, their hands touching. Patience stared at Tom; he gazed back. Their breathing slowed, became synchronous; without realizing it, Tom tightened his large hand around Patience's small one.

Patience began to feel as though her life was slowing down. Heat suffused her face. She licked her lips, her gaze still locked with Tom's; she slowly began to move, as though to extricate herself from him. Imperceptibly, his grasp upon her hand tightened. He began to draw her toward him and she moved willingly, albeit unthinkingly, lips parted and her tousled hair falling across her eyes.

"Hey," whispered Tom. "Hey . . ."

"Uh, Mr. Lone?" a plaintive voice interrupted him. "Can we have our ball back? Please?"

Patience and Tom looked up to see a ring of kids staring down at them. The two adults looked at each other, embarrassed, then began to laugh.

"Sure," said Tom, getting to his feet. He tossed the ball to one of the boys. "I think we're done with it now."

He picked up his coffee cup and walked with Patience back to the Community Center building.

"So," he said when they reached the door. "Any chance of a rematch?"

Patience looked at her feet shyly, then smiled. "Maybe," she said. "How 'bout I call you?"

"How 'bout you make absolutely sure you do that?" said Tom in agreement. They looked at each other, then Patience nodded by way of farewell. Ducking her head, she turned, giving him a last sideways glance, and left.

TEN

That night Patience fell into a troubled sleep of confused dreams in which the moon raced across a violet sky and small, swiftly moving creatures, only half-glimpsed, leaped and fought mock battles at the edge of a sluggish river where cattails and tall reeds rustled in the night wind. The rustling grew louder, the sounds of fighting punctuated by shrieks and an insistent, thudding sound. Patience groaned, turning in her bed, then suddenly sat up. The dream was over; the strange moonlit vista disappeared into the familiar sight of her studio, drafting table, bookshelves.

Only the noise remained, louder than it had been just moments ago.

"*Another* party?" muttered Patience, and said a very bad word. She grabbed the clock on her nightstand, stared at it blearily, dropped it and glared at her apartment door.

"I. Don't. Think so," she said through gritted teeth. She stumbled from bed, yanked on her bathrobe, then went out into the hall and knocked loudly on her neighbor's door.

Seconds later it was flung open. There stood her neighbor, his long hair pulled back with a leather headband, his tattooed, shaved chest exposed above a wide leather belt and some sort of leather-and-silver kilt. Patience blinked, then looked beyond him to see other people dressed just as outlandishly.

A costume party. Her neighbor's attire was obviously an attempt—a lame one—at dressing like a Greek hero.

"Look," she said, forcing a smile. "Could you please turn it—"

"Undress, dress up, or piss off," he snapped, and slammed the door in her face.

Patience stood frozen in disbelief. Then, slowly, disbelief turned to cold fury. She dragged her fingers down the door's surface, her nails like claws digging into the wood. She let out a long, low hiss.

Then, suddenly, she smiled, a wicked, knowing smile, and quickly returned to her own apartment.

Dress up or piss off, she thought with quiet glee. *Well, what if I get dressed up and pissed off?*

She began going through her closet. Slowly at first, then with growing impatience, she pulled out one outfit after another and threw each on the floor.

"'Dress for success,'" she said disdainfully, as she surveyed the heap of sensible yet elegant, yet utterly uninteresting blouses and trousers and skirts before her. "Tried that. Didn't work. Now, how about this—dressing for *excess*?"

She stood on tiptoe and reached for the closet's top shelf. A large, shiny, white gift box was there, its resplendent red ribbon still in place. A card dangled from the ribbon, covered with large, loopy letters.

Open in case of dating emergency! Love, Lance and Sally

Patience yanked the lid off the box. Inside, nestled in red tissue paper, was the black leather outfit and gloves her friends had given her for her birthday the year before. She'd seen it, of course, but she'd never worn it. The price tag still hung from one sleeve—"In case it's not the right size," Sally had said; "In case it's not the right color; like, maybe you want scream- ing scarlet?" Lance had added helpfully.

Now Patience held up the tight leather jacket. She grabbed the price tag with her teeth and, with a small sound that was almost a snarl, ripped it off. She tore off her nightclothes with the same vicious glee, then pulled on the leather pants. The supple material was snug and surprisingly warm; like slipping into fur. She put on the jacket next, sleek and body-hugging as the pants were; last of all a pair of high, open-toed black leather boots. She spun on her heels and stared at herself in the full-length mirror.

"Oooh. *Pretty*," she cooed, then bared her teeth. "But not enough of a fashion statement . . ."

She stalked across the apartment to her drafting table and grabbed a pair of scissors, a box of soft pastels, and two jars of pigment. Then she strode into the bathroom.

Snip, snip! Patience chanted wordlessly as the scissors sheared away her long curls. She kept at it until she liked what she saw in the mirror: a sleek hel- met, cut close to her skull. She opened one of the jars of pigment and dug her fingers into it, carefully worked the color through her hair, streaking and spiking it a deep, rich red, the color of claret. She wiped her hands on her arms, leaving reddish tiger stripes, then reached for the box of pastels. The sticks were soft and friable, soft black, ultramarine blue, saffron yellow.

Patience leaned forward until her face nearly touched the mirror. With her sure, practiced, artist's hand, she began carefully but quickly to draw a long, black line above first one eye and then the other. She drew back a little, squinting in approval, then drew a second line above the first in ultramarine, arching up past her eyebrow. Then she drew another line beneath each eye, finishing with a black dot at the outer corner, and dabbing a bit of saffron yellow in the center of each dot. When she was finished, she took a step back and surveyed her work with approval.

"Patience Phillips, Queen of Denial," she said, grinning, "meet the new you, the Queen of the Nile."

The exaggerated Egyptian makeup didn't mask her beauty; it enhanced it. Almost as an afterthought, she dabbed one finger in the jar of carmine pigment, then touched it to her lips. The pigment was cold and stung slightly, but she liked that.

A *little bit of pain is good*, she thought. *Makes you feel like you're alive, not half-asleep. And now . . .*

Her wicked grin widened as she whirled, stiletto heels clicking loudly as she strode toward the window of her apartment.

Now it's time to give my neighbor a little wake-up call!

She flung the window open and stepped fearlessly

out onto the sill. She bent into a half-crouch, hands splayed at her sides, then made a spectacular leap across the alley to land upon her neighbor's window-sill. In one fluid motion, she grabbed the window and pulled it open, then leaped feetfirst into the middle of the revelry.

"Holy—!" someone yelped as Patience hit the floor and immediately straightened, glaring at the partyers.

"Batman," she snapped. "I'm Batman. Oh, never mind."

She sniffed at them disdainfully as she strode through the room. People gaped. She was an extra-ordinary figure—her tight leather outfit an unnatural extension of her skin, her spiked hair and Pharonic makeup giving her a striking, even sinister, mien.

She waltzed into the next room, her nose wrinkling at the stench of cigarette and marijuana smoke, and scowled at the deafening thunder of heavy metal blaring from the speakers. A small crowd sprawled across the low-slung furniture, young men and younger women scantily dressed in glittery costumes—biker chicks, ersatz big-haired rock musicians, toga-clad frat boys, girls in fishnet stockings and feeble efforts at sultriness. Patience gave them all the once-over twice, and began to strut casually around the room, knocking things off tables and flicking at lit cigarettes and drinks with a crimson-nailed finger.

She hesitated in front of a flickering candelabra, leaning forward as though to blow out the candles. Instead she gave it a playful swat that sent it toppling onto a floor pillow.

"Look at the pretty yellow flower!" Patience exclaimed, dancing backward to avoid the flames. Shocked partygoers swore and stamped out the fire, but Patience had already turned her attention elsewhere.

"Didn't your mother ever tell you no black leather after Labor Day?" she said to a guy dressed as a heavy-metal drummer. Daintily, she reached for the pair of studded leather gloves draped over his belt. The drummer watched in numb disbelief as she took the gloves, snapped them in his face, then pulled them on. She flexed her fingers approvingly, leaned forward to run her leather-clad fingers across his face, then walked them down his chest to where his belly protruded slightly over a wide, big-buckled belt.

"Love the paunch, sweetie," she purred in a sultry voice. "Give me a man with meat on his bones . . ."

Abruptly she turned from him, her lip curling in disdain. She stretched out her arms, admiring the addition of the sleek leather gloves. Ignoring the stares of onlookers—outraged, curious, aroused, amused—Patience slowly turned. She gazed measuringly at one of the stereo speakers.

Then, so quickly that afterward some of the observers weren't sure they'd actually witnessed it, her fist shot out and smashed into the speaker.

The music grew very slightly less deafening. Patience wrinkled her nose.

"Still too loud," she said.

She glided over to a table covered with the party's detritus. Beer bottles, wine bottles, empty liters and half gallons of cheap whiskey, Scotch, vodka, gin.

Fastidiously, as though plucking a blossom, she lifted a whiskey bottle and sniffed it.

"Ugh," she said, grimacing. She glanced at a wide-eyed woman costumed as a flapper. "You should save this kind of stuff for stripping paint, darling."

Patience stepped past the woman to where the CD player was surrounded by stacks of disks. She held the whiskey bottle above the stereo and poured its contents over the controls. There was a faint hiss, followed by static and the sound of frying circuitry. The music began to distort.

"Uh, that doesn't sound so good," someone announced drunkenly.

"I'm surprised you can tell the difference," said Patience, and gave him a suggestive smile. "I think it's a real improvement."

With an explosive roar the stereo burst into flame. Sparks cascaded everywhere as party guests shrieked and retreated to the room's corners. A cloud of foul black smoke rose from the stereo. The smell of singed circuitry and burned wire filled the air.

"What the hell—" Patience's enraged neighbor staggered into the room, pushing his guests aside. When he saw Patience, he drew up in a cold fury. "*You*?"

Patience arched her back and looked at him coyly. "Me—*ow*."

He stared at her in disbelief. When he could finally tear his gaze away, he began to turn, taking in the chaos of the apartment around him.

"Jesus! Are you out of your *mind*?"

Patience assumed a thoughtful pose. She cocked her head, considering his question, then without warning grabbed him by the belt and jerked him toward her. Her lips almost brushed his as her piercing gaze held his.

Then she shoved him backward. With a muffled shout he crashed onto the bottle-covered table. Glass and liquid flew everywhere as the table collapsed beneath him. Patience stepped over the mess, leaned down, and hissed into his ear.

"*Yes.*"

She straightened, held out her gloved hands again, admiring them. Her brow creased as she made a little moue of concern.

"Time to accessorize." Her eyes narrowed as she surveyed the stunned revelers. "Anyone going my way?"

Several mesmerized young men began to step forward to volunteer. Before they could, Patience's attention was diverted. In one corner of the room a set of steps led down to a small open space that adjoined a garage door. Something gleamed down there, black and chrome; she sniffed, and scented well-oiled leather. Pushing aside her volunteers, Patience ran to the steps and stared down.

"Never mind," she announced. "I found my ride."

She vaulted down the stairs, pausing for an instant to admire her neighbor's motorcycle. She ran her gloved hand over the leather seat, stroked the engine case, then in one smooth motion swung herself behind the controls.

"Hey!" shouted her neighbor. "That's my—"

Patience kick-started the engine. As it roared to life, she leaned forward and punched the button that raised the garage door. With a blast of exhaust and the screech of burning rubber, she lifted a hand in farewell and thundered out onto the street.

"Now, *why* exactly haven't I borrowed someone's motorcycle before now?" Patience asked herself as the bike rocketed down the block and onto the city's main drag. She wove crazily in and out of traffic, testing her skills. "I was *born* for this!"

She laughed exultantly, eyes shining as she observed the alarmed looks she got from other late-night drivers. She raced down the main street, yanked the bike into a sharp turn, and tore down a narrower side street. Like an arrow, the motorcycle shot toward the spot where she and Sally had paused that morning. Patience's grin widened as the bike skidded to a stop, sending clouds of dust and gravel into the air. One stiletto-heeled boot knocked the kickstand into place as she swung herself onto the sidewalk.

"Diamonds are a cat's best friend," she sang sotto voce. She stood in front of the jewelry store, hands on hips, surveying the window display, then cocked her head.

Inside the store a flash of light appeared, shone momentarily, then went out. Seconds later, the sound of breaking glass made Patience frown.

"Hey, no fair—that was *my* idea."

Stealthily she slipped into the alley beside the store. At the back, hidden between two Dumpsters, she found a rope ladder. She shimmied up it expertly until she reached the roof, then stepped silently toward a skylight. A jagged opening showed where and how the thieves had broken in. Beside it, the snipped line of a security alarm dangled in the empty air.

"Amateurs," Patience sniffed. She flicked dismissively at the alarm wire, then swung down through the skylight.

The store was dimly lit by rows of fairy lights strung between glass display cases. A man wearing a hooded mask was working his way methodically among these, breaking the front of each case with a sharp tap of his handgun. A second man worked behind him, snatching up necklaces, bracelets, rings, and earrings with a gloved hand, and shoving them into a black cloth bag. In the back of the store, a third man knelt before a locked steel case of drawers. The brilliant blue gleam of a blowtorch showed where his hand moved back and forth across the steel. At his side, tools spilled from a canvas sack.

Messy, messy, thought Patience. Her face crinkled in distaste. *Sloppy, and careless, too! Standards at Burglar School have gone right down the tubes. . . .*

Ghostlike, she stepped behind the man crouched before the steel cabinet. A warm breath stirred in his ear.

"Huh?"

Startled, he turned.

There was no one there.

In front of a glass vitrine, the second thief continued to stuff his bag with goodies. Unseen, a black-gloved hand snaked across the floor. Leather-clad fingers lightly grasped the black bag. With a soft, slithering sound, the bag slid across the floor and disappeared. The burglar hesitated. He glanced over his shoulder, but saw nothing but his comrade continuing to work on the steel cabinet.

Meanwhile, at the front of the store, the remaining thief busied himself with emptying another display case. A slender, shadowy figure stood behind him, like a black moth drawn to the glittering jewels at his feet. The black cloth bag now covered her face, with two small slits where she had torn the fabric to see through. The man remained oblivious, grunting to himself as he held up a rope of pearls, then shoved it into his pocket.

"*So* unprofessional," breathed Catwoman.

The man froze. He held his breath, but hearing nothing, lowered his head once more. Catwoman moved with him, her sinuous grace mocking his clumsy motions. She was close enough to be his own smaller shadow, separated by a scant inch of empty air. But every time he paused, imagining he heard something, she would freeze, a smile playing across her face beneath the mask.

"Idiot," she whispered, and this time he *did* hear. "Look behind you . . ."

With a gasp he whirled, gun leveled in an unsteady hand.

But Catwoman had already disappeared.

Quickly the thief turned back to the case. His hand shot inside, then drew back. From his fingers dangled the diamond claw necklace. He stared at it, gloating, then looked around to make sure no one else witnessed his triumph. When he looked back at his upraised hand the necklace was gone.

"What the—?"

Dumbfounded, he stared across the room, to

where the second thief was climbing the stairs. A shadowy feline figure appeared at his side. Around her neck glowed the diamond claw necklace. She smiled at the first man, lifting her hand in a coy little wave.

"You!" he exploded. He drew his gun and took aim at her.

"What the hell are you doing?" shouted the man standing alone on the steps. Catwoman was nowhere to be seen. He glared at the other thief, then drew *his* gun. Behind him someone began walking down the staircase.

"There's somebody here—" the third thief hissed.

"*What*?" the others demanded in unison.

"You boys need to learn some manners," a woman's voice called down from the mezzanine. The three burglars craned their necks, straining to make out the slim form perched, catlike, on the railing. "You think you can just barge in here and take all these beautiful things that don't belong to you?"

The three men raised their weapons. Catwoman stretched calmly, then pointed at them with her gloved hand. "Why, what a *purrfect* idea."

A volley of gunshots. Plaster sprayed down from the ceiling, and broken glass. With a single leap, Catwoman vaulted from the mezzanine. The burglars fired after her fleeing form, but she was too quick. More glass rained down on them as the sound of gunfire echoed off into silence.

"What the hell was *that*?" one of the men shouted.

"Watch your language!" sang out Catwoman as she leaped forward, kicking him in the head. "Do you kiss your mother with that mouth?"

The man went flying into the second thief, and the two crashed onto the floor. Catwoman scampered up a post, leaping from there to the top of a display case. One of the thieves raced after her, gun raised, trying to get a bead on her. She jumped onto another display case as he fired the handgun again, then lunged, lightning-fast, past the bullet.

"Safety is our Number One Concern," she purred, crouched atop a vitrine. Without looking, she reached for the wall behind her, grabbed a string of fairy lights, and yanked it from the molding. She leaped from the display case, somersaulting as she cracked the lights like a whip. "My safety, that is, not yours—"

The string of lights slashed at the first gunman's face. Like a string of firecrackers, each bulb exploded, sending showers of sparks into the air. The thief yelped, struggling to shield his eyes as Catwoman drop-kicked him. His gun went flying as he hit the floor with a thud.

"Now let's see what's behind Door Number Two," she cried, turning to face the second man. He lunged for her, groaning as she kicked his legs out from under him. With a hiss of pleasure, Catwoman did a flip, delivering another kick to his head. As he struggled to crawl away, she pounced on him, hands poised to claw at his face; then she looked up.

"Oh, so you want to play with kitty, too?" she sneered, as the third thief loomed above her. She did another backflip, kicking him in the chest so that he groaned and crashed down beside his comrades. His gun went flying from his hand, sliding across the floor until it came to rest beside the first man. He blinked, then woozily started to get up.

Patience watched him, shaking her head; then dove between his legs, grabbing the gun and jumping to her feet before he could register her presence. With a calm smile, she coldcocked him.

"Are you a man or a mouse?" she asked, then watched him topple to the floor with the others. She swept up the fallen jewels, depositing them into one of the back swag bags, then started out the back door.

But before she disappeared she paused to look back into the room at the unconscious thieves. A smile played across her face as she answered her own question with a derisive hiss.

"*Mice,*" she said, and melted into the shadows.

ELEVEN

Early the next morning, the bad karma fairies were hard at work in the Hedare Building. Laurel Hedare stepped crisply out of the elevator from the parking garage, her pale gray linen suit already wilting from the humidity outside. What greeted her in the lobby did nothing to lower her temperature.

Everywhere workmen were clambering up and down banks of scaffolding, busily changing the signs suspended from the walls and ceiling. Only hours before, Laurel's refined image had gazed coolly from medallions and billboards.

Now Laurel's profile was gone. In its place, Drina's Medusa curls snaked across every placard, and Drina's sultry eyes gazed down upon the people hurrying across the lobby to their offices.

Laurel stopped dead in her tracks. She stared up at the new graphics, her face impassive. When her husband crept up behind her and gently touched her shoulder, she didn't so much as flinch.

"Don't be sad, darling," he said, his voice low and teasing. "No one can defeat Father Time."

He turned her toward him and ran a finger over the skin beneath her eyes. This time she did flinch, as George conceded, "Though you did put up a hell of a fight. Beau-line works wonders, doesn't it?"

Laurel stared at him. Finally she said, "Yes, it does."

George gave her a mirthless smile. "I have a busy day ahead of me. And tonight drinks, then dinner. Don't wait up."

"Oh, don't worry—I stopped waiting a long time ago, George," Laurel responded in silky tones.

George ignored the barb. Still smiling, he turned to leave, then stopped. Irritation creased his face as he added, "Oh—and lunch tomorrow? Cancel it, too."

Laurel raised one perfect blond eyebrow. "Problems?"

"I doubt it. But Slavicky won't stop calling. These scientists are worse than models. You have to coddle them like children. I'll have Wesley reschedule."

Laurel nodded, distracted, as her husband walked away. Only when she looked up did her expression harden, as she stared at the plasma screens and watched as, one by one, her face winked out from each of them, to be replaced by Drina's simpering features.

Another image filled Patience's dreaming mind, that of a calmly smiling, cat-headed woman sheathed in a robe like a column of silk. The cat's elliptical pupils flared black-green against emerald irises, as the woman lifted a hand that suddenly struck out at Patience, gold-tipped claws tearing at her breast. With a cry, Patience started to wakefulness.

She blinked, surprised to find herself lying at the foot of her bed. With a groan, she turned and pulled something from the jacket she still wore—the long metal spine of a brooch that had pierced the leather to prick her bare skin beneath. She stared at it, bemused, then quickly sat up.

The floor around her shone and glittered and gleamed as though it were aflame. But there was no blaze there save the blaze of jewels winking in the morning sunlight. Emeralds, pearls, lapis beads and tourmaline, rubies and yellow topaz and diamonds. Feeling as though she were still dreaming, she picked up a diamond ring and absently put it on her left hand, shook her head, and put it on the other hand.

"Better on the right," she murmured.

Suddenly her eyes widened. She stared at the ring, then at the jewels everywhere around her.

"I'm *not* dreaming," she said.

Horrified, she yanked off the jersey mask that still covered her face and threw it across the room. In a panic she scrambled to her feet and began grabbing jewels, stuffing them into a paper bag.

Last of all, she found the diamond-claw necklace, lying atop her bureau. She picked it up and held it above the bag's mouth, the claws turning slowly and giving off lambent sparks. For a long minute Patience stared at it, biting her lip. Then she opened her hands and let it fall.

Only at the last second did she move the bag aside, so that the necklace dropped silently into the bureau's half-opened top drawer. Patience's expression grew pained. She hesitated, clutching the bag in one hand; with the other slammed the drawer tight.

* * *

"Now this, this was a *very* nice piece . . ."

The proprietor of Marsden's Jewelry Store sat at a long table, ruefully flipping through a book of photographs—his shop's entire inventory, carefully filed for insurance purposes. His finger stabbed at a picture of an emerald-studded onyx brooch. The brooch was shaped like a leaping panther; the emeralds formed its spots, scientifically inaccurate but a striking example of Mr. Marsden's taste for the exotic. "And this, this is another nice piece, also gone. One of a kind, from Egypt. Lucky I got insurance."

He looked up at the sound of a tinkle from the front door. "Closed!" he shouted, as the door softly closed again. With a sigh, Mr. Marsden turned back to his inventory.

"Now, this is weird," remarked one of the forensics technicians from a corner of the room. She was dusting boot prints, but looked up when Tom Lone approached her, frowning.

"What?" he asked.

"These boot prints." She settled back on her heels and pointed her brush at the floor. "See here? The front of the sole is missing, so the toes stick out. Like paws. Paws in stiletto heels."

Tom stooped, peering at the bootprints. He shook his head and glanced at a scrawled page in his notebook.

"So . . . an unarmed female, working alone, takes out three armed pros, then walks away with the jewels. In Manolo Blahnik footwear. This is a hell of a profile."

"My kind of girl," remarked one of the cops as he walked by.

"My kind of detective," the forensics tech said with an admiring glance at Tom Lone. "I appreciate a guy with a working knowledge of women's fashion."

Tom shrugged. "What can I say? I'm a man of varied interests."

He looked at the bootprints again, brow furrowed. "She wears freaky makeup, and some kind of leather suit . . . she has *paws*, she calls the perps 'mice' while she beats them senseless . . . and she purrs."

The forensic tech frowned. "She *purred*?"

"That's what the perps said." Tom straightened and looked around the room. "Anybody else want to take this one?"

"Hell, no!" chorused the other cops.

"Rhetorical question," muttered Tom, and sighed.

"Yo, Tom. Check this out."

He turned and crossed to where the cop stood by the front entrance. He wore latex gloves, and pointed at something lying just inside the door: a white box with a brown paper bag atop it. A single word was scrawled across the bag.

SORRY.

Gingerly, he picked up the bag and opened it. Mr. Marsden peered over his shoulder and let out a gasp.

"My jewels!"

Tom shoved past him, throwing the door open and stepping outside. The sidewalk was empty. He looked one way, then the other.

Nothing.

Angrily, he strode back into the store. "Did anyone see anything?"

The assembled cops shook their heads. Mr. Marsden beamed.

"No, but look—they're all there. I think so, anyway. And see . . ."

He pointed to where the cop was carefully lifting the box's lid with a pen.

Lone stared at him, waiting. The cop frowned, then looked up at Tom with a bemused expression.

"Well, what is it?" Tom demanded impatiently.

The cop tipped the box toward him so that Tom and the others could see its contents.

"Cupcakes."

TWELVE

I would like to be there, were it but to see how the cat jumps.
—Sir Walter Scott, *Journal*, 7 October 1826

Patience ran the last few blocks to Ophelia Powers's house, heedless of the odd looks she got from passersby. She bounded up the porch steps and began battering frantically at the door. When it finally swung open, she stared at the woman inside with pleading eyes, breathless and unable to speak. Ophelia stared back, and after a moment, nodded and motioned for the distraught young woman to enter.

But once inside, all Patience's restraint fell away. She began to talk compulsively, sharing every detail of her last twenty-four hours with the surprised (but not *that* surprised) Ophelia.

"Please. You have to help me. I don't understand what's happening to me!"

Ophelia listened, fascinated, as Patience spoke. And watched, even more fascinated, as Patience restlessly *stalked*—jumping from coffee table to couch to windowsill, completely unconscious of her bizarre behavior. The cats watched too, unblinking and wide-eyed, occasionally swatting at the young woman's ankles as she leaped lightly past curious tabbies and kittens.

"I don't even know why I did it—really, you have to believe me—but I took them back."

She paused and shot Ophelia an anxious look. "I swear I did."

Ophelia stared with penetrating blue eyes. Patience faltered, blushing, and added, "Well, mostly."

"I''m sure they appreciate that," Ophelia said in a tart voice. "Mostly."

"Please." Patience crouched at Ophelia's feet, pleading, then hopped onto the coffee table. "What's *wrong* with me?"

Ophelia looked absently at the cat purring in her lap. As though she hadn't heard Patience's question, she remarked, "Did you know that a cat cannot see what is directly under its nose? No, it's true. They have tremendous eyesight, but if something is right under their nose, they don't even know it's there."

Patience said nothing. Ophelia glanced at her, nodding. "That's my favorite table."

For the first time, Patience realized she was standing on top of a coffee table. Mortified, she stepped down, smoothing her hands against her sides. Ophelia gave her a sharp sideways look, then seemed to decide on taking another tack.

"Do you like books, Miss Phillips?"

Without waiting for an answer, she stood and walked out of the room. Patience followed, her gaze still pleading. They walked down a long, book-lined corridor that opened onto a larger, book-lined room, two stories high, a sort of literary atrium with a balcony running along its upper level. Ophelia indicated a spiral staircase leading to the second level. She began to climb, Patience at her heels.

"This is where I keep my research books," the older woman explained as they reached the upper level. Patience looked around, impressed.

There were certainly many books here, but there were even more artifacts, plunder from a lifetime of travel and collecting and research. Painted leather shadow puppets, carven Garudas, bronze Buddhas and silver Hindu deities; silk kites shaped like butterflies and dragonflies and phoenixes; Bunraku figures and Tibetan prayer flags and Oaxacan skulls of plaster and human hair.

And masks. Patience had never seen so many masks. Leering Ojibwa masks of carved wood, Balinese demons, Kabuki lions; featureless, rather sinister faces of molded leather the color of mahogany. Patience stood staring, her anger momentarily replaced by amazement.

Ophelia walked briskly to a library table that overlooked the floor below. On the table was a stack of volumes—a few crumbling leather folios, a few moldering old books from the nineteenth century, the rest more recent publications with dust jackets glossy and iridescent as beetle wings.

It was one of the latter that Ophelia picked up now, holding it so that Patience could read its spine. *Bast*, by Ophelia Powers.

"The goddess Bast," said Ophelia.

"You wrote this?" asked Patience.

"I was a professor for twenty years, until I was denied tenure. Male academia . . ."

Carefully Ophelia set the book upon the table and

opened it, gesturing for Patience to join her. "There's something here I'd like you to see."

Ophelia pointed to the frontispiece, a color photograph of a restored Egyptian temple. Bas-reliefs carved in sandstone, life-sized faience paintings propped against the walls; a few small, mummified forms wrapped in linen and reeds.

And, in the center of the room, a huge golden statue of a woman with a cat's head, emerald lozenges for eyes, her arms upheld in a welcoming pose.

"Bast is the daughter of the Egyptian sun god, Ra," Ophelia began in a low voice.

As she spoke, the Mau, Midnight, jumped onto the library table to stare with implacable green-gold eyes at the feline goddess's graven image. When the living cat turned its head to stare at Patience, the young woman's eyes widened.

Midnight looked just like the cat in the temple.

"The Maus are sent by Bast," Ophelia said. "They are her messengers."

Patience swallowed nervously, then looked at Ophelia once more.

"Bast is a rarity. A goddess of both the moon and the sun. She represents the duality in all women," Ophelia went on. "Docile, yet aggressive. Nurturing, yet ferocious."

Patience shook her head. Her mouth tightened, as she reached past Midnight to grab the book's cover and close it.

"So, what . . . what does she have to do with me?"

Ophelia gazed at her, seemingly unconcerned by Patience's rudeness. "Western culture has never truly accepted female empowerment," she said, as though the younger woman hadn't said a word. "The powerful woman threatens the patriarchy. She is self-possessed; she holds the secrets of birth and death within her. She can give birth to entire nations, with but a single man as father. She can hide her children's paternity as she hides her own wisdom, allowing her mate to believe he alone holds the powers of procreation and survival, creativity and inspiration.

"But his power is an illusion. It was hence, and it is now. That is why the patriarchy rages and makes war, not just upon other men, but upon our kind as well. That's why they threw down her temples and destroyed her cities. That's why they burned her at the stake.

"And that is why they denied her tenure—though I guess I got off easy, huh?"

Ophelia's gaze flickered. She allowed herself a small, self-mocking smile.

But the smile was lost on Patience. She took a step toward the older woman, almost threatening, her voice desperate. "Ophelia . . . *please* . . ."

Ophelia shook her head. She pointed at the book. "Docile, yet aggressive. Nurturing, yet ferocious. These dualities form the very nature of Bast—as they do of all women."

Patience pushed at her in frustration. "Stop it, stop it! This is all bullshit! I want to know what happened to *me*!"

Ophelia stared at her unblinkingly. "The priestesses of Bast were murdered."

"I don't have anything to do with that."

"Yes, Patience," whispered Ophelia. "You do. Patience, the priestesses were *murdered.*"

By now, Patience had backed Ophelia against the balcony railing.

"I don't *care!*" shouted Patience. Her voice rose to a howl of frustration and rage. Ophelia stared at her, her own expression unreadable, then she slid from the younger woman's grasp. With surprising agility, Ophelia grabbed Patience's arms and spun her around, pinning her to the rail.

"How can you *not* care?" she cried. "Don't you see? Don't you *understand*? T*hey died.*"

For the first time, Patience seemed to hear the other woman. She blinked, shaking her head as though awakening from a bad dream. "Died . . . ?"

Ophelia looked keenly at her. "What happened the other night?"

Patience tensed. "I don't remember."

"Do you want me to tell you?"

Patience said nothing. Finally, in a frightened voice, she replied.

"Yes."

"You died."

"What?" Patience shook her head furiously. "I didn't die! I'm right here! You're . . . you're crazy, you're a crazy cat lady!"

And then it was as though she was plunged into nightmare again. Her nostrils filled with frigid water, her arms flailed helplessly against black rapids and knife-edged rock.

"You *died.*" Ophelia's voice echoed dimly through a whirlpool's roar and the sound of Patience coughing and gasping for breath. "You died, but you were reborn. Resurrected."

Patience drew a shaking hand to her face, struggling against the undertow of that terrifying memory. "No! You're out of your—"

"By the goddess! By her messenger—by the Mau!"

Patience's body went limp. Dread and horror clawed at her, the slow realization that this was real—that *all of it* was real. The drowning, the black vortex that had been her own death, the sound of gunshots and the thick choking taste of her own blood mingling with river mud and icy water in her windpipe . . .

And not only that, but what came after: a numb memory of small, soft faces and glittering eyes, the moon spinning overhead and the touch of a small rough tongue upon her face, her lips, her eyes. Her terror as she fled across the marshland and escaped the snarling junkyard dogs; her exhilaration as she stalked into a room full of strangers at a party, a room full of jewels and more strangers—and she laughed at them, too. As though they were less than she was, less than human—animals, prey. M*ice.*

She turned her head. Perched on the balcony rail was Midnight. The Mau's eyes gazed into hers, wise and cold yet welcoming.

Yes, that gaze said, as clearly as if the cat had hissed the word aloud. *Resurrection.*

That was when Ophelia took a deep breath and, with all her strength, shoved Patience off the balcony.

In midair Patience screamed. And twisted, her body sinuous as a ribbon uncoiling. When her feet struck the floor she fell into a crouch, her scream deepening to an outraged, inhuman snarl, her fingers splayed like claws as she stared at Ophelia standing on the balcony above her.

Ophelia shouted, "Midnight saved you."

All that mindless, instinctive fury suddenly drained from Patience Phillips. Her body grew limp; she leaned back, still on her hands and knees, stunned.

"But you are not alone, child. They've saved others before you. Look," urged Ophelia. "On that table, beside you."

Patience struggled to her feet and crossed to the table. It was covered with pictures. Some were drawn on old parchment; others were old mimeographs or Xeroxes, others clipped from newspapers or magazines. There were a few black-and-white or color photos strewn among the rest. Patience began to look at them, dully at first, then with growing fear.

"They are all examples of *feligyny*," Ophelia called down in a low voice. "*Feles*, the Latin for cat; *gyn* from the Greek for woman. A hybrid word; as you are now a hybrid being."

Faster and faster Patience flipped through the pictures. A Japanese woodcut of a naked woman with elongated eyes and ears, her mouth opened in a snarl; a drawing done in sumi ink of another woman slinking through a forest of bamboo trees. Curatorial photographs from a museum collection of cat masks; a Betty Page–style pinup from the 1950s; a blurred surveillance shot of a woman perched calmly upon a high-rise, the crescent moon behind her like a silver diadem.

"You are a *catwoman*, Patience," Ophelia went on in a low, commanding, voice. "But you are not the first. The phenomenon goes back centuries; millennia."

Patience stared horrified at a sepia image of an Egyptian sarcophagus, its face that of a sleeping feline. "You're saying that . . . that I died and . . . turned into . . ."

Her voice broke. "Oh God. You're saying I've lost my *mind* . . ."

"You've lost *nothing*!" cried Ophelia. "A fractured, fragmented, insecure young woman died—yes, that's true! But look what has been returned whole!"

"But . . . but what do I do now? If I'm not Patience anymore . . ."

Patience grew very still. She looked at the picture in her hand, then at the woman on the balcony above. Ophelia began to walk quickly along the railing, her voice rising, fervent.

"Patience—there is no longer any separation between the truth of *who* you are and the truth of *what* you are. You are just discovering this truth. Now you must embrace it."

Patience's face was tilted toward Ophelia, but the catwoman's eyes were unseeing; tranquil.

"I died," she said softly. "I was reborn. . . ."

She looked down at herself, slowly, as though she had never gazed upon her own body before. She clenched her fingers, then relaxed them; stretched her arms and rolled them back and forth, her body supple, fluid . . .

Feline.

"Every sight, every smell," crooned Ophelia, as

though reciting an incantation. Her face radiated a joy that Patience could suddenly begin to feel herself. "Every sound—all are now incredibly heightened. Fierce independence. Total confidence. Inhuman reflexes—you feel like you can do anything, Patience . . ."

As she spoke, Patience crouched, then leaped toward the balcony. She grabbed the railing and swung herself over, as easily as though she'd stepped off of a curb. She began to laugh.

". . . and you *can*," Ophelia finished triumphantly.

Patience stood, flexing her arms. She went into another half-crouch, then sprang forward. Her leap took her high into the air, her feet grazing the vaulted ceiling as she spun, then landed, impossibly far from where she had started, at the other end of the room. She bounced up and down on the balls of her feet, not even winded; looked down and saw a small dark form leaping to join her.

Midnight.

Patience smiled and leaped again. The Mau followed her, and the two began a feline ballet, leaping from table to chair to balcony, bounding to touch the ceiling, then spinning in midair to barely touch ground before springing off once more. The Mau made one final, gravity-defying jump from the balcony rail to the top of a glass-fronted cabinet. Here the cat paused, turning to cast her green-gold gaze upon Patience where she still stood on the floor.

"What do I do now? I'm not Patience anym—," she started to ask.

"You *are* Patience," said Ophelia Powers. She crossed to where the young woman stood and looked up at the wall beside the Mau. A dramatic reproduction of an Aztec mask hung there, supple leather shaped into a stark, Symbolist version of a jaguar's skull. "And you are Catwoman. Duality personified."

Ophelia reached for the mask and took it from the wall, then turned and held it out to Patience. "*Accept it, child. You've spent a lifetime being caged. In accepting who you are, you can finally be free.*"

Patience stared at her. Then she took the mask.

"Thank you," she said. She looked up to where the cat sat watching the two women from atop the cabinet. "And Midnight—thank you, too."

And Catwoman sprang to an open window, crouched, and leaped down to the street two stories below.

THIRTEEN

> *The cat in gloves catches no mice.*
> —BENJAMIN FRANKLIN, *Poor Richard's Almanac*

"Well," Patience said to herself with grim delight. "There certainly *is* more than one way to skin a cat. . . ."

She was back in her studio apartment. In front of her, the drafting table was littered with torn scraps and curling fragments of leather. She picked up the scissors and made another adjustment to the leather mask she'd liberated from Ophelia's collection.

"I hope you don't mind, Bast or whatever your name is," she said, lifting the mask to peer through the two slashes she'd made for eyeholes. "But I need something that looks a little more modern. And a name that's a little easier to pronounce . . . like, say—*Catwoman*."

Her lip curled. Her hand closed around the diamond-tipped claw necklace. She drew it toward her face, regarded it appraisingly before suddenly, violently giving a snarl and ripping it apart. Claws went flying across the drafting table. Catwoman looked at them coldly, then quickly gathered them. One by one, she slashed each diamond-tipped claw through a finger of her leather gloves, until she had ten lethal, shining talons. She turned her hands this way and that, admiring the effect, then shoved her chair away from the desk, exposing her legs in her skintight leather pants. Swift as a striking cobra, her hand tore at the leather. Catwoman hissed, the sound somewhere between pain and pleasure, and when she was finished raised her hands, curling her fingers in delight.

Tiny droplets of blood clung to the tip of each diamond talon. Blood threaded its way across arabesques of skin exposed where she had ripped away the leather. She stood, stretching her legs to admire the interplay of black leather against warm flesh. The pattern resembled the Mau's jagged tiger stripes.

She'd made a few other improvements to her wardrobe as well. The leather jacket was now a halter. Its sleeves now served as gauntlets covering her forearms. She'd found two belts she'd never had much use for; now she wore them across her torso like bandoliers. She ran her gloved, spiked hands across her abdomen, then bent. Her claws tugged at the open fronts of her stiletto boots, tearing them so that her toes could move more freely.

"When the cat's away, the mice will dance," she sang to herself. "Gotta make sure I can keep up with them."

She grabbed the black jersey bag she'd kept the necklace in and tied it around her sleek head in a do-rag, then pulled the modified jaguar mask across her face. Her movement sent something falling from her drafting table and she whirled, hackles raised and claws curled to attack.

But it was only Patience Phillips's design for the Hedare logo, drifting toward the floor. With a vindictive hiss, Catwoman slashed at it in midair. A blizzard of bloodied paper fragments eddied behind her as she strode to her open window and climbed outside. Silently she crouched there, scanning the street below before looking up at the rooftop opposite. With a long, slow smile, Catwoman stretched, then leaped into the night.

Two nights before, it had taken her nearly an hour to reach the Hedare factory. Now, racing along the city's rooftops like a panther, she made the journey in a quarter of that time. She was approaching the industrial waterfront near the plant, when suddenly she stopped.

She was five stories above street level, atop an abandoned factory not yet converted to artist's lofts or dance clubs. In the distance she could see plumes of white smoke rising from the Hedare facility. Her nose wrinkled as she made a low sound of disgust and repressed fury.

But then came that sound again, so faint she had almost forgotten it was what arrested her in the first place: the *flick* of a match striking sandpaper.

Catwoman's head swiveled. Her hooded eyes fixed on something in an alley below. A stretch Hummer, idling in the darkness. As she watched, a figure stepped from the limo. She saw a face momentarily aglow, a spurt of flame beneath his mouth as he held the lit match to a cigarette.

Armando. One of the men who had tried to kill her in the factory.

No! *Scratch that*, Catwoman thought, letting her breath out in a low hiss. The sound of a gunshot echoed through her memory, and water thundering through a spillway. *One of the men who* did *kill me . . .*

Her eyes narrowed. She watched as Armando took a few quick drags on his cigarette, then tossed it into the underbrush. He turned and ducked back into the Hummer. With a low roar, the limo swung back into the dark street and began to make its way toward the waterfront.

Catwoman followed, tracking the Hummer as it wove through a labyrinth of derelict streets and between crumbling buildings. It finally stopped in front of a long, low, windowless warehouse beside the murky river. Incongruously, a line of people stretched in front of the warehouse's single door. A red velvet rope stretched between two brass stanchions, and behind the rope stood a bullnecked man the approximate size of a Home Depot.

"Interesting," murmured Catwoman. She watched as the Hummer came to a stop. Its doors opened and Armando stepped out. Swaggering, he proceeded to the front of the line. The bouncer tugged at the watch cap covering his shaved head and glanced at a clipboard. He nodded, gave Armando a flamboyant bow, then unhooked the velvet rope and let him through. With a nod, Armando walked inside the club.

Catwoman waited until the stretch Humvee lumbered off to join a long line of a dozen other parked limousines. Then she made her way down the side of the building, slinking off to find a way to enter the club unseen.

Minutes later she was inside. The deafening throb of techno surrounded her, the vast, dim space ignited by intermittent lightning as strobes flashed and people screamed in delight from the dance floor. Mirrored balls hung from the ceiling; there were mirrors on the walls, and behind the cages where young men and women writhed in time to the pulsating music. A few people did double takes as Catwoman strutted past them, her face hidden behind its sleek mask.

"Daddy, buy me one of *those*," a young woman whispered into the ear of her older, well-heeled escort.

"Only if she's had all her shots," he replied, staring after the feline woman in a daze. "Here, kitty!" he called drunkenly.

Catwoman froze. Slowly she turned on one stiletto heel, then leaned forward. Her arm extended until one hand cupped the man's chin. Her diamond-tipped claws tightened around his chin, and her forefinger tapped the pallid skin until a fleck of blood welled from it.

"You weren't talking to *me*, were you?" she purred.

The man's terrified eyes bulged as he tried to shake his head. "N-no," he gasped in a muffled voice.

"I didn't think so," Catwoman said silkily. She dropped her hand and blew a kiss to the young woman. "Be careful what you ask for," she said mockingly. "I don't think you're quite ready to upgrade from a housecat to a jaguar."

She spun, and sashayed off into the crowd.

She could have tracked Armando by scent if she'd

wanted to—his aftershave, the reek of tobacco, his acrid sweat, heightened now by the faint musk of excitement aroused by his surroundings.

But Catwoman didn't have to rely on her heightened sense of smell. Instead she simply followed him, a lithe shadowy figure darting between dancers and drunks, nimbly avoiding contact with all of them. When Armando sidled up to a bar, she stood casually, a few feet off, watching as he slid a hundred-dollar bill across the zinc bar surface.

"I've been here all night," said Armando, raising an eyebrow. "Right?"

The bartender took the bill and slipped a beer into Armando's hand. "Absolutely."

"Keep the change," said Armando, and moved off into the crowd. Catwoman watched him go, then slipped up to the bar where he'd stood, swaying slightly to the music. The bartender lifted his head, then blinked.

"Whoa! What can I do for *you*?"

Catwoman tapped her nails on the zinc bar. She cocked her head, seeming to ponder the question, then said, "White Russian, no ice. Hold the vodka and Kahlúa."

The bartender blinked again. Catwoman's piercing green eyes stared at him from behind her mask. He suddenly caught himself and turned, hurrying to fill her order.

At the other end of the bar, a man raised his hand.

"I'm buying," he said, and sidled up alongside Catwoman.

"Suit yourself," she said, without looking at him.

The man continued to stare at Catwoman, even as

his girlfriend materialized behind him, a skinny blonde wielding a martini the color of the sky over the Bikini Atoll.

"Earth to slut," the blonde snapped. She sidled up to Catwoman and lay a proprietary hand on her boyfriend's shoulder. "He's *taken*."

Catwoman didn't look at her, either. "Slut to bimbo—you can have him."

The bartender reappeared, bearing a shot glass brimming with white liquid.

"Cream—straight up," he announced, and set it before her. Catwoman's taloned hand curled around the glass. She raised it to her lips, knocked it back in one long swallow, then dropped the glass back onto the bar. She licked a stray droplet of cream from her upper lip.

The pick-up artist still wasn't giving up.

"Can I help you with that?" he asked. His girlfriend scowled at Catwoman.

"How did trash like you get into a club like this?" she sneered.

Catwoman smirked at her. "One man's trash is another man's treasure."

She turned to look back out over the dance floor. Armando had taken a seat on a private, raised platform that gave him a commanding view of black-haired twins gyrating to the music. As Catwoman started moving toward him, the man at the bar beside her reached after her, his hand deliberately brushing the back of her leather trousers.

"Hey—" he began.

With a hiss, Catwoman whirled, her taloned fingers a scant millimeter from his face.

"Not *for touching*," she snarled.

The man made a strangled sound and fell back against the bar. His girlfriend gave him a cold look.

"She's way outta *your* league," she said disdainfully, and watched with a mixture of begrudging admiration and apprehension as Catwoman stalked off onto the dance floor. "Outta the whole *human* league, maybe . . ."

Catwoman edged between the dancers, her moves somewhere between a slink and a strut. The music seemed to grow louder, more intense, as she reached the center of the floor; her body reacted as well, as almost unaware she began to arch her back and give way to the propulsive beat. Not noticing the looks she got from all the men around her, and a good many of the women; not conscious of her own abandon as she whirled and lunged, her lithe form a black flame barely contained by her leather catsuit.

Because even as she appeared to have given herself over completely to the music, her expression beneath the leather mask was grim, and her eyes remained fixed upon one goal.

Armando.

He sat alone on his viewing platform, his attention wavering between the dancer gyrating a few feet away from him, and the feline woman commanding the floor below. Catwoman slipped in and out of the crowd, blind to the men whose gazes remained riveted upon her. At the bottom of the dance cage she paused, then grasped one of the columns that supported it and clambered up.

"Your dance card full?" she asked slyly.

The dancer froze in mid-gyration. Her outfit was

like a bad imitation of Catwoman's: clunky platform boots, torn fishnet stockings, shiny black bustier supporting pneumatically enhanced breasts, thick makeup that couldn't disguise the dark circles beneath her eyes.

The two women stared at each other appraisingly.

Catwoman lifted her chin. "So where'd you get the costume? Frederick's of Halloween?"

The dancer pursed her lips, striking a defiant pose, but it was useless. She was seriously outclassed, and knew it.

Catwoman shook her head, cocking a thumb at the dancer's outfit. "Leatherette, honey? It just looks so *cheap*. You should always splurge for the real thing"—she ran her hands along her thighs, conscious of Armando's hungry stare—"leather moves when you do; it *breathes* with you. Makes all the difference in the world . . ."

Suddenly she spied a bullwhip coiled around the dancer's belt. Catwoman licked her lips covetously, extended one graceful, diamond-tipped hand toward the dancer.

"Kitty want whip," she purred. "Gimme. *Now.*"

The dancer gasped and stumbled backward as Catwoman snatched the whip from her belt. She ran her hands over it greedily, then cracked it a few times. On the floor below the crowd laughed and applauded, egging her on.

She crouched, then leaped toward the edge of the stage as she sent the whip snaking through the air above her. "Where's Helmut Newton when you need him?"

She grasped the center pole that thrust up through

the stage floor and began to swing around it, using the bullwhip to keep herself anchored. She clambered to the top, pausing to grin down at the ecstatic crowd watching from the dance floor, then began to descend upside down, catlike, the whip trailing behind her. Her gaze, cold and merciless, was fixed on Armando.

Hell hath no fury like a woman drowned, she thought grimly. *Good thing some of us have nine lives. . . .*

Her body tensed. Without warning, she sprang from the pole, landing just a few feet from where Armando stared at her, entranced. Her eyes locked with his. She raised the whip and cracked it again.

Whooosh!

The steel tip missed him by inches. Armando swallowed, still gazing transfixed at the woman before him. She moved invitingly, the warmth of her supple body at odds with the icy resolve of her stare. She drew the whip slowly, enticingly, through her gloved fingers, then with a smile stepped forward and gently looped it around his neck.

"It takes two to tango," she said with a suggestive twitch of the whip. "How 'bout we practice a few steps?"

She stepped backward onto the stage, gently pulling him with her. Armando followed, dazed, not even looking at the envious crowd observing him. Catwoman moved soundlessly across the small raised stage, heading toward a door that opened onto the backstage dressing area. One stiletto heel kicked the door open, and she entered. Armando followed helplessly.

"Something seems a little fishy here, don't you

think?" she said. She began to reel him toward her, looping the whip over her arm. "Mmmm, looks like I hooked a big one. . . ."

His body hovered scarcely an inch from hers. Catwoman stared at him lasciviously. Quicksilver-fast she grabbed him by the collar, turned, and kicked open a door marked EXIT, and shoved him outside. He flew out into the alley, sprawling onto the ground ass-first. Catwoman sprang after him, landing square on his chest.

"Ouch," she said, with pretend concern. Armando's head slammed against the pavement. "That felt *good*. Was it good for you, too?"

Armando shoved her off him, fumbling in his jacket for something. His expression melted from red fury to raw fear.

"Finders keepers," announced Catwoman.

She lifted her arm fastidiously. Two diamond-tipped claws grasped the barrel of a handgun. She let it dangle there for a moment, staring at it in distaste.

"I think it makes me look fat," she said at last, and tossed it into a metal trash bin.

With a muffled shout, Armando lunged after the gun. Catwoman yanked on the whip still looped around his throat, drawing him toward her. Before he could catch his breath she stepped backward, flicking the whip so that he spun from it like a top, slamming into a wall.

"Do you know me?" shouted Catwoman.

Groaning, Armando staggered to his feet again. Catwoman leaped toward him, her high-heeled boot nailing him in the stomach. He toppled facedown onto the gritty pavement. Catwoman jumped onto his back, grabbed him by the hair, and twisted his head so that he was staring at her. A seam of blood trickled down his cheek, but his eyes were hateful and unrepentant.

"*Do you know me*?" she repeated, her voice rising. "Because I *know you*."

"What do you *want*?" Armando grunted angrily.

Catwoman's hold on his hair tightened. Remorselessly, she pounded his face against the pavement, her words coming out in furious gasps.

"The other night you killed somebody."

Slam.

"She was a *good person*. She was a *friend* of mine."

Slam.

"*Why*. Did *you*. Kill *her*?"

Armando shook his head desperately. Catwoman heaved him onto his back, one hand around his throat, the other pinching his tongue between two claws.

"What's the matter?" she hissed. "Cat got your tongue?"

She dragged him to his feet, still holding his tongue. He flailed helplessly, making useless gargling sounds.

"Bet you saw *that* one coming," Catwoman sneered.

With one swift motion she kneed him in the gut, let go of him, and stepped back, watching coolly as he collapsed into a heap. Catwoman stared down at him.

"This'd be a lot more fun if you'd play along," she said, her tone veering between boredom and annoyance. "Now—I'm going to ask you nicely. One . . . more . . . time . . ."

She straddled his chest, her claws poised an inch from his bulging eyes. "And then? I'm going to stop acting like a lady."

"I just do what I'm told!" Armando gasped in a strangled voice.

"Not for much longer, you don't."

The claws moved closer. Armando groaned and shut his eyes.

"I don't even know your friend!" he cried hoarsely. "They just told me to flush the pipes. That's all. I didn't *know*—"

One claw descended to touch his lip, momentarily silencing him. Her green eyes grew wide, almost maddened. When she finally spoke, her voice came out as a prolonged yowl.

"Wh*yyyyy*?"

Armando shuddered at that inhuman cry. "I don't know! Maybe she heard something she wasn't supposed to hear!"

Catwoman's lip curled back in a snarl. "Yes? But *what*?"

"I don't know, I don't know—" Armando took in her crazed look and began to babble helplessly. "Beau-line! There's something wrong with Beau-line!"

Catwoman looked taken aback. For a moment she was silent. She looked back down at Armando.

"And Hedare is covering it up," she said. It was not a question.

Armando nodded frantically. Catwoman gazed at him in repugnance and got to her feet.

"Well, ain't that a kick in the head," she said.

Her boot lashed out, landing in the middle of his forehead. Armando slumped against the pavement, out cold.

Catwoman surveyed him disdainfully. "Men. They always fall asleep at the good part."

She gathered her bullwhip, coiled it around her belt, and left.

FOURTEEN

It took her only minutes to reach the Hedare factory. Rage spurred her, and the knowledge she held now like a weapon.

There's something wrong with Beau-line, Armando had said.

Yeah. Just like there's something wrong with a world that drives women to prize youth and beauty above other things—like a deadly dropkick, Catwoman thought as she made her way along the outside of the plant.

The moon had already set, leaving the clouded sky dark and starless. A few more lights twinkled in the factory windows than had shone there two nights ago, but Catwoman didn't notice. Her mind was elsewhere, brooding on Armando's words; her senses were elsewhere, too, sifting through the night as though it were a deck of cards and she was seeking the ace of spades.

I ran that way, she thought, racing alongside the building without looking overhead. *Then out through there* . . .

She darted across the desolate loading area,

strewn with wooden skids and Dumpsters, flattened cardboard cartons and broken glass. *And came out* . . .

Abruptly she halted.

"Here," she said.

Below her she could see the mouth of the immense outflow pipe. Carefully she climbed down the stony precipice, swinging herself to a small outcropping where she paused before jumping to grab the bottom of the pipe. She swung herself up, as though doing chin-ups, and peered suspiciously inside.

This time there was no raging torrent to carry her away. Instead a thin trickle of brackish-looking water threaded its way down the center of the tunnel. Catwoman sniffed. Her nose wrinkled in distaste. She pulled herself up a little more, and some of the water dribbled onto her face, seeping beneath her mask.

"*Ugh*," she snorted, coughing and spitting as she tried to shake the water from her. She let go of the pipe and scrambled back up to the loading area. "That could strip paint from a wall."

She made her way back toward the factory. She didn't bother with a door. She found a pipe leading to the rooftop and shimmied up it, then ran soundlessly until she found a skylight. She prised it open, slipped inside, and let herself fall.

Bingo!

She was in the R&D wing. She darted down one corridor and then another without hesitation, her feline instincts recalling the route she'd taken the other night as though she'd done it a hundred times. Only when she reached the door to Dr. Slavicky's office did she hesitate.

Something bad happened here, she thought. Her skin

prickled. Dr. Slavicky's words, only half-remembered, rushed through her memory.

It *launches next week . . . there will be no turning back*.

"No turning back," she whispered. She took a deep breath, then pushed the door open and entered.

"Holy . . ." she breathed.

The lab had been trashed. Papers were strewn everywhere, torn and wadded into heaps. Computers had been thrown across the floor like oversized blocks tossed by a gigantic child in a tantrum. Catwoman picked her way among shattered monitors and jagged bits of circuitry, stooping to sniff tentatively at pools of liquid and the remains of a glass crucible.

Whoever had done this didn't stop with the computers, either. All the lab equipment had been destroyed, a welter of broken tubes, petri dishes, and bottles. She stepped over a chair that had been splintered, looked up to see the cracked lozenge of a video screen dangling from the wall—the same screen she had glimpsed the other night.

She drew her breath in sharply. Unbidden, the images returned: a lovely young woman's face suddenly fracturing into corrosive shards of flesh. Catwoman gave a low hiss and started to turn, when she saw something else sprawled on the floor amidst the wreckage.

A corpse.

She gasped. She darted toward the body, crouching above it and turning it toward her. Jagged black starbursts showed where he had been shot repeatedly in the chest. Blood pooled around him, staining his crumpled lab coat. Ragged cloth flapped across one limp arm, where the torn lab coat still bore an embroidered name.

Dr. Ivan Slavicky.

Catwoman reached for the lab coat's pocket. Abruptly, she tensed, snatching her hand back. She cocked her head, listening.

Sirens.

Her eyes narrowed. The sirens' wail grew closer. Startled by another sound, she looked up and saw an elderly man standing in the doorway. He wore a dun-colored uniform and carried a broom, holding it protectively before him as he stared at her in horror.

"Please," he whispered. He shook his head. "I won't—"

Catwoman looked around desperately. Trapped!

The janitor began to edge back toward the door. Before he could reach it she lunged toward him, tossing him aside as she raced out into the corridor.

FIFTEEN

It was turning into a long night for Tom Lone, as well. He knew something was up when he entered the station for the graveyard shift. The detectives working in the bullpen barely glanced at him, but he could hear repressed snickers and a few muttered remarks as he passed. His steps slowed as he approached his desk, carrying his evidence bag with the paper bag in it. He stopped, shaking his head, and let out a muted groan.

Piled on his desk were cat toys—a catnip mouse, a little plastic ball with a bell inside—alongside stuffed plush kittens, a bobblehead cat, a shag-covered scratching post. Tom picked up a red rubber mouse and squeezed it.

Squeeeeak!

He turned and looked at the other detectives. Their heads were bent over their desks, their mouths pursed as they tried not to smile. Tom did his best to look stern and unamused, but it didn't work. He gave the rubber mouse another squeeze and tossed it aside, then moved a stuffed cat off his chair and sat, placing the evidence bag on the desk in front of him.

"Got her yet, Lone?"

"Yeah—did you catch Catchick?"

The first detective looked peeved. "I thought we'd decided to go with Catbroad."

"We did." The other detective shrugged. "But it seemed kinda, you know, derogatory."

The first detective rolled his eyes. "Well excuse *me*, Officer Oprah."

"You two?" Tom broke in. He pointed at first one, then the other. "You're why I work alone."

He turned back to his desk, and was reaching for the evidence bag when another detective walked over and dropped a file in front of him.

"Tom? I hate to give you more work when you're so, uh, *busy*—but this just came in. From that Slavicky homicide down at Hedare. Maybe you want to take a look?"

"Sorry, Bob. I was just thinking."

"Nasty habit." The detective glanced at the collection of toy cats and grinned. "But it looks like you're working hard at breaking it."

"I met somebody," Tom went on, almost to himself.

"Yeah?" A flash of interest passed over Bob's weathered face. "Like, a girl?"

"Yeah." Tom hesitated, then asked, "Would your wife crawl out onto the ledge of a building to rescue a stray cat?"

"Maybe. If the cat was carrying a pizza."

Tom stared at him, then shook his head.

"Thanks, Bob," he said dryly.

He turned to pick up the Slavicky file. As he did, his gaze fell on the decorated cardboard coffee cup Patience Phillips had given him the previous afternoon. It stood in a place of honor between a high school basketball trophy and a photo of his parents. Tom looked at it for a moment, smiling, then picked up the evidence bag from the jewel heist.

"Huh?"

He frowned. The bag's top was open. Through the gap he could see the paper sack the jewels had been returned in. Slowly he pulled it out, his curious frown turning to genuine puzzlement, then concern. A single word had been written across the bag.

SORRY.

Tom looked from the bag to the coffee cup. He picked up the latter, turning it in his hand until he was staring at its simple message, a single word surrounded by scrolls of flowers and leaves.

SORRY.

Tom blinked. He shook his head.

"Nah, that's crazy," he said under his breath.

He turned his attention back to the Slavicky file. But a few minutes later he found himself looking at the bag again, and the cup.

SORRY.

It wasn't the same handwriting; at least, it wasn't *exactly* the same handwriting.

But it was similar enough that a connection lodged in Tom's mind. He didn't like it, but there was no putting it off now. He swore softly, then reached for his phone and punched in the forensics lab.

"This is Lone. I've got something I'd like you to look at. . . ."

An hour later he was down in Forensics with one of the department graphologists. Two images were projected on a screen in front of them—the word SORRY from Patience Phillips's cup, and the same word from the jewel heist bag. The graphologist stood with her arms crossed, looking thoughtfully at the screen as behind her other specialists busied themselves.

"So." Tom shifted in his chair, trying not to look anxious. "Were they written by the same person?"

"Hm." The graphologist directed her laser pointer at the screen. "Well, there is a similarity. The shape of the S, this loop on the Y . . ."

The laser pointer's glowing red bead hung above the offending letters.

". . . but this first one . . ."

She pointed at the projection of the coffee cup. "The broad spacing of the letters on this are indicative of loneliness. The O—it's reaching out, insecure, afraid of being rebuffed. It's the handwriting of a people pleaser. Whereas *this* one . . ."

She indicated the word SORRY on the bag that had held the stolen jewels.

"Look at the harsh stroke of the Rs here. *Very* self-confident. Defiant, almost angry. The O . . . this one doesn't play by the rules."

"So." Tom let his breath out, relieved. "They're two different people."

"Very much so." The graphologist turned off the projection monitor. "Still, keep in mind, this isn't an exact science. But put those two women in the same room?" She looked at Tom and shook her head. "You've got yourself a hell of a party."

She began gathering papers, slid a form across the table for Tom to sign. "Got a big weekend planned, Tom?"

He looked up at her and grinned. "I do now."

SIXTEEN

A package arrived for Patience early the next morning, via courier. She opened her door warily, fearful of something from Hedare, or worse, the police department.

But there was only a uniformed young FastFlight Express deliveryman, still yawning as he waited for her to sign for her package.

"It only came from 'cross town," he said, handing her a copy of the signature form. "But I guess someone was in a hurry for it to get here."

"I guess so," said Patience, perplexed, and closed the door. She stepped absently over her leather suit, sat down at her drafting table, and stared at the large envelope's return address.

Dr. Ophelia Powers
197 Lilac Street

"Huh." Carefully, Patience opened the packet. A heavy book slid out, its dust jacket slightly worn. The cover illustration was a photograph of a golden cat statuette, superimposed over a woman's face.

The Cat Who Walked By Herself:
Avatars Of The Feline Goddess
By Ophelia Powers

She turned the volume over. On the back was a photograph of Ophelia Powers—a much younger Ophelia, by thirty years at least, smiling as she held a cat that was a dead ringer for the Mau.

It couldn't possibly be the same cat—could it?

Do cats live to be that old? wondered Patience. She opened the book and glanced at the introduction.

> *My hope in this volume is to entertain and enlighten curious readers with fictionalized accounts of events that, while certainly not historic records, do indeed have their roots in the real world and the real lives of women of civilizations past. . . .*

In the room behind her, the kettle began to sing. Patience stifled a yawn and went to make herself some tea, then settled back at her desk. She had much to do this morning—a visit to Sally, first of all—but she was intrigued by the book, and the implicit message that, whatever knowledge it contained, Ophelia was anxious that it should be in Patience's hand as soon as possible. She flipped through the first few chapters, and came to a photograph of an ancient fresco of young girls bowing before a regal woman seated upon a throne.

THE LADY OF THE BEASTS, blazed the chapter heading. Patience read on.

SEVENTEEN

THE LADY OF THE BEASTS

Kalliste, 1647 B.C.E.

It was autumn, the season when the saffron-gatherers made their way up the grassy, stone-scattered slopes of the island they knew as Kalliste, the Beautiful Place. For some of the girls—and Aktana was one of them—it was not the Beautiful Place so much as the Place of Sorrows, and the temple where Aktana spent her days and nights was the Palace of Suffering, though that was probably too melodramatic a term for what was mostly a life of ease, spent wearing pretty clothes and memorizing arcane rituals.

Aktana was an acolyte of the Lady of the Beasts, the high priestess of the island that thousands of years later would be known as Thera: fear. Like all of the other acolytes, Aktana had no family save those she served at the temple. Girls of good background were married by the time they were Aktana's age, fifteen. Many of them left Kalliste to live with their husbands on Keftiu, the great island that was the political and cultural center of their world. As Kalliste became Thera, so one day Keftiu would be called Crete, but now it gave its name to an island empire scattered across the Aegean Sea from Keftiu to Anatolia.

Aktana had never seen Keftiu. She would never have a husband—not that she wanted one. Infant girls whose mothers died in childbirth were given to the Lady of the Beasts. They were considered to be orphans, for only very wealthy widowers had any use for a daughter. For them, a daughter might one day become currency, to be traded on Keftiu.

But Aktana's father was not a wealthy man. At least, she didn't believe he was. She had never met him; she did not even know his name.

"Hurry up!" called one of the other girls.

The rest of the group had already scaled the mountain that was the island's heart. Foul-smelling steam sometimes escaped from fissures upon the hillside, and near these spots no crocuses bloomed.

But Aktana and the other girls were on the south side of the mountain. Here purple crocuses were clustered in stony hollows, as though the Lady of the Beasts had walked there, strewing Tyrian pigment from a basket. The *real* Lady of the Beasts, that is: the Goddess, and not her mortal and very worldly representative, the priestess Ilis. Ilis was back at the temple, still asleep or playing with her makeup in front of the polished onyx mirror that had been the latest gift from one of the Egyptian envoys who came to Kalliste to trade.

Aktana scrambled up the mountainside to catch up with the rest of Ilis's acolytes. There were seven of them, all dressed like Aktana in the gauzy skirts and blouses they wove themselves from linen and wool brought to Ilis as offerings. The dyes and pigments arrived at the temple the same way, in baskets and amphorae borne from Keftiu and Egypt; the results of all these offerings could now be seen as the girls made their way to the mountaintop. Their clothes were lovely—not even Aktana could argue with Ilis's fashion sense. Their long skirts were of woven bands of Egyptian blue and ochre, scattered here and there with bright yellow flowers dyed of the same saffron the girls were picking now.

As they worked they gossiped—who was sleeping with whom, who had fallen out of favor with Ilis, who had borrowed someone's gold hoop earrings and not returned them. Aktana listened, smiling but saying little. Their gossip bored her, just as Ilis's antics bored her. Aktana wondered sometimes if all goddesses were as shallow (or inattentive) as the Lady of the Beasts, who (according to Ilis, anyway, and as evidenced by the carven seals of chalcedony and alabaster the priestess used in her correspondence) spent Her immortal days sitting upon a distant mountaintop, attended by lions and spotted cats, winged dogs and clouds of honeybees, as She awaited Her next offering.

Which, of course, would be given to Her representative here on Kalliste: namely, Ilis.

"You'll miss lunch if you don't hurry," Lyssa, one of the older girls, remarked. She peeked into Aktana's basket. "Over there's a patch no one's harvested yet," she added in a kinder voice, gesturing to a large rock surrounded by nodding crocuses.

"Thanks," said Aktana. She wandered over to the rock, tall stands of bristling dark green rosemary brushing against her skirts to release their sharp piney smell. Aktana crushed a stalk between her fingers and ran them across her cheek, then turned to the business of gathering saffron.

And it *was* a business, for all that Ilis termed what the girls did a sacred ritual honoring She Who Nurses Lions. The crocuses bloomed in autumn, each small, slender, purple-throated blossom yawning open, the bright stigmas protruding like slim yellow tongues, each one scarcely larger than a thread. The stigmas were coated with pollen, an astonishing brilliant orange, and it was the job of the acolytes to pluck the stigmas from each flower, carrying them in baskets back to the temple. There the contents of each basket would be poured into a single large woven container, big enough for a girl to hide in; the saffron would be dried, then sold or traded throughout Keftiu and Egypt, to be used in making pigments and dyes for paintings, frescoes, clothes, makeup.

But in weight and mass, the harvest from any single crocus was no more than a few golden hairs plucked from a child's scalp. So the acolytes of the Lady of the Beasts worked from a few hours after sunrise till dusk, gathering the precious gold from each flower. If you attempted to pluck the stamens too early, the pollen was damp with dew and would be wasted, sticking to fingers and clothes; too late and twilight fell, and the girls were in danger of falling prey to the same lustful men who would watch them from the corners of their eyes during temple gatherings. Not everyone who arrived to worship the Lady of the Beasts came for religious reasons.

But there were no men around now; certainly none that Aktana could see. She knelt among the stand of crocuses, the small purple flowers nodding in the morning wind, and began to gently pinch the yellow threads from each violet throat. It was tedious work, but better than tending the fires back at the temple; better than waiting on Ilis, whose whims and bad temper were legendary (to her acolytes, at least). She could hear the other girls singing and laughing elsewhere on the hillside, and Aktana smiled, joining in softly where she worked. Her fingers became gilded with pollen, her long skirts dusted with gold. The sun was warm but not too hot, the breeze sweet and scented with rosemary and the sea. Soon enough they could break for lunch, olives and goat cheese and bread, washed down with some resinous yellow wine one of the other girls had surreptitiously taken from the offering room at the temple.

"The Lady didn't mean for us to starve," the girl had said when she revealed the small amphora. "Or die of thirst, either!"

For now, it was enough that Aktana was warm, and alone with her thoughts.

But not alone for long.

Mrrrrow.

Aktana stopped, a crocus blossom caught between her fingers, and looked around. The wind had shifted, and the other girls were now higher up the hillside, their laughter faint.

"Hello?" Aktana looked around but saw no one.

But she'd heard—something. She wiped the sweat from her face, leaving a long streak of yellow across her forehead. The heat of midday had brought out honeybees and a few autumn-loving butterflies, and the scent of honey rose from late-blooming gorse.

And there was another smell, too. Aktana wrinkled her nose at a faint reek of sulphur. Still, there was no sign of smoke that she could see. She turned back to the crocuses.

Mrrrooooowwww.

The noise was louder now, and more plaintive. Aktana stood, shading her eyes; heard the cry again. It seemed to come from a large rock a few yards off. Gorse grew thickly here, and as she walked toward it she was careful to hold her skirt up, to keep it from tearing on the thorns.

Mrrrooow!

"Ah, poor thing!" Aktana crooned. "How'd you get here?"

An animal had become trapped in the gorse thicket. A cat, one of the tawny sand-cats the Egyptian traders sometimes brought from their homeland to sell in Kalliste's markets. They were desert animals, larger than the cats that prowled the alleys of Kalliste, and not easily tamed.

But they were beautiful, with pale gold coats and golden eyes—and very, very sharp white teeth.

It was the teeth Aktana was regarding now, with some apprehension. The sand-cat had somehow gotten itself tangled in the thorny gorse. She could see streaks of blood on its sleek fur. One of its front paws was wedged between two branches, and the thorns cut cruelly into its flesh.

Mroooow!

The sand-cat's teeth were sharper than the thorns. Aktana stood and stared at it, musing.

"If I help you, you won't bite me, will you?" A child had been bitten by a sand-cat in the market and died of the bite. Ilis said this was because the child had been evil and the Lady of the Beasts was punishing it, but Aktana had thought this was nonsense—the boy had been only four years old, incapable of any evil beyond trying to stroke a wild animal. His wound had grown black and foul smelling, and some bad humor had no doubt burrowed its way into his flesh, completely independent of the Lady's doing.

Still, Aktana was wary of anything like that happening to her. She stared at the animal, and it cried out even more piteously. Its golden eyes stared back at her imploringly, but also with something that almost seemed like a command.

Aktana bit her lip. All animals were sacred to the Lady of the Beasts, but few were as sacred as lions. And what was a sand-cat but a small lion? The animal began to struggle once more, more desperately now, and the thorns pierced its skin. If she left it, eagles would find it and devour it alive—she could already see them gathering above her. Quickly, almost without thinking, Aktana ripped a strip of linen from the hem of her skirt. She wrapped it around her hand and arm, then very cautiously reached through the thorns to the struggling animal.

"Now then, now then, calm down," she murmured. Her fingers reached through the gorse, and she winced as thorns tore at the cloth to prick her fingers.

But, miraculously, the sand-cat grew still. She let her hand rest upon its smooth back for a moment, feeling its heart racing, as though water flowed beneath the surface of its skin. Then she slid her hand beneath it, and slowly began to work it free.

It took several minutes. The cat became so limp that for an instant she feared it was dead. But its golden eyes, though they narrowed, remained watchful and fixed upon her.

"There!" With a sigh of triumph, Aktana sank back upon her heels. She cradled the sand-cat, then gently put it upon the ground. "Now, be careful you don't do the same thing again!"

She had thought the cat would bound off. Instead it sat and calmly began to clean itself of blood and dirt. Aktana watched it for a minute. Then, still wary—it *was* a wild animal, after all—she stood and began to walk away.

After she had gone a few steps she stopped and looked back. The cat paused in its toilet and stared up at her. Aktana smiled. Then she made a fist, drew her hand beneath her chin and bowed.

"Please give your Mistress my regards," she said, and then hurried back to join the others.

Ilis was in a bad temper when the girls returned late that afternoon.

"The bull beneath the waters is moving," she announced, as the girls began pouring the contents of their baskets into the enormous basket that stood before Ilis's throne—the Lady's throne, although when Ilis sat there, she made a point of appearing haughty and powerful enough that it was difficult to imagine anyone else ever taking a seat on the raised stone platform. "At least that's what they're saying in the city. I didn't notice anything. Did any of you?"

The girls shrugged.

"Not really," said Lyssa.

Aktana thought of the sulphurous odor she'd smelled on the hillside, but said nothing. She also didn't mention the fact that, judging from her disheveled hair and the odor of honey wine, Ilis had probably spent the day in bed with her latest lover. In which case, she would no doubt have mistaken the earth-tremors that signaled the sea bull's waking for something else.

"Good." Ilis yawned. She glanced at the temple doors, where two guards had been turning away petitioners. "I'm exhausted—I've been praying all day, so maybe it's working."

Aktana tried not to roll her eyes. Ilis's "prayers" to the Lady were a notorious euphemism for sleep or lovemaking.

The high priestess smoothed the front of her robe and glanced into the huge basket. A small mound of saffron threads covered the bottom. It would dry before tomorrow's harvest was gathered and added to the heap. "That looks like good work, girls. Thank you."

She looked at the acolytes who stood waiting for the signal to leave. "You may go now. All except . . ."

Her gaze swept the room. It settled on Aktana, who groaned inwardly.

"*You*. Aktana. I need someone to stay here all night and keep the Lady's fire burning. And there may be more petitioners if the bull remains restless, so make sure you don't let the fire go out."

"Yes, Mistress," Aktana said. She bowed resignedly. The other girls gave her sympathetic looks as they filed from the temple. She could hear their relieved laughter once they were safely outside, running to the long, low, stucco building where they lived.

"Very good," Ilis said absently. She stooped to run her hand through the saffron threads, then straightened and started to leave. At the door she paused, looking back at Aktana and seeming for the first time to actually see her.

"What happened to your skirt?" Ilis asked.

Aktana looked down, chagrined, and fingered the cloth where she'd ripped off a strip of linen to help the sand-cat. Ilis didn't care for animals, and she was afraid of cats. "They *watch* you," she'd said once to Aktana, who suspected there were many things Ilis wanted to keep secret. "Like they always know something you don't know."

Aktana made a silent prayer to the Lady, asking forgiveness for lying. "I . . . I'm sorry, Mistress," she said to Ilis. "I must have torn it while climbing."

Ilis shook her head. "You must be more careful, Aktana. Maybe you can work on your weaving tonight. That will keep you awake."

Put me right to sleep, more likely, thought Aktana, but she said nothing.

As it turned out, not even weaving could make Aktana drowsy that night. Ilis's fears about fretful petitioners turned out to be groundless. A solitary old woman appeared as the sun was setting, and gave

Aktana a small wooden platter with some olives and flatbread and tomatoes.

"For the Lady," the old woman said. She drew the woolen shawl back from her head and smiled at Aktana. "But I think you will have to eat it for Her."

"Thank you," said Aktana. She took the platter, offered an olive to the woman, and began to eat. The Lady's fire burned on a small open hearth made of flame-blackened stones. It gave off little smoke but a pleasant heat, and smelled sweetly of the fragrant woods Ilis liked to burn: apple, olive, cedar. "Would you like to sit here and warm yourself? It's getting dark."

The woman shook her head. "No, daughter. But thank you." She gazed curiously at Aktana as she ate the olives, licking her fingers delicately after each one. "You are not afraid here, by yourself?"

Aktana looked up in genuine surprise. "No." She glanced at the temple's plaster walls, painted with blue waves and gaily leaping dolphins, crocus flowers and swallows, the lovely portrayal of the Lady of the Beasts that Ilis had modeled for years earlier, when she was not much older than Aktana was now. "It's beautiful in here," said Aktana. "I love it. And the Lady protects me."

The old woman stared at her. "Yes, she does," she said softly. "But you should take care—down in the city, they say the bull in the sea is waking. The sailors are making petitions to him, rather than the Lady."

"I will be careful." Aktana looked at the temple ceiling high overhead. There was broken mortar between some of the beams, where earth tremors had shaken them loose.

The woman inclined her head and left.

Aktana yawned. It was still so early! She poked at the fire's glowing bed of coals and tossed another bit of wood onto it, then turned to her weaving.

Hours passed. As the night grew long Aktana dozed, leaning against her loom with a linen shawl as a pillow. Each time, she woke before the fire went out, and fed it more branches. Now and then she would stand and stretch and go outside, in hopes that the cool night air would revive her. Usually it was fresh and sweet, scented of the sea below and the lingering smell of wildflowers and woodsmoke.

But tonight the air smelled thick and fetid. Aktana stood on the temple steps, staring at the sky. The stars glimmered feebly, all but hidden behind a strange gray veil.

That can't be my smoke, thought Aktana, frowning. *The Lady's smoke . . .*

She glanced at the temple roof, saw the familiar wisps of white rising from the opening above the Lady's hearth. *And it's not fog, either . . .*

The strange mist seemed to emanate from the stars themselves. "But the stars wouldn't smell this bad," Aktana said aloud, trying to buoy her confidence. "Phew."

She went back inside, closing the door tightly behind her. She busied herself with the fire, dipping a few stalks of dried rosemary into a water jar, then tossing them onto the coals in hopes that the scent would mask the sulphurous smell from outside. She had just settled herself back on her thin mattress beside the hearth when she heard it.

Mrrrrow.

Now what?

Aktana sat up, sighing in exasperation. She peered through the twilit space of the temple but could see nothing. The sound came again, and again; louder each time, and more persistent. Aktana stood, taking the staff Ilis left for the girls' protection. She had just taken a few steps from the hearth when a small, pale figure with glowing golden eyes appeared, like a vagrant path of smoke.

"Oh!" Aktana gasped, clutching the staff to her. "It's just *you* again!"

It was the creature she'd saved that morning on the mountainside—the sand-cat. It must have followed her inside. Aktana stared at it in the near-darkness, and the cat stared back, its eyes like the coals burning on the Lady's hearth.

"You can't stay here," Aktana said at last. Lady of the Beasts or no, Ilis didn't permit animals in the temple—they were unpredictable and messy, besides which they made Ilis's beautiful dark eyes redden and her nose swell. "Here now, I'll let you out . . ."

She crossed hastily to the door—the cat looked larger in the dark, and its huge golden eyes were downright uncanny: They didn't seem to trap and reflect the light so much as burn from within, as though there were live coals inside its skull. The thought made Aktana even more uneasy. She flung the door open, smacking the staff on the ground several times for emphasis.

"*Go*," she said.

To her astonishment, the cat went.

But at her feet, it stopped. It gazed up at her, and

now there really *was* something uncanny. Because as clearly as though a gong had been rung beside her ear, the girl heard a voice.

"*Come.*"

Aktana looked around nervously. There was no one there. Overhead, the unsettling haze smirched the midnight sky. The stink of sulphur had grown stronger. At her feet, the cat sat on its haunches and let out a low, insistent growl; once more that command sounded in Aktana's ears.

Come.

The cat stood. It looked over its shoulder at the girl, then started to walk down the hillside. After it had taken only a few steps, it stopped and looked back at her again.

Come.

Aktana shook her head, dazed. She felt as though she had drunk the libation that Ilis prepared each summer for the harvest festival, a potent brew of herbs and fermented honey that brought on visions, and usually, a horrible headache.

And, in fact, Aktana's head *was* starting to throb. The stench of sulphur, or whatever it was, was making her feel sick and dizzy. She turned to go back inside.

As she did, the cat attacked her. Leaping through the air with such swiftness that Aktana had no chance to flee or even cry out. She fell, the animal clawing at her breast, shredding her linen blouse until its claws bit into her flesh.

Then Aktana *did* scream. It was as though the flames from the hearth had escaped, to burn her skin away: heat rippled from where the cat clawed at her, heat and pain—though almost instantly, the pain subsided. As it did, the cat leaped away. Aktana gasped, struggling to sit up. She drew a shaking hand to her face, then looked down.

Her clothes were in tatters. Her breast ached as though she'd been branded.

Yet there was no blood, not even the faint marks of bruises. The sand-cat had clawed her mercilessly— but the claws had left no mark.

Aktana looked up, frightened, to where the cat stood watching her. Its golden eyes stared piercingly back at her through the night haze.

And suddenly it was as though she herself was a gong that had been struck. Her ears rang with sound: the hiss of the coals from the hearth in the temple behind her; the susurrus of nightwind in the tall stalks of dry grass; the nearby rush and sigh of waves on Kalliste's shore. Not just sound but scent over- whelmed her: the comforting odor of the sand-cat; the blood-warm smell of pigeons roosting in the temple's eaves; salt and cool earth—

But most of all, the smell of fear; of fire-riven rock and sulphur. It was so strong now that it was like a sound or a color, flooding Aktana's senses. The very ground beneath her seemed to vibrate so that she reeled, her hand flailing at the air for her staff.

But the staff had fallen and rolled away. Aktana looked around desperately and saw only the sand- cat watching her.

And once more it opened its mouth, baring sharp white teeth and a slender red tongue as it spoke to her—

Come. Now. Or you will die.

At the sound of the command Aktana's flesh burned anew, as though scored with flame. This time, when the cat turned and began to run down the hillside, Aktana followed.

She should have had difficulty finding her way in the dark; should have stumbled and fallen a dozen times, a hundred, over unfamiliar stones and brush, because the cat took no path that Aktana knew.

But she did not fall. Instead, she moved as the sand-cat itself did, swiftly and smoothly, sliding through brambles and gorse, catching herself when a crevice or gulley opened suddenly underfoot. As she raced downhill, the stench of smoke and sulphur did not disappear, but the smell of the sea grew stronger, and with it the reek of rotting mackerel and cuttlefish. The smell should have sickened Aktana. Instead her mouth watered, and when at the bottom of the hill the long white shingle appeared before her, she began to run madly toward water's edge, the sand-cat just a handsbreadth before her.

"Batta!"

A man's voice shattered Aktana's running reverie. She stopped, breathing hard, and found herself a few yards from where an Egyptian trade-ship was moored on the beach, a weatherbeaten pier leading the last few feet to shore. Several men were raising its sails. To the east, a dull red glow burned upon the horizon: dawn, a pending storm. Several Kallistean fishing boats were already plying the waters.

But on the deck of the Egyptian ship a man stood, cradling the sand-cat in his arms.

"Batta!" he scolded it. "You were nearly left behind."

For the first time he looked down and saw Aktana panting on the stony beach. "My pardon," he said quickly, as the cat leaped from his arms to the ship's rail. "I didn't see—"

He stopped, his face creased with concern. Aktana stared at him, still dazed, then looked down and saw her torn clothes, her arms and legs scratched from thorns.

"Are you all right?" The man swung himself over the rail onto the rickety pier, and walked quickly to where Aktana stood. "By the Sun! Did *she* do that to you?"

He looked back to where the cat sat on the ship's rail, washing itself unconcernedly.

"N-no," said Aktana. She blinked, looked around as though waking from a deep sleep. "I . . . no!"

Her eyes widened. "I should be at the temple! I— oh, Ilis will beat me for sure!"

She turned to run, but the man grabbed her arm.

"Wait," he said, gently but firmly turning her back to face him. "You said Ilis—do you mean the priestess?"

"Yes." Aktana began to shake her head. "Oh, what I've done, what I've done! She'll sell me down to the docks for sure—"

"The priestess? No child of Bast would ever dare harm one of her initiates!"

"Bast?" Aktana's face grew miserable. "I know nothing of Bast. Ilis serves the Lady of the Beasts— but mostly she serves herself. And when she finds me gone . . ."

She began to cry. The man stared at her, perplexed. Then he gazed at the mountain looming above them, and after a moment Aktana looked up as well. A dark gray haze clung to Kalliste's slopes. The Lady's temple, usually a brilliant white, like an alabaster stone fitted into the green mountain, was not even visible through the foul-smelling mist.

"This is an evil thing," the man murmured. From the ship behind him, the cat mewed softly. "I have been coming here for many years, but of late it seems that the gods have abandoned this place."

He turned to look at Aktana. "You say you serve a priestess, yet what priestess would teach her acolytes such fear? There is no goddess here anymore, child. Or if there is, She grows angry—"

He pointed to the smoke clouding Kalliste's summit. "The goddess of my country does not speak thus. But I am not going to wait to hear what it is that *your* goddess has to say."

Gently he touched Aktana's shoulder. "Batta has been consecrated to the goddess of my country. She has accompanied me on many journeys, and always I have returned home safely. That she has brought you here is no accident, child."

His expression grew kindly. "I have a daughter no older than you. I would not like to think of her alone in a temple that has been abandoned by its Mistress."

From on board the ship several voices called out urgently. "Mal'tan! We will lose the wind!"

Mal'tan nodded. "I'm coming." He looked at Aktana. "I promise you safe passage to Keftiu—that is my next port. No man on my ship will lay a hand upon you. Batta will see to that—as will I."

Aktana hesitated. She looked back up the hillside to the Lady's temple—

No, Ilis's temple. Whatever else this man was, he had the gift of clear sight. Aktana knew as well as he did that the Lady could not be pleased with Ilis's neglect. She looked down at her torn clothes, and then at Mal'tan.

"If I come with you . . . ," she began, then faltered.

Mal'tan completed the question for her. "What will become of you?" Aktana nodded silently. "You have the look of one who has been educated—I hope your mistress saw to that, at least. You will be schooled with my own daughter. I have only one child; a curse, many have thought, but I see now it is the wisdom of the Goddess that it was so."

"*Mal'tan!*"

"We must set sail." Mal'tan swung back onto the ship's deck. The cat, Batta, remained on the rail, staring at Aktana. "If you would come, do so now." He held out a hand for the girl. She cast one last glance back at the temple, then clambered on board.

She had never been on a ship before. Her grief at leaving her home country was softened by the sheer novelty of her surroundings, and by the need to keep out of the way of the ship's crew. As though to underscore the fact of Her protection, the sand-cat followed Aktana everywhere, even sleeping with her at night in a hammock slung from the beams belowdecks. Mal'tan was kind to her, as were the other sailors—there were only a dozen of them—who all seemed to have children of their own in their home country. These were not the cruel men Ilis had warned her acolytes against; while Mal'tan assured Aktana that there were indeed dangerous men to be found in every port, not every one was to be feared or hated. She spent her days dreaming on deck, or exploring the vessel's hold, where huge jars of honey for embalming were stored, along with bricks of beeswax and, yes, small but precious terra cotta vials of dried saffron. Mal'tan and the other men taught her phrases of their own language, and Mal'tan opened a packet he had purchased for his own daughter, a blue-dyed girl's shift woven of linen and wool. The fabric was coarser than what Aktana was accustomed to, but she had never felt anything so fine against her skin.

They were five days out of Kalliste when they made landfall on the westernmost shores of Keftiu. It was dawn. Mal'tan had left three men to guard the ship, and was walking up a high rocky hillside with Aktana, Batta at their heels, when suddenly he stopped.

On the northeastern horizon, the sky grew scorched with black clouds. A flicker like crimson lightning seemed to shatter the sky.

"Run!" shouted Mal'tan.

As though echoing his cry, a thunderous roar tore through the air. Batta leaped uphill, racing toward a low stone building.

"There!" cried Mal'tan. He grabbed Aktana and pulled her after him. "In there—"

The building was long and narrow, windowless, though there were small slits in the walls where the stones did not quite fit together. A storage building. Aktana jostled in the darkness past tall terra cotta amphorae, as Batta cried insistently.

"Cover your mouth," commanded Mal'tan in a

muffled voice. He had already yanked his shirt over his own face. "Quickly."

The entire building trembled, then grew still. Waves of heat seemed to batter against the stone walls. Terrified, Aktana tried to peer out through one of the slits.

Black rain was falling. Black rain and gray ash, and scattered sparks. A stench of sulphur and scorched rock wafted through the cracks in the walls. Outside, something fell flaming through the air. The horrified Aktana saw it was the body of a seabird. She recoiled, and Mal'tan put his arm around her.

"It is as I feared," he whispered through the folds of cloth covering his face. "The goddess has taken her revenge upon Kalliste. . . ."

They waited for days inside the storage building, breaking into the amphorae to drink wine and feed on handfuls of honey. The sand-cat caught mice, and lapped stagnant water from a tiny declivity in the rock. Outside, the black rain fell, and fine white ash sifted down over the countryside. When at last a fitful yellow sun shone, Aktana and Mal'tan emerged into another world, a grim, ghostly landscape sculpted of white ash like snow, and Batta left small footprints as it led them to join the other survivors atop the mountains of Keftiu.

Ophelia Powers's note: Nearly five thousand years ago, the civilization of the people we call the Minoans was destroyed in the cataclysmic eruption of Thera, their island capital. It was one of the most devastating volcanic events of recorded history, and probably inspired Plato's account of the legendary island of Atlantis. Frescoes and stone seals found

on the island, now called Santorini, indicate a culture that
may have been matristic, with a goddess figure who has be-
come popularly known as the Lady of the Beasts.

Patience closed the book thoughtfully.

"Well," she said. "You don't tug on Superman's
cape, you don't spit into the wind . . . and I guess you
don't mess around with the Cat Goddess. Whoever
She is."

She glanced at her watch.

"Oh my god—Sally'll *kill* me!"

Hurriedly she began to dress, then headed for the
hospital.

EIGHTEEN

> *Beauty is as Summer fruits, which are*
> *easy to corrupt, and cannot last.*
> —FRANCIS BACON, *Essays*, 1625

Sally sat propped up in her hospital bed, avidly watching the morning news.

"... *Dr. Ivan Slavicky, head of research and development at Hedare Beauty, was found dead at the scene* ..."

A file shot of Dr. Slavicky filled the screen, then the camera cut away to a field reporter standing in front of the desolate Hedare factory, emergency vehicles and fluttering yellow police tape in the background.

"Just as I always suspected," Sally remarked with satisfaction. "I miss just one day of work and *everything* goes to hell."

She reached distractedly for the plastic tray that held her breakfast, glanced at the grayish sludge that passed for oatmeal, and grimaced. As she did, there was a knock at the door. Sally looked up to see Patience standing there, holding a small overnight bag.

"I'm not too early, am I?"

Sally stared at her friend in astonishment. Instead of her customary, if elegant, uniform of neutral-colored blouse and skirt, Patience wore a black sleeveless tank top and sunflower yellow cargo pants. Her cropped hair was sleek against her skull, showing off a pair of chunky topaz earrings.

"First: Wow," Sally breathed. "You look *amazing*. Second, this guy is *really* good for you. Bet you're glad I pushed you into it. Props to Sally, right?"

Patience smiled. "Props to Sally. I mean that, too—I'm meeting him later. A street fair down at the place he volunteers."

"He volunteers, too?" Sally pretended to faint. "Wow! A genuine Good Guy."

Patience nodded. "A genuine Good Guy." She crossed to sit at the edge of Sally's hospital bed. "But now I want to know about *you*. Are you going to be okay?"

Sally sighed. "Well, they still don't know what it is. And there's a good possibility it could be life-threatening. So in the interest of public safety and hospital policy they're releasing me anyway." At Patience's stricken look she laughed. "No, really—I *do* feel better. Maybe I should lay off the chocolates and Cosmos more often."

She pointed at the TV. "Check this out. Some crazy chick in a cat suit murdered Slavicky last night."

Patience froze, then looked warily at the TV. She had a brief glimpse of the factory exterior, the on-the-scene reporter mouthing the usual blather about justice and inexplicable violence.

Then a police artist's sketch of the suspect popped up—a masked woman with the penetrating eyes and pitiless expression of a psychopath. Patience blanched.

Talk about having a bad hair day! she thought in chagrin.

The footage switched abruptly to George Hedare, standing in front of the Hedare corporation headquarters, addressing a crowd of reporters.

"Mark my words," he intoned. "The actions of this lunatic will not keep Beau-line off the shelves. We will launch next week as scheduled."

George stared into the camera and waggled his finger portentously. "Because we owe it to the women of this country. Because we owe it to the memory of our fallen comrade."

Patience scowled and switched the television off.

Sally snorted. "What a phony. Like George ever cared about anyone on God's green earth but George."

Absently she reached for her purse on the bedside table and pulled out a small vial of Beau-line. She opened it, then shook her head in consternation. "Damn! I'm almost out."

Patience looked at her friend. Armando's garbled words came back to her in a rush.

Beau-line! There's something wrong with Beau-line!

"Let me see that," she said sharply. She took the bottle from Sally and examined the label. "Sal— those headaches. How long have you been having them?"

Sally shrugged. "I dunno. A few months, maybe?"

"Do me a favor. Stop using this."

"But why?"

Patience read the bottle's slogan aloud. "'*Beau-line: To Be More.*'"

She stood and crossed to where an orange biohazard waste container stood by the bathroom door.

She opened the container, dropped the Beau-line bottle inside, and slammed the container shut.

"Why?" she said, and turned to look at her friend. "Because you're enough, Sally. Just the way you are."

In the mansion she shared with her husband, Laurel Hedare sat staring, transfixed, at her own reflection. Around her were all the pretty trappings of wealth. A marble bathroom the size of a train station waiting room, with a Latin inscription carved above the entrance. PULCHRE! BENE! RECTE!—Beautiful! Good! Perfect!

The marble countertops held Slavonica crystal containers for cotton balls, bath salts, tissues; a bouquet of freesia and lilac in an antique Wedgwood vase; handmilled lavender soaps from Provence, each stamped with Laurel's profile; linen facecloths with monograms embroidered by nuns in a Swiss convent.

All lovely, all fabulously expensive, all utterly trivial.

Laurel leaned forward, transferring her gaze from the wall-to-wall mirrors to a magnifying mirror. Her fingers traced a line beneath her eyes, drew another line down the side of her mouth. She frowned slightly, then forced a smile. Slowly she reached for a large bottle of Beau-line on the counter.

She poured a small amount into her palm, glanced down at it, then dumped the entire contents into her hand. She lifted her head to stare again at her image—a hundred reflections, a thousand; numberless Laurels staring back at her, turning and smiling into infinity everywhere she looked.

She began slathering the pale fluid onto her face,

carefully at first, then faster, with manic, almost de-monic, intensity.

She who is beautiful is more formidable than fire and iron. . . .

The door behind her opened. Laurel's house-keeper stood there, embarrassed at having intruded.

"Mrs. Hedare . . . I am so sorry . . ."

Laurel looked up and smiled. "Don't be." She hesi-tated, then said, "Why don't you take a break, Maria. Join me for a cocktail."

The housekeeper shook her head. "I'm sorry, Mrs. Hedare. My family . . ."

"Oh, of course." Laurel waved at her lightly. "You go ahead."

Maria closed the door.

"Family," murmured Laurel. "Nothing comes before that. . . ."

She gazed sadly into the mirror, and reached for another jar of Beau-line.

NINETEEN

The day was cloudless and warm, perfect weather for the Rainbow Center's annual street fair. Patience met Tom Lone at the Community Center, and the two immediately set off to sample the rides and games of chance that had been set up in the parking lot. A crowd of eager children trailed them, laughing and talking excitedly.

"Did you check out that Dragon Coaster?"

"No way I'm getting on that thing!"

"What about the Ferris wheel?"

"No way!"

An hour later, most of the children clutched stuffed animals, all courtesy of Ms. Phillips.

"Well, you should have no trouble with this one, anyway," Patience said to Tom. She nodded to where water guns beckoned.

"Been a while since I've had to polish off my sharpshooter badge," Tom said with a grin. "Hanging out with you, I'm starting to feel like my reflexes are a bit slow—better start going to the gym more often."

He went first, taking aim with the water pistol and

shooting a stream of water into the mouth of a plastic clown. It took him three tries, but the balloon above its head finally popped.

"Three tries, that's a keychain," the carnie said, tossing him a tiny plastic trinket. Several of the kids laughed.

"That's it? No wonder you wouldn't show us your gun the other day!"

Tom grinned good-naturedly and handed the water gun to Patience. "Ladies last."

"Now you'll see how it's done," she said, and winked at the watching children. She settled herself on the edge of the rail, pointing the water pistol at a plastic cat's head topped by a green balloon, then pulled the trigger. A spray of water shot right into the cat's mouth. The balloon popped and a buzzer rang, as the watching children cheered.

"Got it in one!" the carnie shouted. He grinned at Tom. "Seems like you got a new partner, Detective! This is for the lady—"

He handed her a stuffed tiger. Patience tossed it to one of the few kids who wasn't already clutching a prize.

"Aren't you supposed to let me win?" Tom asked, pretending to be hurt.

"I'm not that kind of girl."

"No? What kind of girl are you?" Tom countered suggestively.

Patience smiled. "A loser."

"This is a definition of the term I'm not familiar with." Tom looked at the kids and grinned. "Okay, you lot—go get yourselves some cotton candy."

The kids ran off. Patience and Tom wandered

through the maze of trucks and carnival games, ignoring the cries of barkers trying to lure them to roulette, Whack-A-Mole, the Dragon Coaster and Monster Mouse.

"Hey, win the pretty lady a goldfish! Three balls, three tries—you can do it!"

They halted in front of a brightly striped tent. Behind a barrier stood neatly arranged pyramids of metal milk bottles. The carnie held out a hand clutching three baseballs.

Tom shook his head. "Uh uh. I'm not going to embarrass myself again. Ladies first."

Tom took the balls and gave one to Patience. She threw it. It tore through the air and knocked down two milk bottles. Even the carnie looked impressed.

"Nice heater," said Tom. He hesitated. "Can I ask you a question?"

"Who did my hair?"

"I like it." Tom smiled and handed her another ball. "You worked for Hedare. Anybody have a grudge against the company?"

The question jolted Patience. The ball left her hand too fast and went wild, missing the bottles completely. She looked out of the corner of her eye at Tom, who was gazing nonplussed at the remaining milk bottle.

"George Hedare isn't the nicest man in the world," she said cautiously, and drew her hand back to throw the third ball.

"Someone was murdered at his factory last night."

Whump!

The final ball went flying straight toward the

barker's head. He ducked, and it smacked the back of the tent.

"Aw. Walked him," said Tom.

"Sorry!" Patience yelled. She turned to Lone. "George has a *lot* of enemies. He fired me."

"I heard."

Patience looked at him in surprise, quickly decided to play coy. "Am I a suspect, Detective?"

Tom took a handful of balls from the barker, wound up and threw his first. It caromed into a pyramid, sending metal bottles flying.

"Winner!" yelled the barker.

Patience smiled, then looked over her shoulder at Tom. He was staring at her, serious expression softened by the warmth in his eyes.

"No," he said, as the barker held out a small glass globe holding a goldfish. Tom waved it off. "You're not a suspect."

Patience nodded vaguely. Her eyes were on the goldfish. As Tom began to turn away, she licked her lips and reluctantly resisted the impulse to grab the fishbowl.

"How about a snack?" she suggested.

They walked to a concession stand. Tom bought cotton candy and handed it to Patience, then got himself a hot dog. They walked aimlessly around the fairground, Tom finishing his hot dog in a few bites. He then watched mesmerized as Patience twirled the cotton candy around her fingers, licked the sugar from her fingers, then attacked the rest of the cloud of pink sticky stuff until it was all gone.

"I didn't think anyone over the age of nine was allowed to eat cotton candy," he said as she gazed sadly at the now-empty paper cone. "That stuff'll kill you."

"But it looks so *pretty*."

"All right. Here's something else I always thought was off-limits once you turned eighteen."

Tom pointed at the Ferris wheel. "You game?"

They waited in line with dozens of noisy kids. Parents and more children stood behind the gate, watching as the riders boarded the cars in ones and twos. It was a tight fit for Patience and Tom, but they squeezed into the car, slid the safety bar down, and laughed giddily as the rattletrap contraption lifted them up.

"*Hold on tight!*"

A chorus of excited squeals and laughter came from those watching on the ground. The antiquated wheel groaned and creaked as it turned, the cars swinging gently back and forth as they rose. Patience sat, delighted, while Tom watched her with obvious pleasure.

"Look!" His eyes widened in mock awe as he pointed. "You can see all the way . . . across the street."

They had nearly reached the top of the ride's trajectory. With a sudden lurch, the machinery ground to a halt. The car swung gently back and forth. Tom looked at Patience.

"Oops," he said. "Might be up here for a while."

Patience snuggled closer to him. "You in a hurry?"

"Uh uh."

Tom shook his head, gazing intently into her eyes. They turned toward each other, faces nearly touching, and Tom's hand crept over hers. Patience's eyes

half closed, her lips parted as she lifted her face to
him—

"Mommy!"

A heartrending wail rang out above them. Patience
peered over Tom's shoulder, to a car that was opposite theirs, and slightly higher up. A solitary boy sat in
it, terrified, looking around wildly as he screamed.

"Mom—!"

On the ground a frantic figure ran from the crowd
to stand below the car.

"I'm right here, baby! It's all right, I'm here!"

"Mommy, get me!"

Tom and Patience stared at each other. At that moment the Ferris wheel gave a sickening lurch. The cars
rocked back and forth as the central mechanism
groaned and twisted, sending the cars swinging crazily.
Patience and Tom grabbed the handrail to keep from
being thrown out, as around them the air filled with
screams.

"One of the gears slipped—," Tom yelled to Patience, then turned to shout at the hysterical little
boy across from them. "Hang on, kid!"

"Hold on!" Patience called. "They're getting help!"

But no help seemed in sight. Below, the crowd
seethed in turmoil. A carnie fought with the opera-
tions lever, trying to keep it still, but it clanged madly
up and down like a piston.

"It's out of control!" Patience looked from the
struggling carnie to the frantic boy behind them. He
gripped the rail of the car, his cheeks white, and wet
with tears, his face nearly rigid with terror. Quickly
she took the measure of the fretwork of gears and
metal scaffolding that supported the wheel.

I *can reach him*, she thought, edging silently toward her side of the car. I *can save him*. . . .

But not without Tom seeing what she was up to. He, too, was trying to get a fix on exactly what had gone wrong.

"That's the one!" he exclaimed, and pointed to where a metal gear ground uselessly, sending off sparks. He looked at Patience. "You hang on, too."

She looked at him, not understanding. "Tom?"

Before she could say more, he clambered from the car, hanging on to the shaft. As he did, the wheel gave another heart-dropping lurch. The boy's car dipped forward. With a shriek, the boy tumbled out, grabbing the safety rail. Echoing screams came from the ground.

"No! *Help him, help him!*"

In the middle of the machinery, Tom inched toward the stuck gear, eyes intent on keeping his balance. He didn't see the child dangling a few yards away, not yet.

But Patience did. Without a glance at the distant ground, she jumped to the rail of the empty car directly above hers, grabbed it and swung herself onto the wheel's scaffolding. As she did, Tom crawled with agonizing slowness down the central rail to the wheel's hub.

By now the entire structure was shaking. A second carnie ran to join the first, but not even two of them could control the broken lever. High above them, Tom kept hold of the central rail and continued his climb toward the hub. As he did, the violent oscillation of the wheel caused a crossbar to loosen; it sheared off its restraining bolt, and the crossbar began to rock free. Tom grabbed it, tearing it from its mooring. He continued to climb, with more difficulty now that he held the crossbar tightly in one hand.

"*Mommy, help!*"

The hysterical screams of the little boy turned to terrified whimpers. He clung to the broken safety bar, his legs dangling uselessly in the air.

Got to reach him, Patience thought with grim resolve. She gathered all her strength, no longer caring who might be watching her, then leaped past startled riders to the child. Her feet barely touched first one car and then the next as she bounded upward until, with a last powerful lunge, she landed atop the boy's car. Her hand shot out to grab his wrist.

"Gotcha!" she breathed. She felt how weak his grasp was—a few more seconds and he would have been gone. "You're safe now."

She held him in her arms, lifting him into the car beside her.

But still the Ferris wheel continued to jolt wildly. Riders screamed, as Patience looked around in dismay.

This entire contraption is going to shake itself to pieces, she thought, fighting to keep her expression calm for the child's sake and holding him more tightly. *And there's not a damn thing I can do to stop it. . . .*

But Tom Lone could. He pulled himself hand-over-hand until he reached the wheel's center hub. There was a smell of scorched metal and singed wood. Gears whined and shrieked deafeningly as sparks fell in a cascade onto the wooden struts below. Tom straddled one of the rails that radiated from the hub. Gritting his teeth, he leaned forward, still holding the crossbar, then with a quick feinting motion jammed it between the madly spinning gears.

Immediately he recoiled, shielding his face in case the gears flew apart. There was an earsplitting squeal as the gears bit into the crossbar; then silence. The shaking stopped.

Below, the crowd erupted into cheers. Tom shook his head, limp with relief, then began the long climb back down to earth.

Patience hugged the little boy to her. "It's okay, baby," she said comfortingly. "Scary ride, huh? But on the bright side? He's always gonna remember our first date."

The boy smiled weakly. He huddled closer to her in the car, still trying to stifle his tears, when with a heart-lurching sound the car suddenly broke loose.

With muffled screams, both the boy and Patience fell. Patience grabbed the crossbar, clinging to it with all her strength; at the same time her legs reflexively snapped shut, catching the child. He wrapped his arms around her knees.

Patience looked around for the safest way out, her fear overcome by her feline instincts.

"I got you!" a voice called.

She looked down to see Tom Lone standing atop a ticket booth directly below them. He motioned at two carnies, who began to manually turn the Ferris wheel's gears.

The wheel slowly turned, lowering Patience and the boy until they were within Tom's grasp. He held out his arms, reaching for the boy.

"I got ya," he said.

The child twisted to stare up at Patience, silently

asking for reassurance. She smiled and nodded. He let go of her and fell into Tom Lone's waiting arms.

Moments later Patience landed safely. She watched as the little boy ran to his tearful mother.

"Thank you—God bless you, both of you!" she said to Tom and Patience, as her son embraced her.

Patience smiled. She turned to see Tom staring at her.

"You are amazing," he said. "How did you—?"

Patience ran into his arms and held him tight. A circle of excited bystanders and carnies surrounded them, all talking at once.

Patience smiled, then let Tom gently steer her away so they were on their own. Well-wishers called congratulations and grateful thanks as they walked across the carnival grounds, heading toward the Community Center.

"I'm not sure how you did it, but I'm impressed," he said when they were alone.

"Tom. I *saw* how you did—and so am I." Patience squeezed his hand. "You were amazing."

"Well, sure. But how did you—?" He stopped, overcome by something more than relief and astonishment: the way Patience felt in his arms. "Are you okay?" he asked in a softer voice.

"Safe and sound," Patience murmured, and snuggled closer to him.

"So," said Tom. "Cotton candy. Check. Carnival Ferris-wheel rescue, also checked."

He glanced down hopefully. "So . . . we should celebrate. How about dinner? Unless . . ."

Patience shook her head. "I'd love to. I *want* to. But I can't. Not tonight."

Tom looked crestfallen. "Oh."

"I've got work to do."

"I thought you lost your job."

"Well, yeah, I did. But you know, I'm gonna need a *new* job. So, I, mmm, should probably polish up my résumé?"

She knew the excuse sounded lame, but it was the best she could do.

Tom just stared at her. Finally he nodded. "Okay. I got work, too. Crime is being committed even as we speak. I should go make the city a safer place."

Patience smiled. *This guy is great*, she thought.

"That sounds like a nice way to spend an evening," she said softly.

"But will you promise me something?"

"Sure."

"Don't make me wait too long till we see each other again. It's not that I mind thinking about you all the time? But"—he sighed, and their eyes locked—"it's starting to interfere with my work."

TWENTY

Patience returned to her apartment feeling as though some of the helium from the carnival's balloons had leaked into her veins: she actually caught herself *running* up the stairs. She swept up her leather costume and mask from where she'd tossed them the night before, then stopped.

The late afternoon sun glinted off the cover of Ophelia's book where it lay upon her drafting table, making the image of the cat statuette appear to blaze. Patience stared at it, then, still carrying her outfit, crossed to the desk and sat.

I'm just going to take a peek, she told herself, then smiled. *It's not like I'm doing anything wrong—it's only a book!*

She closed her eyes, opened the volume, and let its pages flip through her fingers. After a moment she stabbed at a page at random, then opened her eyes and began to read.

THE POET AND THE INKMAKER'S DAUGHTER

Heian Japan

In the reign of she who became known as the Dark Willow Empress, there lived in a far-off city a poet by the name of Ga-sho. He lived as all poor poets do, upon memories and tea-dregs, but what sustained him most of all were thoughts of a certain young woman, a maid to a lady-in-waiting to the Dark Willow Empress. This young woman had no name, at least none that Ga-sho knew of. He had glimpsed her only once, as she followed the litter bearing her mistress along a canal and then over a bridge at the city's edge. The hem of her kimono was spattered with mud and rotten waterweeds, but her face—what he could see of it, anyway, as she kept her head down and her long sleeve held before her cheeks—was exquisite, with skin as fine and white as rice paper and long-lashed eyes like chrysanthemum blossoms. As he stood aside on the bridge to let her pass, he caught the strong fragrance of *kurobo*, sweet incense, trailing her like a warm wind. For this reason, and the beauty of her eyes, in his thoughts he called her Fair Flower.

Ga-sho had inherited a small sum after his father's death, enough to keep a tiny room in the very darkest quarter of the city. Here, before a brazier no bigger than his cupped hands, Ga-sho wrote his poems upon scrolls of rice paper. All of his verses praised Fair Flower's beauty, her gentleness, her devotion and her virtue (though mostly he wrote of her beauty). He did not know that the young woman he loved was in fact bad-tempered and shrill, with a voice like green sticks breaking; that she gambled with the other maids and had amassed a considerable debt, which she had absolutely no intention of paying; that she snored, and her breath often stank of plum wine, even in the morning; that she had for some time now been trysting with a handsome gardener in the Dark Willow Empress's employ; and that she dallied also with the gardener's cousin, and occasionally with the cousin's best friend, who worked in the lower kitchen. (The name they had for her was less flattering than "Fair Flower," and I will not reveal it here.)

No, Ga-sho's poems took none of this into account, and that is perhaps for the best. That which is true often makes for very bland reading.

Poor as he was, Ga-sho kept a cat. She was a fastidious creature, bobtailed as cats of that time and place were, with pale aquamarine eyes and black front paws; not as beautiful as Fair Flower, perhaps, but with far better manners. The most remarkable thing about her was her color: a strange, deep reddish brown, the color of new bronze tinged with blood. Such red cats were considered to have special powers by the superstitious, and were called *Kinkwaneko*, Golden Flower, but Ga-Sho, while a sentimental sort when it came to women, was not particularly superstitious. He called her Clean-ears.

The red cat slept beside Ga-sho and kept him warm at night. In the morning, she gently woke him by nudging his cheek. When the poet ate, he always saved bits of fish for his companion. When he had little money for food, or forgot to eat, Clean-ears would slip silently as a sigh from his tiny room and make her way to the city docks. An hour or so later she would return, bearing a fish, or perhaps a prawn, that she would lay upon the poet's wooden pillow. Always she would politely refuse to dine until he was finished, and in return he was careful to save for her the choicest parts of the head, particularly the eyes, to which the red cat was very partial.

One of the few people Ga-sho could afford to do business with was an inkmaker whose shop was not far from the poet's cramped room. The inkmaker was a poor man himself, but poverty had made him neither kindly nor patient toward those who owed him money. Rather, he was mean-spirited, craven to those with more wealth than his meager savings, and to one person at least he was downright cruel.

This was his stepdaughter, Ukon. He had married her mother under the misprision that she had a small fortune; upon discovering that she did not, he had hounded her to her death (or so it was believed in that part of the city, where gossip ran hot and destructive as the fires that often broke out during the winter months). Ukon's mother was also reputed to have been a fox-fairy, and for several weeks after she died the inkmaker kept a cudgel by his bed, in case her vengeful spirit returned to harm him.

But either because she was not a fairy, or because she feared for her daughter's well-being, the ghost did not appear, and poor Ukon was left alone to her fate. Neighbors could hear her piteous cries late at night when her stepfather beat her—bamboo-and-rice-paper walls do little to hide such things—but no one moved to help her. A man's daughter, even a stepdaughter, was his own concern. So, as her father spent his days and nights drinking with his customers and creditors, the brunt of the work of making ink was left to his stepdaughter.

It was Ukon who tended to the small stove where red pine wood and red pine resin were burned, all through the autumn and winter months. It was Ukon who then scraped the resulting soot from inside the stove, placing it in a bowl to which she added fish glue. The fish glue she made herself, begging fish bones from the docks, then boiling them on another stove. It smelled horrible, so she added plum and peony blossoms, and sometimes even sandalwood, if she could afford it. She mixed the fish glue and the soot together on a wide wooden plank, kneading the thick paste until it became soft and pliable as sweet rice cakes, then pressed the soft ink into wooden pattern blocks, square and round and rectangular. But the ink could not be left in the pattern molds, or it would crack as it dried. Ukon had to very carefully remove the blocks of ink, transferring them to wooden boxes filled with damp charcoal. Here the sumi ink would dry slowly, for days or even weeks, and Ukon had to replace the charcoal as it dried. Finally the sumi was dry enough to be wrapped in rice paper and hung to cure for another month, in the little shed in the alley behind the shop where she and her stepfather lived. Only then would Ukon carefully mark each sumi stick with her stepfather's mark, wrap it in fine paper, and pile them all in neat stacks in the rear of the little shop. Her hands and fingers had become so stained by sumi ink that they never washed clean, nor did the rank smell of fish bones ever leave her skin; rather than help her, though, her drunken stepfather only mocked the girl.

"You will never win a suitor," he said disdainfully, staring at her black hands. "I will be lucky if you don't frighten away the few customers we have—"

And he cuffed her fiercely on the cheek, sending her reeling back to where the largest ink blocks awaited cutting.

Now, I have written that no one ever moved to help Ukon, but that is not quite true. Because the girl, poor and miserable as she was, yet possessed a kind heart, and like the half-strangled rosebush that still reaches toward a thread of sunlight, so did Ukon strive toward charity. As there was not a single human being in that quarter as poor and unhappy as she, Ukon's kindnesses by necessity were directed toward other creatures, smaller and even hungrier than herself. So she would rescue crippled crickets trapped in their bamboo cages when the boys grew bored with them and tossed them aside, and save grains of rice to feed half-starved sparrows in the winter snow. And she would secretly feed a cat that often showed up in the alley behind the shop, a small red cat with a puffy bobbed tail like a blossom past its prime. It was drawn like other strays by the smell of rotting fish that rose from the ink shed. But it was smaller than the other cats, and milder-tempered, and Ukon made a point of saving fishtails for it, and fish bones with bits of flesh still adhering to them like hairs to a brittle comb.

It was on one such afternoon, late of a winter day in the Eleventh, or Frosty, Month, that Ukon made one of her furtive forays into the alleyway.

"Ah, *suteneko*," she crooned, stooping to stroke the red cat behind its ears. "Poor *suteneko*, pretty *Kinkwa-neko*—you are so cold! Here—there is hardly anything, but . . ."

She held out her ink-blackened fingers, and the cat licked the flakes of fish from them gratefully.

"She's not a stray, you know."

Ukon whirled, frightened, and backed against the flimsy wall of the shed. She lowered her head automatically, as she would in deference to any customer, but she also raised her arm, as though to protect herself from a blow.

Peering through her fingers she saw, not the threatening figure of her drunken father, but a young man in frayed robes and worn wooden shoes.

The poet, she thought, recognizing him by the ink stains on his sleeves and his hollow cheeks. Slowly she lowered her hand, but remained where she huddled against the wall, heedless of the sleet pelting down on her bare head.

"She stays with me," the poet went on matter-of-factly. " '*Suteneko!*' " he said chidingly, and bent to pick up the cat. "She thinks you're a stray!"

He stroked her head, blowing into her pointed ears, then looked at Ukon. "I call her *Kuri-ryoumimi*," he said. "Kury-ri."

"Ah." Ukon smiled tentatively. " 'Clean-ears.' "

The poet smiled back at her. But his smile died as he took in her blackened hands and red face—red and chafed from crying, and still bearing the marks of her stepfather's blows. "I . . . I was in the shop, but saw no one," he said apologetically. "I need some more ink. But I can come back tomorrow—"

"No, no," Ukon cried, and hurried back inside. "My father is gone on an errand"—in fact, he was drinking at the tavern—"but I will get whatever you need."

She busied herself with finding and wrapping several rectangular blocks of ink. The poet had asked for the cheapest kind, which was all he could afford, but as she began to pull the ink from its shelf, Ukon suddenly hesitated. She glanced over her shoulder to make sure he could not see, and that no other customers had entered the shop. Then she swiftly replaced the inexpensive sumi stick with a chrysanthemum-shaped block of the most expensive ink her stepfather sold, scented with geranium leaves and tinted a deep vermillion. She wrapped it in a second sheet of rice paper, so that the poet would not see its value and refuse it. Then she hurried back to the front of the shop.

"Here," she said, bowing as she handed it to him.

And as she gazed at him, her face reddened even more, though not from fear or pain. The poet took the sumi ink and stared back at her musingly.

She is nothing like Fair Flower, Ga-sho thought. There is no fragrance here but the reek of boiling fish guts, and her hands are black as my cat's paws, and her skin is as red as— well, as red as Clean-ears's fur. And everyone says the old man beats her. . . .

And yet her smile was sweet, her voice low, her gaze gentle. And she had shown kindness to a stray cat. . . .

"Thank you," he said, too quickly, then turned and left.

That night Ga-sho wrote a poem in praise of the

inkmaker's daughter. He could not, in good con-
science, compare her to a flower, or even a blossom-
ing weed. But the Japanese have many poems that
honor cats, and so he began by comparing her to
Clean-ears. After some time spent thus, his thoughts
began to move from feline virtues to more feminine
ones, and he found himself composing verse that (to
his own mind, at least) was at least as fine as those
poems inspired by Fair Flower. He recited the best of
these several times to Clean-ears, who sat washing
her paws (which became no whiter than Ukon's palms)
beside the lamp.

> *Red cheek, raven hair,*
> *Her hands night-shaded and raw—*
> *I would know her name!*

He took a sheet of paper, withdrew the sumi stick
he had bought that afternoon, and unwrapped it.

"Ah!" The poet's eyes grew wide and wondering. He
held up the blossom-shaped ink block, glossy, with a
telltale reddish tinge. He felt his cheeks grow hot,
and looked furtively aside at the cat, as though to
make sure she did not notice his blush.

But the cat was gone. And so, smiling to himself as
he ground the vermillion ink on his inkstone and
licked the sable tip of his brush, Ga-sho began to
record his poem.

Meanwhile, Ukon was waiting up for her stepfather
in the back of the shop, where her bed was a thin pal-
let on the floor. She dared not sleep before he returned; in any event, her thoughts were too full of the

young poet to be at rest. So she busied herself tending the small hearth that heated the shop, and removing dry sumi sticks from their rice husks and wrapping them in paper.

It was past midnight when she heard the sound of stumbling footsteps in the alley, followed by the creaking of the door as it was pulled open.

"Father," she called softly, going to greet him.

Her stepfather stumbled into the room, robes awry and his thin hair disheveled. Ukon drew up alongside him, trying to help him keep from falling.

"Lazy bitch!"

He struck at her furiously, but in his drunkenness he went flailing wildly, bashing against one thin wall. Ukon ran to his side, but he lashed out at her again, striking her so that she fell, weeping, by the hearth.

"You have been seeing men in here," he gasped, struggling to his feet. "The old woman next door said she saw that layabout from the next street—"

"He was a customer, most watchful of stepfathers," Ukon pleaded. "You must remember him, he is the poet—"

"Poet! He is worthless, as you are! Whoring like your mother before you!"

But at the word "customer" his eyes had gone to the metal strongbox where each day's accounts were kept. He grabbed it, shaking it; opened it, then glared accusingly at Ukon.

Oh no! She covered her face with her hands. Her delight in serving the young poet had blinded her to duty—she had forgotten to get payment for the ink stick!

"Father," she stammered, but it was too late. He

began beating her with the strongbox, battering at the poor girl's face and shoulders until she collapsed onto the floor in a heap.

"I will find this poet and kill him," she heard her stepfather mutter thickly as he flung the metal box aside. "That I will . . ."

Ukon was too weak to do more than pull herself to a corner, watching through swollen eyes as her stepfather lurched out the back door into the alley. But soon sheer exhaustion washed over her pain, as with time the tide will cover a littered beach, smoothing out the soiled sand and, for a little while at least, making the world seem at peace. So it was that Ukon fell into fitful sleep upon the dirt floor, one arm still flung protectively over her poor battered face.

She woke to a low voice calling her name.

"Ukon . . . Ukon, you must wake!"

She raised her head groggily, the torn sleeve of her robe catching on the edge of a small table, and looked up. In her dreaming she had half-imagined the voice belonged to the young poet.

But as she blinked in the darkness she saw a woman standing before her. She was older than Ukon, her neat coif showing wisps of gray beneath thick black hair lacquer; for an instant, Ukon thought it was her mother. Then she saw that while the woman's pointed face had the same piquance as her mother's, her eyes were a very pale gray, like seawater, and she wore a kimono of deep scarlet silk, a color her mother would never have worn.

"You must come with me," the woman said, calmly but with great urgency. As Ukon began to stammer a question, she raised a hand, its palm smudged as black as Ukon's own. "There is no time—come!"

Ukon got to her feet. Her ears rang from the blows her stepfather had given her, and she thought she could hear another sound, oddly familiar, but the strange woman did not give her the opportunity to look around the shop for its source.

"This way!" she hissed; grabbing Ukon's wrist, she dragged her out to the street. They began running along the narrow way, their wooden shoes sliding in the sleet and dirty snow. As they ran, Ukon began to hear agitated voices behind her, and then a sudden shout.

"Fire! *The inkmaker's shop is on fire!*"

"Aiie!" With a cry, Ukon stopped and looked back. From the alley behind her stepfather's shop rose a plume of smoke. Abruptly the wind shifted, carrying the smell of burning pine. "He must have overfilled the stove in the shed! I must go—"

"No." This time the woman's voice was a command. Her hold on Ukon's wrist tightened. Her breath as she pulled the girl to her smelled of rotting fish. "Your life there is over. You will come with me now. Do not look back again."

In a daze, Ukon turned and let herself be led along twisting alleys, away from the inkmaker's shop. A great clamor of gongs and bells now arose from the streets, as people signaled that the quarter was in danger of burning; as dozens of men raced toward the shop carrying wooden buckets of water and sand, few noted the inkmaker's stepdaughter hurrying in the opposite direction, a small red cat at her side. Afterward, those who *had* seen her running displayed neither recrimination nor much remorse for her leaving her stepfather to perish in the flames. His cruelty and drunkenness were well-known; the fire, which had indeed started in the shed, was contained to his quarters, and no one else was harmed.

Ukon followed the strange woman to a narrow street where she had never been.

"Here," the woman said, bowing as she gestured at the door. "Here you will find safety."

And before Ukon could protest, or give voice to her questions, the woman was gone. The poor girl stood shivering in the snow, tears once more springing to her eyes, when suddenly the little door slid open, and who should be standing there, yawning and rubbing his face, but the young poet, Ga-sho.

"Why . . . ?" He stared at her in disbelief. Ukon dropped her head, abashed and ashamed, and had begun to turn away when he grabbed her hand. "Don't go! Please, come in. You look half frozen, and"—his voice dropped, and he chuckled—"and look who you've found! Kury-ri, you naughty creature. . . ."

He bent to pick up the red cat, which had appeared out of nowhere to rub against the filthy hem of Ukon's kimono. "Where have you been?"

He held the cat to his breast and looked at Ukon. "She ran off after I saw you—she's been out all night! But please, come in."

And he stood aside so that Ukon could enter.

They did not marry immediately, and for a while there was some mild scandal over the fact that the inkmaker's stepdaughter had found a home in the poor poet's rooms. But the tongues of that quarter soon enough found other tales to wag about, and by the time Ukon and Ga-sho were wed and had a baby due, the red cat had given birth to a litter of kittens of her own.

And, while the strange woman who had saved Ukon was never seen again in that district, for years afterward the descendants of the cat called Clean-ears—red-furred, black-pawed, gray-eyed like their mother—were said to be lucky. Because how otherwise to account for the success the poet had, and the long and happy marriage he and Ukon endured? Such things did not come often to the poor people of that time, any more than they do to us today!

Ophelia Powers's note: In medieval Japan, red bobtailed cats were known as Kinkwa-neko, Golden Flower. They were thought to assume the forms of beautiful young women, and to help young girls in distress.

TWENTY-ONE

It was nearly eight o'clock before Patience finally put aside Ophelia's book and got down to her night's real work—breaking into the Hedare mansion. The sprawling mock-Victorian building sat atop a knoll surrounded by oaks and weeping willows. A cast-iron gate crowned by a scrollwork H formed the entrance, with ten-foot brick walls to either side. A security camera was mounted on top of one of these. Cat-woman stood safely out of its field of view, her bull-whip uncoiled. She ran her gloved fingers lovingly over its length, then expertly stepped back and sent the whip flying.

Its metal tip knocked the camera to one side. Cat-woman quickly wound the whip around her hand, then stuck it back into her belt, its end trailing behind her like a tail. She leaped onto the wall, landing on all fours, jumped down and ran through the trees' shadows toward the house.

The grand front door was brightly lit, but there were no other lights on, save a dim glow at one window on the second floor. A tall trellis was fixed to the house beneath it. Catwoman climbed up the trellis, then jumped onto a wide ledge. She crouched and peered inside.

"George's study," she said beneath her breath. "I'd bet on it."

She extended her diamond-tipped forefinger and traced a small circle into the glass. She tapped the circle and it popped out, falling silently onto the carpet inside. Catwoman reached in, her hand closing on the window latch. She unlocked it and pulled the casement open, then jumped inside.

She landed on a thick Baluchi rug, woven in rich shades of burgundy and indigo and violet. The walls around her were paneled in fumed oak; there were carved bookshelves, heavy Mission-style furniture, a huge leather chair and matching ottoman, an oak rolltop desk and the faint underlying musk of expensive cologne and hand-rolled Cuban cigars—

George's office, absolutely.

Catwoman strode to the desk and began yanking out drawer after drawer. She flipped through a box of Zip disks, checking the label of each one before tossing it aside.

Nothing.

"Damn," she muttered. "Maybe downstairs—"

Swiftly she turned and headed out into the corridor. As she did, a figure emerged from the darkness, swinging a golf club.

WHAM!

The nine iron connected with Catwoman's skull.

Without a sound, she crumpled and toppled down the stairs, struck the landing, and sprawled motionless across the floor.

A light came on, revealing a slender figure at the top of the stairs, brandishing the club like a sword—Laurel Hedare, in a pose incongruous with her sleep-tousled hair and silk pajamas. She crept cautiously down the stairs, club raised. When she reached the prone figure of Catwoman, she nudged her tentatively with her foot, then leaned in to study her more closely.

"You picked the wrong house," said Laurel.

Without warning, Catwoman sprang up. She snatched the club from Laurel's hand and tossed it down the stairs.

"I'd love to play, but I don't have time," Catwoman snapped as Laurel warily backed away.

"You're that cat. The one who killed Slavicky."

"Now, Laurel. You shouldn't believe everything you see on TV."

"What do you want?"

"Is the 'man of the house' at home?"

Laurel recovered herself, running a hand self-consciously across her hair. "Why on earth would *he* be home?" she snapped. "I'*m* here."

"Too bad he missed me." Catwoman leaned in toward Laurel, her voice sultry. "I hear he loves pussy . . . cats"

Laurel met her eyes. Then she ducked, darting beneath Catwoman's arm and heading for the stairs. Before she reached them, Catwoman pounced on her, and the two tumbled down together. When they reached the bottom, Catwoman was on top, trying to catch her breath.

"If you've got a problem with him, maybe we can work it out?" pleaded Laurel. "Girl to girl?"

"Oh, that'd be *fun!*" Catwoman said mockingly. "We could make s'mores and do each other's hair and talk about boys—"

"Or . . . ," said Laurel. She arched her back, suddenly thrust Catwoman from her, and scrambled to her feet. "We could skip the snacks and makeovers and talk about whatever the hell it is that you *want.*"

"I want to talk to your husband," Catwoman said, and stood. "Man to cat. If he ever comes home again, tell him I know all about Beau-line."

Laurel froze. "What about Beau-line?"

"Beau-line. It's disease in a jar. Wouldn't caulk a sink with it."

"Nonsense. I've been using it for years."

"Drop the habit." Catwoman held up her claws, preening. "Or not. It's your funeral. Because whoever killed Slavicky, did it to keep Beau-line's toxic little secret. And Slavicky wasn't the first."

Laurel looked startled but did her best to hide it. "You're suggesting that my husband is . . . a murderer?"

"I'm *suggesting* that you tell me where he is, so I can ask him myself."

Laurel stared at her, deliberating. Finally she said, "I should be shocked. I should protest his innocence, tell you he would never do such things. . . ."

Catwoman's eyes narrowed. She had a sudden vision of a body plunging from the waste tunnel at the

Hedare factory into the torrent below, but she said nothing as Laurel went on.

"But the truth is, that man's capable of anything."

Her voice trailed off. Slowly but resolutely, she crossed to a side table and pushed aside a cell phone, then began to sort through a stack of mail. She turned, holding out a glossy turquoise invitation.

HYDROPOLIS: *An Aquatic Fantasy*
Opening Night Benefit
By Cirque de Lune

Catwoman looked at the card, then took it. Once again her eyes locked with Laurel's, but this time there was a powerful undercurrent of complicity; a kind of recognition between the two women.

"Thanks," said Catwoman.

Laurel nodded. She looked down, composing herself, then gave Catwoman a determined look. "If this is true, I won't be a party to it. I want to help. Is there a way I can reach you?"

Catwoman read the address on the invitation— the city's main performance center. She thought for a moment, then snatched the cell phone from the table.

"I'm not listed," she said. "Hit me up on your cell."

She turned and headed for the door. Only when she opened it did she pause, looking back at the slim, fragile-looking blond woman standing in that vast house.

"Take care of yourself, Laurel," she said in a low

voice. "Not everybody gets nine lives. For what it's worth, I'm sorry."

Laurel shook her head. "I built my life around him."

"It's time to get your own," said Catwoman, and was gone.

TWENTY-TWO

"What are we seeing, George?" Drina simpered for the crowds of paparazzi and security men as she sashayed into the performance center lobby. "Another benefit play?"

"Less seeing," retorted George. He flashed a cold, professional smile. Camera flashes lit the night around them, and he took Drina's arm. "More *being seen.*"

Drina giggled, and let George escort her into the main theater complex.

Just a few yards away, Catwoman was making a more furtive entrance. She crept through the bushes, looking for a way in; finally spied a two-story glass atrium fronted by ficus trees. She used the trees as a springboard to scale the facade, leaping onto a second-floor balcony.

"Doesn't anyone ever lock their doors anymore?" she muttered, and slipped inside.

But Catwoman's entrance was not as subtle as she'd planned. On the ground, a uniformed cop witnessed the entire display—with enough amazement that it wasn't until Catwoman had disappeared that he fumbled for his walkie-talkie.

"You're not gonna believe this!" he gasped, and started running.

Inside, Catwoman was slinking along a wide, crimson-carpeted hallway. A crowd of security personnel hovered around the formal stairway that opened onto the second floor.

No *go that way*, she thought, and bared her teeth in frustration. She turned and ran at a half-crouch to where a velvet rope blocked another narrower corridor. A sign dangled from one brass stanchion.

PRIVATE BOXES.

She slipped past the rope and made a beeline toward a door. She opened it silently, crept inside, and halted.

The box was plush, all velvet and gold tassels. A single silver-haired couple in formal wear and enough diamonds to outfit an emerging nation sat mesmerized, watching what was onstage.

And for a minute Catwoman stared too, momentarily riveted by the explosion of light and color and sound. Aquamarine and cerulean scrims set the underwater theme, enhanced by giant painted tropical fish that floated above the stage floor—clown fish, parrot fish, angelfish, glowing electric eels and ultramarine octopi. Trapezes and tightropes were strung between the bobbing fish, and a troupe of nearly naked acrobats shimmied up and down and across, leaping and falling from bungee chords as the audience gasped and applauded. Just offstage, huge fans were turned so that long banners and streamers of emerald and jade and indigo fluttered and rippled in their wake.

Catwoman blinked, and reluctantly tore herself from •the entrancing undersea vision below. She waited until the music rose to a loud pitch, then stepped silently into the shadows behind the couple. She scanned the theater until she found what she was looking for—

George Hedare and Drina, sitting in the President's Box. Heavy velvet drapes were swagged to either side. George was watching the performance raptly. Drina snuggled up against him, bored.

"I think this is a total waste of time," she began.

"Don't," said George brusquely. "Remember—*no thinking.*"

Drina stood in a huff and stormed out of the box. George shook his head and turned back to the performance.

Awww. Poor guy's probably not used to being without a woman for more than five seconds, thought Catwoman. *Better do something about that . . .*

She darted to the front of the box, ignoring the astonished expressions on the elderly couple.

"Is she part of the show?" the man asked his wife doubtfully.

"Check out the encore," Catwoman advised, and climbed out onto the gilt molding that framed the box. She clambered up, grabbing on to a frieze that wrapped around the hall's ceiling. The wood-and-plaster decorations fortunately were mounted on steel girders. She swung herself on top of this, then crawled along just inches from the ceiling, until she reached the proscenium.

The President's Box was opposite her now, on the far side of the stage.

Let's hope it's dark enough up here, she thought, and looked dubiously at the brilliant display of writhing bodies and luminous color below. *At night all cats are gray, right?*

She took a deep breath, then edged across the proscenium arch. Beneath her, the performers wriggled up and down tightropes. The music swelled and started to build toward a grand crescendo, and the luminous tropical fish slowly started to rise toward the ceiling. When Catwoman glanced out at the audience, she saw several people in the front row pointing at her and grinning.

They think I'm part of the show! she thought. *The cat stalking aquarium fish—but I've got bigger prey than that.* She glanced back down and saw an usher staring at her in alarm. *Uh-oh . . .*

Catwoman scowled as the usher turned and rushed toward an exit. *No Ocean Delight tonight. Better hurry!*

She reached the edge of the proscenium. Just below, George Hedare sat alone in his plush seat, yawning. Catwoman crouched, then jumped, landing in the empty seat beside him.

"Right on time," she whispered. "I love this part."

"What the . . . !"

"Like my nails?" Catwoman leered, holding up her diamond-tipped claws. "I just had them done."

She slashed him across the cheek. He cried out, clutching his face, but the music drowned out his voice. He staggered from his chair and stumbled for the exit, but Catwoman got there first. She shoved a chair against the door, blocking it, then advanced on him.

"Ooh, my bad. You can take the cat out of the alley, but you just can't take the alley out of the cat. But, you know, red's a good color on you." She inclined her head to where blood dripped from his cheek, staining his white tuxedo shirt. "Want to see more?"

"Get your paws off me this instant—"

She grabbed him and slammed him against the wall, yanking one of the velvet drapes to hide them from view.

"No, please—" George pleaded.

"I know all about you, George," Catwoman said in a deceptively calm voice. "I know you're a cold-blooded killer. I know you're willing to poison millions of desperate women just to make a buck."

"*What?*"

"I *know about* Beau-line. I know it's poison and I know you're covering it up. And so did my girl Patience. That's why you killed her."

The door began to rattle. Catwoman's head swiveled as she heard voices shouting in the hall outside. George choked, then gasped, "What? I *fired* her—"

She slid a hand around his throat, her claws digging into his skin as her voice dropped to a whisper. "Sad, isn't it? That your last words will be a lie. Oh well—"

With a crash, the door flew open. A half dozen uniformed cops streamed in, guns drawn. With a hiss of frustration, Catwoman threw George aside. She jumped to the edge of the box, and paused.

Below, more cops were charging down the aisles toward the stage. All were armed. Catwoman looked behind her.

Only one way out . . .

She leaped toward the stage, grabbing a trapeze. Around her the *Cirque de Lune* performers registered shock, but continued their performance as the leather-clad figure swung from the trapeze to an acrobat clinging to a bungee cord. She landed on his back and immediately sprang off into the rafters, while the audience erupted into cheers.

Hey, maybe I should quit my day job!

Catwoman swung from one sandbagged rope to another, slashing so that the bags fell on the cops swarming the stage. She scrambled higher into the grid of catwalks high above the stage floor, jumped onto the light grid, and began to run.

"*Stop right there!*"

She froze at the familiar voice. Scarcely an arm's length away, Tom Lone climbed a ladder toward the grid. His gun was trained on her, and it didn't take a ballistics specialist to see that he had a clear shot.

"Come down. *Now,*" he commanded.

Catwoman stared at him with cool green eyes. "You know nothing about cats. We come when we feel like it, not when we're called."

Tom pulled himself onto the grid. He approached her slowly, stepping gingerly along the grid. Below, the spotlights cast a blinding glare on the stage, but here all was thrown into shadow.

"You're under arrest—"

He stepped toward her, his weight falling on a two-by-four. The board creaked, then gave way. Tom swayed, losing his balance, but before he could fall Catwoman sprang, grabbing his gun arm and pulling him upright.

He stared at her; she stared back. Then she snatched the gun from his hand and tossed it into the darkness; grabbed his tie and pulled him slowly, inexorably, toward her.

And kissed him, leaving a bright crimson imprint upon one cheek. Then she spun and bounded off, walking with ease along the narrow metal railings. Tom blinked, then continued his pursuit, walking warily, one foot right in front of the other, until he reached the end.

There was a steel-mesh platform here, twenty-five feet above the stage. Catwoman stood in the corner, looking from Tom to the stage floor. A crowd of armed cops waited there, guns aimed at her.

She was trapped.

Tom moved toward her, still wary, but confident now that she had no way out. He pulled a pair of handcuffs from his vest. Catwoman's eyes narrowed.

"What? Don't I get dinner first?"

"They'll feed you in your cell."

He lunged at her. She dodged, kicking his leg out from under him.

But Tom recovered quickly. He rolled, then planted a kick in her midsection. Catwoman gasped in pain.

"Someone likes playing rough," she hissed. As Tom lunged toward her again, she jumped, grabbing an overhead electrical cable, and swung out of reach. Tom kept coming—he was going too fast, and flailed helplessly to keep from plunging over the railing. Catwoman twisted around on the cable, adjusting her weight so that it swung back toward him like a pendulum. As she approached, she wrapped her legs around his neck, saving him from falling, then drew him back to the center of the platform. He grasped her legs, trying to pull her down—

And snapped the cable.

The stage lights went black amidst shouts and confusion from below. Sparks flew everywhere as Catwoman and Tom Lone thudded onto the platform together. With a low hiss, Catwoman snatched the cable in midair, catching it just before it struck the grillwork.

"Careful!" shouted Tom. "If that thing hits the metal, we're both fried!"

Catwoman held the spitting cable above her head like a torch. She drew her head alongside Tom's and whispered, "I knew I felt a spark between us."

Then she turned and flung the cable away, so that it dangled free, safely out of reach of the grid but still sending out showers of sparks. Tom took this opportunity to grab her, snapping one handcuff around her wrist, then the other around his own, locking them together. He knocked her to the metal floor and spun her around, his hand yanking at her mask.

Catwoman slapped him away, then pinioned him. "Please—it's our first date!"

"Oh yeah?" Tom gave her a cold smile, pretending to join her game. "Don't flatter yourself, lady. I'm taken."

Catwoman smiled back. "Really?" she asked, taunting him. "Does she know about us?"

"There *is* no 'us.' Just a cop and a cat he's trying to collar."

"Is your girl purr-fect, like me?"

"She's not like you at all."

He struggled to push her away, but Catwoman kept her thighs locked around him.

Catwoman smiled and purred, then squeezed her fingers together and, in a single, fluid motion, slipped her hand out of the restraining handcuff.

Catwoman smiled. Then she booted him, knocking him backward, and jumped to her feet.

The echo of heavy feet made her glance to either side. The cops had made their way up onto the catwalk, blocking every possible exit.

She backed away, leaped, and grabbed the power cord still dangling from the ceiling. She hung on to it carefully, then began to shimmy down, jumping at the last moment to the floor.

Cops surrounded her, a dozen guns all aimed at the same lithe figure. She continued to hold the power cable like a Fourth of July sparkler. The cops looked at one another uneasily, when she suddenly broke away, still holding the cable, and darted to a wall.

"Show of hands!" Catwoman looked meaningfully at a circuit breaker on the wall beside her. "Who can see in the dark?"

She looked around, daintily raised her own gloved hand, then swung the cable into the circuit breaker. "Oops!"

There was a blinding flash, a thunderous *bang*! Sparks cascaded down onto the stage as the theater was plunged into darkness. Panicked screams echoed from the rows of seats—the performers were long gone—and a chorus of grunts and curses from the cops stumbling blindly backstage. Catwoman took a few careful steps toward the stage door, then made a mocking bow.

"Thank you, ladies and gentlemen," she said. "The pleasure has been all mine."

Then she darted outside.

TWENTY-THREE

O tiger's heart wrapt in a woman's hide!
—WILLIAM SHAKESPEARE, *Henry VI, Part III*

"This is a disaster! A total disaster!"

George Hedare tore through his study, yanking cartons from shelves and searching frantically through them. His face had been bandaged, and his cell phone was pressed gingerly against the wads of white gauze. "No, you don't understand—this could destroy us," he shouted. "How does she know all this, anyway? Who is she and what—"

"Problems?" asked Laurel.

He stopped abruptly, looked up to see his wife standing in the doorway, arms crossed. He switched off the phone and tossed it aside, then stared at her accusingly.

Laurel stared back at him, her gaze unruffled. "It's all right, darling," she said. "Don't be scared."

"You have no idea! We are on the brink of ruin! And your brilliant advice to me is, '*Don't be scared*'?"

"No."

Laurel walked right up to him, until she was inches from his face. "My advice to you is quit the self-tanning, stop pretending Viagra is a vitamin, resist the urge to date children born on the same day they invented cell phones, and *for God's sake*, George, for just once in your miserable life—*be a man.*"

George went white. He stepped toward his wife and slapped her, hard, across the face.

Laurel didn't even flinch. Instead she stood impassively as her husband recoiled in pain and fear.

Because when he struck her, his fingers didn't meet warm, yielding flesh.

It was as though he'd crushed his palm against a granite slab. He grimaced, clutching his limp hand, and looked at his wife as though he had never seen her before.

Laurel stared back, unblinking, her eyes remote. In a way, she didn't see him: the man before her had crossed a line, and she wasn't going to follow.

Without speaking, she turned and left.

It was late afternoon when Patience woke the next day. She yawned, rolling over and kicking the covers aside.

It's too early! she thought, though the clock showed it was nearly four. She rubbed her eyes, then glanced down at Ophelia's book on the floor beside her bed.

"Mmmmm. Just one more," she murmured, and picked up the book. "That way if I ever actually *see* Ophelia again, we'll have something to talk about . . . besides Catwoman."

She opened it, and began once more to read.

MIDITYI GOES HUNTING

This a tale of the Sundarbans, the Country of the Beautiful Trees—the *sundari* trees which grow in the southern delta of the Ganges River. In this land as well are found the vast mangrove swamps and forests, and off the coast the Drowned Lands, mangrove islets that appear, then mysteriously melt back into the Sea of Bengal like so many morning fogs. Fishermen ply their way among the mangrove islands, for between the shadowy tree-knees, crabs hide and scuttle. Farther out in the water, the men drag great nets to catch the great tiger prawns which taste so sweet when roasted over an open fire with cumin seeds and fenugreek.

But men step warily among the Drowned Lands, for that is where the tigers prowl. That is where Bonobibi the tiger goddess dwells, protector of the forest, as she is the protector of children and of the helpless. And in that lovely though haunted place it is not just children who are helpless, but women, whose lives and voices can be as silent as the screams of the tiger's prey. For it is well-known that no one ever hears the tiger strike: he devours even the voices of his victims, so that they leave no trace whatsoever, not a drop of blood, not an echo upon the salt-smelling air.

And so it is that the history of the women of the Drowned Lands is as much a secret as the place where Bonobibi lays her tawny head to sleep.

In those days upon an islet in the Drowned Lands there lived an elderly widow named Midityi. I will call her that, though in fact if you read the old tales of that time and place, you will seldom see a woman named; she is always called simply the Widow, or the Bride, or the Daughter, or the Mother. Never is she given her own name, and so I will make sure you know Midityi's.

Midityi was not old as we reckon it, only a few years past childbearing age, but in the Drowned Lands she was considered ancient. She was considered cursed, as well, for while she had made a comfortable marriage to a fisherman, and was fond of her husband as he was of her, still she had borne him no children, not even a daughter whom she might have married off, and whose husband might then have given Midityi a few more cowries to spend on cooking oil and spices.

Midityi's own husband, alas, had died several years before. He had been out plying the sea in his small, nimble boat when an estuarine crocodile, easily three times the length of the little craft, had tipped it over and eaten the luckless fisherman. Witnesses said that the crocodile was so huge it surely must have been Shiber Kuma, Lord Vishnu's Crocodile; but to the fisherman it made no difference whom he was eaten by. He was dead, and his grieving widow was left with only their small home, barely more than a shack, and the remnants of the fishing boat when they were washed ashore. With the bits of wood she reinforced her home; the remnants of net that she gathered from the muddy shore she repaired, so that she might at least be able to catch *saphari*, the minnows that dart in the shallows of the mangrove-knees. When she went wading in the muddy flats she wore a necklace of *rudrashka* beads, so that Shiber Kuma would know she was under Siva's protection. She was a pious woman, hard-working and, if anyone had bothered to look, still quite lovely.

But as she was a widow, and poor, no one paid Midityi any mind at all except to pity her. This they need not have done, because though she was poor, still she knew the best places in the marsh to fish and drag nets for shrimp, which hollow trees held honey, which drowned roots hid crabs and shellfish. And she knew which trees to avoid, because venomous kraits and vipers nested in their crotch, and she knew to rub her eyelids with tamarind leaves to discourage the tiny flies who would lay their eggs there, to hatch fifteen years later and blind the unwitting.

Most of all, she knew to leave offerings for Bono-bibi, the guardian of the forest, and to Dakshineroi, the monstrous Father of all Tigers, whose uneasy peace with Bonobibi did not always extend to Her followers.

One evening, Midityi was in front of her tiny house, cooking the head of a large *rui* she had caught that morning in a freshwater pool nearby. The smell of frying fish and hot oil made her mouth water. As she stirred the ancient cookpot, she gazed into the twilight encroaching upon the clearing where her house stood, violet shadows overtaking the canopy of *sundari* trees and mangroves, the cries of kingfishers settling for the night and the insectile silhouettes of long-legged herons and egrets roosting in the marsh. The birds seemed restless this evening—they would light upon a mangrove branch, sitting there with wings outspread like a cormorant's, but instead of folding their wings to sleep, after a few minutes they would take off again, giving fretful cries as they flitted from tree to tree.

"Midityi! Midityi!"

The widow turned in surprise. Running along the shoreline was one of her neighbors, a young woman named Nritoka. Nritoka's husband had often fished with Midityi's husband, and after his death he had shown kindness to the widow, helping her make repairs to her house, and sometimes giving his wife rice and cooking oil to bring to Midityi. When Nritoka lost her first child before its birth, Midityi had given her herbs to staunch the bleeding, and later herbs to encourage the healthy birth of a son. The boy was now six years old, slender and swift as a young chital-deer; and while some in the Drowned Lands called Midyiti a witch for her success, Nritoka was not among them.

"What is it, child? Is the boy ill?" Midityi frowned, standing and wiping her hands on her sari. "Is it—"

The word lodged in her throat. She could not bring herself to name Lord Vishnu's Crocodile.

"No!" Nritoka flung herself, panting, onto the log that served as a hearthside bench. She was beautiful—plump and with cheeks shining with oil—but unaccustomed to running. "Worse—a human crocodile! The Maharajah of Alwar is preparing to go hunting."

"The Maharajah of Alwar . . ." Midityi's hands grew cold. She shook her head, and sat on the log where Nritoka now was warming her hands above the red coals. "He is coming here?"

"I do not know. But yesterday a runner came from the Widows' Village, a boy who said that, two nights hence, the Maharajah's men had come there and dragged off his grandmother, saying their lord would be hunting soon."

Midityi swallowed, her mouth tasting of bile. The Maharajah of Alwar was a man whose legendary cruelty made even strong men flee at the sound of his name. His palace was filled with mounted trophies of the kills he had made over the decades—the rare two-horned rhinoceros, elephants, chital-deer, leopards, wild boar, and fishing-cats, a creature that was rumored to be the last surviving cheetah in the Drowned Lands.

But the prey that the Maharajah desired more than any other was . . . tigers. It was rumored that an entire wing of his vast palace was carpeted with the pelts of tigers; that a tiger's mounted head gazed with ruby eyes from every window; that the Maharajah's slippers were tipped with tigers' claws; and that he slept with a female tiger he had raised from a cub, feeding her on human blood and milk. Midityi had never paid much heed to these tales, because the Maharajah's palace was many miles away.

Yet there was one portion of the evil man's legend which could not be refuted. It is well known that the fiercest, the largest, the most powerful and cunning of all tigers live in the Drowned Lands. They are maneaters, and crave human flesh the way a child craves sugar. Some say the salt water of the delta drives them to madness, but then why aren't the men of that country mad? I believe it is that the Drowned Lands are the kingdom of Dakshineroi, the Tiger Demon, and that in the veins of his tiger sons and daughters, His blood blazes like a resin-dipped torch.

In any event, a tiger from the Drowned Lands was

the Maharajah's most sought-after trophy. No matter that he had an anteroom furnished with their skins, and a tiger-skull crown; the Maharajah of Alwar wanted more tigers from the Sundarbans.

This is how he got them.

In the coldest hour of the dawn, the hour when you can watch the dew-pearls creep onto the reeds like tiny snails, and hear the crabs blink their stalk-eyes in the mangrove-knees, the Maharajah's men would drag an elderly widow or a child to a clearing in the Beautiful Forest. There they would stake the poor soul to a wooden beam, and leave her (for it was nearly always a woman or girl) while they returned to oil the Maharajah's rifles and heat his morning tea. The girl might scream or rave, the old woman might cry most piteously, the children weep . . . it mattered not to the cruel Maharajah.

Nor did it matter to the tiger, as, silent as the dew, the great cat would creep through the trees and high grass. As it leaped upon its prey, the woman's mouth would open in a scream that no one heard, because the tiger sucked the voice from between her lips. With one massive paw it would snap her neck, then dip its head to feed—

And *bang*!

The report of the Maharajah's gun would rend the dawn, sending eagles and godwits alike flying into the lavender sky. The tiger would fall alongside its half-eaten prey. The Maharajah's men and his photographer would run to arrange the trophy nearby beneath a tree, so that the Maharajah could have another picture taken. Then the evil lord would return to his breakfast, and kites and jackals and smaller cats would dine their fill upon the wretched woman's corpse.

You can now perhaps understand the widow's alarm at Nritoka's words. To lure his tigers, the Maharajah had in recent years taken to kidnapping women from the Widows' Village—women who had no sons to give them shelter or succor, widows whose children were too young to fish or hunt for honey in the forest, or gather firewood there.

"Still, I am not in the Widows' Village," Midityi said, and reached to lift the *rui* from the cookpot. "I live here, among my husband's friends. I have my own home. I cook my own food . . ."

She set the fish-head on a wooden platter and offered it to Nritoka. The young woman shook her head, but as the enticing scent grew stronger, she picked off a bit of white flesh and popped the steaming morsel between lips stained red from chewing betel nut.

"I know, Midityi," she said, her mouth full. "The Maharajah was hunting this morning. I could hear the poor woman's cries as I slept. . . ."

Nritoka shuddered. She reached for another bite of *rui* to sustain herself, then went on. "She must have been very strong! She fought the tiger, enough that it fled before the Maharajah could shoot it. He shot her instead, in his rage, but his men have told him that the tigers of the Drowned Lands will not feed upon a corpse, only upon flesh they have just killed themselves. He is here now and wants to hunt, today. And the Widows' Village is too far for him to go to find new prey. . . ."

Her voice trailed off. "I begged my husband to give

you shelter, but he is too afraid of the Maharajah—all of the men are. We are poor people like yourself, Midityi, with children." She faltered, then said, "Some of the men say it will be best if he takes you—that you are a witch. But I do not believe that. So I came to warn you."

Nritoka looked anxiously over her shoulder. "I must get back. My husband knows I have come here, but if anyone else learns it will go badly for both of us. You must fly, Midityi, before the Maharajah's men find you!"

Nritoka grasped the widow's hands and bowed until their foreheads touched.

"Thank you," said Midityi, as the young woman stood and darted back into the forest. She sat, staring at the fish-head on its platter.

Fly? she thought. I *would indeed have to grow wings to escape the Maharajah's hunters!*

She sat for a few minutes, brooding as she finished eating the *rui*—whatever she did, it would be best to do it on a full stomach. When she was done, she poured water on the fire. In the distance, she could hear the twittering of godwits in the trees; something was disturbing them. Quickly she went into her little house.

What to take? She looked around at her few belongings: her wedding sari; a small knife; some dried prawns. She grabbed the prawns and the knife, also her tinderbox. She was starting out the door when her eye fell upon a small bronze charm, a stylized eye with a tiger's tooth where the pupil should be. It was a talisman sacred to Bonobibi, and supposed to serve as protection against Dakshineroi. Midityi's husband had not been wearing it when the crocodile took him; but then, what good would it have been against a crocodile?

Midityi grabbed it and wrapped it in the folds of her sari, then ran back outside.

Already it had grown much darker. She could see where the moon hung above the eastern horizon, a shining crescent like the tiger's tooth. From high up in the branches of the Beautiful Forest came the sounds of roosting birds, but she could hear their unease—something moved among the *sundari* trees.

And yes, Midityi's eyes widened as she heard the sound of branches breaking, and muttered curses as someone struggled through the mangrove forest not far from the edge of the clearing. Without a sound the widow turned and ran into the trees at water's edge.

"Ah—she's gone!"

Behind her the curses grew louder. Several men were slashing at the door of her hut, but Midityi did not pause to count how many of them were searching for her. Her heart pounded as she ran, terrified, through the mangroves. She knew where the paths ran between the high, bent legs of the mangroves, where the marshy ground gave way treacherously, where slumbering crocodiles might lie half-buried in the mud, and where one of the myriad tiny tributaries of the sacred Ganges suddenly emerged from the woods to make its way to the sea.

But she had never ventured into the forest at night. As she ran, she fought to keep from crying out, as hanging vines whipped her face and unseen things scuttled or slithered or crawled underfoot. Her sari caught on the rough bark of trees, her bare feet stumbled over stones and caught between the leglike roots of mangroves. Once, a pair of glowing red eyes made her heart seem almost to halt, but it was only a rhesus monkey that grinned at her before leaping higher up into the trees' welcoming arms.

"*This way! No, you fool, over here!*"

Tears of exhaustion and pure terror pricked Miditiyi's eyes, as behind her the footsteps of her pursuers thudded on the marshy ground. And ahead of her, she could see pinpricks of light where no light should be. . . .

The Maharajah's camp! she thought in despair. *His tents . . .*

She paused, then turned and raced in another direction, away from the lights. Something moved in the darkness directly in front of her: a greater darkness, branches and leaves giving way as before an invisible cyclone-wave; rhesus monkeys shrieked in fear as dirt and dried leaves beat down upon her head. Miditiyi's foot stumbled against a root. With a muffled cry, she fell, sprawling upon the forest floor as her hand instinctively grabbed at the folds of silk at her breast and the talisman hidden there.

"Mo Bonobibi," she whispered, as her eyes filled with tears. *Mother Bonobibi, help me . . .*

The darkness parted. Miditiyi looked up, blinking.

In the forest stood a tiger, more huge and terrible than any tiger Miditiyi had ever seen. Its eyes were the cold, clear green of tamarind shoots, its paws the size of a tree stump. When it opened its mouth, white teeth like a thicket of bones gleamed in the night, and when it roared its breath smelled of sandalwood and cardamom.

"*Who dares to hunt my children?*"

The voice was not a tiger's. Nor was it a man's.

As Midityi struggled to sit up, she saw that upon the tiger's back sat a woman, as beautiful and terrible as the tiger itself. Her sari was of gold and emerald green, her long, unbound hair dark as a cyclone cloud, and streaked with gold like lightning. She wore a necklace of tiger claws around her neck, and a tiger's pelt wrapped around her shoulders.

"Answer me!" the woman commanded. Midityi opened her mouth to speak, but terror had stolen her voice, as surely as the tiger steals the cries of its victims. She held her hand clutched against her breast, and only stared, petrified, at what was before her.

"Who are you to defy me?" The woman raised her hand, and beneath her the tiger tensed, as though it were about to spring.

But then the woman's gaze fell upon Midityi's clenched fist. "What is that?" she cried, pointing.

Midityi opened her hand. In her palm the bronze talisman glistened, the tiger claw a tiny moon shining against sweat-stained skin.

"Mo Bonobibi," Midityi whispered. She dared raise her eyes enough to see the woman staring at her, the tiger stone still between her thighs. "Mother, have mercy on me! An evil man hunts me like a chital-deer."

For a long moment the woman said nothing. Then she nudged the tiger with her legs, so that it took a step forward.

"Who hunts in my forest?" she asked, but now her

voice was calmer, and the threat it held was not toward Midityi. "Who slaughters my children?"

Midityi wondered if the woman referred to the hapless victims of the Maharajah's cruelty or to the tigers, but she had no intention of asking her question aloud.

"The evil lord of Alwar," she said; and raised herself so that she could see the woman more clearly. "He seizes old women and children and uses them to lure the tigers to where he hides. Then he shoots them, and walks upon their pelts."

Bonobibi's eyes narrowed with fury. "Does he think he is Dakshineroi, to behave in this manner? He will learn otherwise. . . ."

Beneath her the tiger growled. Midityi winced at the deafening sound; she wanted to cover her ears, but dared not move. From atop her fierce mount, Bonobibi gazed at the widow. Her expression held mingled disdain and compassion.

She said, "I see that you fear me, as should all who walk in my forest without permission. But while you are weak, you are also brave, as the tiger's cub is brave. So I will treat you as the tiger treats her cub—"

Before Midityi could blink, Bonobibi's hand lashed out at her. Fingernails like claws raked the widow's arms and face. Midityi cried out in fear and pain, as blood seeped into her eyes from her wounds.

"There," pronounced Bonobibi in satisfaction. "So it is my children learn, not only of my own power, but theirs. Use it wisely, daughter. You are the tiger's child now."

Midityi drew shaking hands across her face, wiping

the blood from her eyes. When she looked up, Bono-bibi was gone.

Yet the forest around her was anything but still. As Midityi gazed up in wonder, it was as though for the first time she could actually *see*—as though until now she had only half-glimpsed the world around her.

The trees were alive! She saw armies of insects crawling along the trunks of the *sundari*; blade-shaped things that she had thought were leaves now lifted their wings and drifted into the night air. A thousand eyes, a thousand thousand, stared down at her from the jungle canopy, crimson and green and yellow; and most brilliant of all were the emerald eyes of something that crouched atop a knot of mangrove roots. It watched Midityi silently, then, giving a low roar, it turned and leaped from the roots into the night.

Midityi stood and felt how her limbs, too, had grown more powerful. She flexed her arms, no longer an old woman's arms but the powerful limbs of a hunting creature. She opened her mouth to speak and, yes, the voice that came out was her own voice—but louder, stronger, more confident; even frightening.

But it was not frightening to *her*. Midityi smiled. She gazed at her arms; even in the darkness she could see where the tiger goddess had raked her skin, the long clawmarks leaving stripes of red flesh. But the wounds no longer hurt; instead, they burned as though beneath the skin her blood pulsed to free itself like a river torrent; as though something fierce and hot inside her fought to free itself, to run and leap and kill.

From the near distance came a man's angry voice.

"What do you mean, she escaped? An old woman fleeing in the woods, and my best hunters cannot trap her? Paugh! You are old women yourself! I will deal with this!"

The Maharajah, thought Midityi. Her lips parted in a smile as she flexed her hands and felt how strong they had grown, how the nails were now like talons. She drew a deep breath, her nostrils flaring; scented the smoke from a cheroot, wet canvas, gunpowder, sweat.

And blood—warm, living blood.

"Midityi goes hunting," she whispered, and began to stalk her prey.

It is still told in the Drowned Lands how it was that the wicked Maharajah and his hunters met their deaths; how they were torn to pieces by a single rapacious tiger, its distinctive pawprints showing clearly in the delta mud amidst the chaos and destruction of the hunting camp. Gnawed bones and the remains of the evil man's skull were found weeks later, lodged in the top of a *sundari* tree. But of the the jeweled turban, rings, armillas, and necklaces the Maharajah always wore, there was no sign, and it was presumed these, too, were devoured by the tiger.

But, you ask, what kind of tiger would swallow a king's ransom in precious gems? Well might you wonder, and as well question how it was that the tiger's pawprints were followed to the very edge of the Drowned Lands, before the prints suddenly disappeared—fa! like that!—as though the tiger had suddenly grown wings and sprung into the air. If it did, the only witness to its flight must have been the old woman whose footprints were discovered nearby, but no one in that country had ever had much interest in old women.

After two days' travel, Midityi found her way to the Widows' Village. It was not at all the bleak, despairing place the legends told of, but rather a small, efficiently managed cluster of houses, where women old and young tended to each other and their children with good humor and only the usual amount of disagreement. They welcomed Midityi warmly, not questioning the torn and bloodied state of her sari; nor the strange scars she bore on her arms and face; nor the quantity of jewels she carried, wrapped in the ragged folds of her garment. The wealth she shared with the other women, using it to build a school, and send several of the younger children to university in Calcutta when they grew old enough.

As for Midityi's scars, they faded over time, though they never disappeared completely. And she told no one how they would burn, late at night when she would hear the roar, far-off, distant as thunder above the Bengal Sea, of tigers hunting.

Ophelia Powers's note: There was a real life and notorious Maharajah of Alwar, who was reputed to do terrible things to his people (and animals—he poured gasoline on his favorite polo pony and burned it). Whether or not he ever encountered a were-tiger, I leave to the imagination of my readers.

Patience put the book aside, smiling. Her eyes closed, and she fell into a dream of darkness and fluttering leaves, a roar that became thunder, then gunshots, then the echo of a man's voice saying *Come down, now, Patience . . . Patience, come down . . .*

Then the gunshots resolved into the sound of knocking, and the man's voice rose several octaves.

"Patience? C'mon, I know you're in there!"

Patience got to her feet, almost falling from bed. She looked blearily at her clock, then stumbled to her apartment door and opened it. "Sally?"

"You were expecting Bachelor Number Three, right?" Sally replied breezily, pushing past her into the room. "Well, he'll be here in an hour, and you look like you need some serious wardrobe management assistance."

"Last time I saw you, you were in the hospital," said Patience, yawning.

"That got real old, real fast. Plus I told you they were going to release me."

"Did your doctor give you his home number?"

"No." Sally grinned. "But the duty nurse did—c'mon, let's see if there's anything in your closet that speaks to me."

A little later, Patience was dressed and the two stood beside a heap of clothes that Sally had passed judgment on and found wanting.

"So?" Patience looked at her friend. "Nothing's speaking to you?"

Sally held out a beige, shapeless turtleneck and stared at it with distaste.

"The only thing this is saying to me is 'Arf, arf.'"

She dove back into the closet, emerging with another armful of clothing. "You should be a fashion consultant, Sal. I mean it—you're in the wrong job."

"Tell me about it." Sally frowned, examining a series of identical gray shirts. "Yuck. Did the Fashion Bug explode?" She walked over to the wastebasket and dropped the shirts inside. "You're the lucky one, getting fired. Things were pretty nasty at work today."

"Really?" Patience looked down, trying to hide her unease. "Like how? George and Laurel at each other's throats again?"

Sally shook her head. "No. That's the weird thing. The two of them were in the conference room together this morning, and it was like the Cone of Silence had descended. Totally ignored each other. Like they were in different dimensions."

"I think they are in different dimensions. How the hell could they have ever gotten married?"

Sally shrugged. "George married Laurel for her beauty. The fact that she had brains was a lagniappe."

"And Laurel?" Patience prodded.

"The way I look at it, Laurel suffered from some form of short-term judgment lapse when she married that jerk. It's sad, really. She loved him—God knows why, but she really did. He was her entire world. And she put up with all kinds of stuff I never would have—"

"Drina?" said Patience.

"Among others. But Laurel always held her own—until now. It's like when Hedare started focusing all its research energy on Beau-line, she just caved in to that line of crap about Eternal Beauty. She lost her nerve."

"Or her confidence," said Patience softly. She gave Sally a pointed look.

Sally shook her head. "I know, I know—but I

stopped, okay? Quit cold turkey. I'll never touch the stuff again. No more Beau-line for me—"

"Or Botox."

"Or Botox."

"Or lipo."

"Or lipo—hey, who's getting the makeover here?" Sally tossed an armful of clothing at Patience and turned back to the closet. "Once more into the breach."

Patience stood and pushed her aside. "Enough! My turn!"

A few minutes later she held up two outfits for Sally's perusal. "Which?"

Sally wrinkled her nose, looking from an ankle-length, long-sleeved, polka-dotted dress to an outfit composed of several inches of purple Lurex and green feathers. "Dunno. You want him to take you to church or the Playboy Mansion?"

"Thanks. That's helpful."

She threw both outfits aside and began searching for another. Sally ran her fingers through her hair, then joined in. "Seriously, Patience. It depends. Do you really like this guy?"

Patience hesitated. "I really like him," she said. "But I'm worried that he might like . . . someone else."

"What makes you think that?"

Patience sighed. "Nothing. Forget it. I'm just a freak right now."

She waited, then looked at Sally. "Aren't you going to disagree?"

Sally rolled her eyes. "Look, I'm a freak, like, Thursday through Sunday. Big deal."

"But what if he doesn't like—"

"He can't pick and choose, Patience. Anyone can like you when everything's perfect. You gotta find a guy who still likes you when you aren't."

"I don't know. Things have been *really* not perfect."

Sally stood her ground. "If he wants it to work, he has to like all of you. Love the girl, love her problems."

Patience took a deep breath, dug into a heap of clothes, and pulled out a black-lace-trimmed halter top that left little to the imagination. She held it up for Sally's approval.

Sally laughed. "Maybe not *that* much of you, honey. It's a second date. Okay, outta my way—I know there's buried treasure in there somewhere!"

And Patience stepped aside, and let Sally get to work.

Patience arrived at the restaurant a few minutes early. Tom had made a reservation at an upscale sushi bar, and the maître d' showed her to a small table in a private alcove, beside a wall-sized aquarium holding tropical fish that floated tranquilly in the deep-blue water. Sally—as always—had finally selected the perfect outfit, at once sexy and demure. Patience smoothed her skirt beneath her and toyed idly with the beaded curtain, watching clown fish drift in and out of a cloud of pink sea anemones. She licked her lips.

"Pretty," said a voice behind her.

Patience turned to see Tom Lone. She looked down, blushing. "Thank you."

"You too," he said with a smile. "But I meant the fish. Sorry I'm late. Paperwork. A mountain of it.

There's enough when you catch 'em, but when you don't . . ."

"Tell me about the one that got away," she said.

"Catwoman," he said. "Heard of her?"

Patience nodded and said, "Yeah. Hot. With a whip."

Tom sank into the chair opposite hers, and Patience sat as well.

She looked up as a waiter arrived, bearing a huge tray of sushi. "Um, I hope you don't mind—but I ordered a bite while I was waiting."

The waiter set the immense lacquered tray in front of Patience. She glanced across the table at Tom, then gestured generously at the display. "Please! Help yourself."

Tom smiled. "Thanks, I will. I'm starving."

But not, apparently, as starving as Patience was. Tom meticulously poured a thin stream of soy sauce over wasabi, mixed the two, then carefully picked up bits of sushi and dipped each into the result. Whereas Patience simply peeled the raw fish from its neat bed of rice and popped it into her mouth as though she were eating potato chips. After each mouthful, she carefully licked her fingers.

"Mmmmm," she said, already looking for the waiter to order more. "This is fantastic."

"She kissed me," said Tom.

Patience cocked her head. "Really."

He laughed. "Yeah. What do you think of that?"

"Depends." She smiled. "Do you like bad girls?"

"Only if they like me back," he teased, then went on more seriously. "I'm a cop, Patience. 'Bad' isn't something that tempts me. It's something I lock up."

"C'mon. Good, bad—there's got to be a place in between. It might be a little more complicated than you think."

Tom listened, unconvinced. "How about we start talking about you? What's it like to be an artist?"

"I'm not really an artist. I mean, I went to art school—drawing was the only thing I was good at. But then I got a regular job, in advertising. Then I lost that. So now I don't know *what* I am anymore."

"You're different," said Tom softly. "You're special."

Patience looked at him, touched. And embarrassed. "Thank you."

He stared at her; then they both looked away, suddenly shy.

"You want that piece of toro?" asked Tom awkwardly.

He leaned across the table, chopsticks poised above a bite-sized morsel of raw tuna. Patience's arm shot out instinctively, moving to protect her food; she caught herself in time, smiled politely, then said, "No, of course not—you go ahead."

The infusion of raw fish had succeeded in pacifying Catwoman—for the most part.

But now Patience Phillips was growing increasingly anxious.

Tom stared at her. "I meant what I said before; I want to know more about you."

"You want to know more?"

"Yeah. I want more."

"You know . . ." Patience pushed the tray of fish aside, her eyes locking with his. "I'm not really hungry anymore."

"Neither am I . . ."

He signaled the waiter, still not taking his eyes from hers. Half an hour later, they were in Patience's apartment.

It was past three A.M. when Tom woke. Patience was still sound asleep beside him, the sheets tangled around her slim body. He gazed at her lovingly, smiling as she stirred and stretched luxuriously in her sleep, then he yawned and slipped quietly from the bed, careful not to disturb her.

He stretched, wincing slightly. He could still feel the scratch marks on his back, and thought with wry pleasure that the reserved Ms. Phillips might be able to teach Catwoman a thing or two. He walked drowsily into the bathroom, passing the chair where he'd tossed his clothes, his gun and holster draped over its back. In the bathroom he found a glass on the counter and filled it, took a long swallow. He started back toward the bed, when something sharp pierced his bare foot.

"*Whoa*," he muttered, grimacing in pain. He lifted his bare foot and pulled out something long and sharp, then held it up curiously to the night-light.

A claw.

And not just any claw, but a weapon as potentially lethal as any blade—a cruelly curved, diamond-tipped claw.

Tom glanced quickly at the bed. He stepped back into the bathroom, shut the door, and switched the overhead light on. He began to examine the claw more closely, turning it this way and that; with each passing moment, he felt more and more heartsick.

No, he thought. *Please, no . . .*

He looked up at his reflection in the mirror, slowly turned to stare at the thin raised lines on his back where Patience had scratched him during their love-making. He touched the marks gingerly and winced; shut the light off and stepped silently back into the other room. Shakily, he lowered himself into a chair, and looked over at the sleeping Patience.

His expression hardened. He looked down at the claw, and for the first time realized he was still holding the water glass. He raised it, holding it to catch the faint glow from the night-light.

A crimson half-moon darkened one edge of the glass. As Tom peered at it, he felt the hairs on his neck prickle. Very slowly he lifted his hand, let his fingers fan out across the cheek that had borne the imprint of Catwoman's kiss.

"No," he whispered.

But even before he reached the forensics lab, he knew the answer to his unspoken question was yes.

TWENTY-FOUR

A muffled electronic tone edged its way through Patience's sleeping mind, persistent as a toothache. She groaned, burying her face in her pillow; then, at the memory of Tom's body beside hers, she smiled. Her hand reached out for him as she murmured and turned in the bed.

"Tom?"

Her hand grasped nothing but the rumpled sheets. She sat up, dazed, and looked around her studio. There was no sign of Tom Lone. The clothes he'd flung over the chair were gone; so was his gun.

So was he.

"Tom?" she called again. Desperation rose in her voice, but as she struggled to her feet she heard that electronic tone again.

It came from underneath the bed. Willing herself to wakefulness, Patience knelt and felt under the bed until she found her leather pants. She pulled them out, then yanked a cell phone from the pocket.

"Hello?" she said thickly.

"It's me." Laurel Hedare's edgy voice came through the phone. "You were right. I can't believe it, but you were right. I've got proof. We can stop him, *together*."

Patience stood, still trying to shake her confusion as she looked around the room for some sign of Tom's presence. Her gaze fell upon a piece of paper on the chair where his clothes had been. She snatched it up and read it.

"*Something came up. Will call.*"

That's cold, Patience thought. *Especially considering how hot things were here last night. . . .*

Anger began to nudge away her disappointment and bewilderment. She pressed the cell phone to her head, her mouth tightening as she listened to Laurel with more interest.

"George is announcing Beau-line at a press conference tomorrow," Laurel said. "It'll be on the shelves by Monday."

Patience's hand crumpled Tom Lone's note, her fingernails shredding it. When she spoke again, her voice was low and commanding.

"*Where are you?*"

Catwoman was back.

She found it somewhat easier to get into the Hedare mansion this time.

Don't exactly have the red carpet rolled out for me, though, Catwoman thought as she eyed the locked front door. She hurried to the side of the house and found a partially opened window to the Hedare's living room. Catwoman flexed her claws, then pulled open the window and jumped in to land on the rug-covered floor.

"Thank God you came," cried Laurel in relief. She emerged from where she'd been waiting in the shadow of the doorway.

"What did you find?" said Catwoman.

"Enough evidence to put someone away for a long, long time."

Laurel turned and led the way through the dark, still house. "This can't be easy for you," Catwoman said, with a mixture of admiration and pity.

"I was everything they wanted me to be," she said. "I was never more beautiful. I was never more powerful. Then I turned forty—and they threw me away."

Laurel's voice broke. She paused, composing herself, then said, "You were right—Beau-line is toxic. It's being covered up; almost nobody knew."

"Somebody did."

They came to the door of George's study. Laurel paused, her hand on the doorknob.

"There were reports," Laurel went on. "Overseas testing showed what a disaster Beau-line would be. But it would have been years before the truth came out. The company would have made billions long before that. The stock would have soared—so the reports were buried." She opened the door.

Catwoman started to cross the room to the front of the desk, but Laurel stopped her.

As she spoke she began to back toward the door again. Catwoman's eyes widened with dawning recognition.

"So, George . . . ?" she said.

Laurel shook her head. "He didn't know *anything*—until *you told him*. And once you did, he got curious. He was going to pull the plug on Beau-line. That would have been tragic—for me."

Laurel had reached the door by now. She grasped the frame and paused, staring back at Catwoman. "You see, in a sense you *did* kill him. I mean, he didn't have to die. Well, yes he did. . . ." She smiled, her ice blue eyes shining. "But he didn't have to die *today*."

Catwoman stepped out from the desk and started for her, confused.

And stopped.

Sprawled on the floor in front of the desk was George Hedare's lifeless body. Bullet wounds showed black against his white tuxedo shirt, and there were vicious claw marks everywhere across his face and hands.

Catwoman recoiled in shock. She looked up at Laurel.

"You killed him."

"No one's going to stop Beau-line from hitting the shelves. Not Slavicky. Not George. And certainly not you. . . . But forgive me—I'm being rude."

Laurel reached to pick up something from a table, something wrapped in a handkerchief. "Can I get you anything? Can of tuna? Saucer of milk?"

Suddenly she turned, letting the handkerchief fall as she tossed what it held to Catwoman. Reflexively, Catwoman snatched it from the air.

Laurel smiled. "Smoking gun?" She gestured at the body. "How'd I do? The clawed flesh thing was a little tricky, but I think I pulled it off."

Catwoman gave a yowl of rage. She lifted the gun and pointed it at Laurel.

"It isn't loaded, sweetheart," Laurel said with a smirk. "Remember? You just emptied it into my husband's chest."

With a furious hiss, Catwoman moved toward her. Laurel just smiled and shook her head, holding up a security remote. She pressed a button, and the entire mansion echoed with a deafening alarm siren.

"*Help me!*" Laurel screamed—but her eyes as she stared at Catwoman were mocking and triumphant.

Catwoman tensed. With her enhanced sense of hearing, the alarm's shriek was like flames searing through her skull. Panicked, she looked around the room for an escape route.

"It's the Catwoman!" yelled Laurel in desperation. "She's got a gun!"

Catwoman backed toward the window, but when she looked over her shoulder she could see security guards already racing across the lawn.

Trapped!

She yowled again, fear vying with rage as she turned and bounded past Laurel, out the door. Laurel stepped away, still smiling, and watched her race down the hall.

"Ding dong dell, pussy's in the well," she sang beneath her breath. "Or will be, any minute now. . . ."

Catwoman fled down the corridor, frantically trying to find a way out. At the top of the stairs, she hesitated.

Through the foyer windows downstairs streamed flashing red lights—police cars.

Scratch that, Catwoman thought. The front door burst open, and three security guards rushed inside, weapons drawn. One of them automatically looked upward and spotted Catwoman on the landing.

"Freeze!" he shouted. "Drop the gun!"

Catwoman stared at the gun in her hand, stunned—she'd forgotten she still had it. As though it were ablaze, she dropped it, turned, and ran down the hall, bullets flying all around her.

She turned a corner, gasping, and spotted a small, square gap in the wall.

A laundry chute. Without thinking, she dove head-first into the opening.

Rough wood tore at her skin and leather clothes as she plummeted downward. Seconds later, she flew into the open air, seeming to hang there for a moment before landing on a pile of laundry. She rolled from the soft landing onto the floor and stood, trying to catch her breath.

The room was the biggest laundry room she'd ever seen, bigger than Patience Phillips's apartment, and dim—or it would have been dim if it had been Patience standing there. Catwoman looked around swiftly, her gaze focusing on standing racks of freshly laundered clothes. She strode to the rack and grabbed a track suit, and stuffed it into an empty canvas bag. Glancing down, she saw a row of recently shined shoes. She grabbed some of these as well, turned, and ran to the far wall.

How could I have been so stupid? she thought furiously. *I walked right into her hands.* . . .

She leaped to grab the sill of a tiny window that

looked out onto the front lawn, pulled herself up, and peered outside.

Police cars were everywhere, and security vans.

And an ambulance. Patience watched as a uniformed cop barked orders into a walkie-talkie, directing his men to surround the building.

These guys mean business, she thought, her hatred for Laurel Hedare burning. Carefully she let herself drop back to the floor, and began looking for an exit.

She found it a few minutes later, in the form of a metal bulkhead on the mansion's south side. She looped the canvas bag around her belt, then pushed the bulkhead door open a crack. Before her rolled an expanse of green lawn, willow trees, and the mansion's brick-and-iron walls, all floodlit.

But the coast was clear—at least for the moment.

Swiftly, Catwoman scrambled from the bulkhead, letting the door fall shut behind her. She began to run. As she did, sudden shouts came from only a few yards off, and the frenzied yelping of guard dogs.

Figures a bitch like that would have lots of canine company, Catwoman thought as she sprinted toward the mansion wall. She leaped onto a rose trellis, climbing with ease until she reach a second-floor windowsill. She clambered onto it, guard dogs howling and yelping on the lawn below, then shimmied up a drainpipe, all the way to the rooftop. She raced toward the edge of the roof at the front of the mansion overlooking the circular drive, and lay flat against the shingles, so that she had a clear view of what was below.

An ambulance had pulled up almost onto the front steps. *This one got here a hell of a lot faster than the one they sent for Sal*, Catwoman thought with gritted teeth.

She angled closer to the edge of the roof and peered down.

Two security guards were holding the front door open. A crew of paramedics wheeled an empty gurney down the steps and began loading it into the back of the ambulance.

Looks like George won't be able to take advantage of that expensive health insurance, Catwoman thought. She felt neither gleeful nor remorseful at the thought of George Hedare's death. She felt . . . nothing.

Laurel Hedare was another matter.

Catwoman watched as the paramedics closed and locked the back of their vehicle. She waited until they had climbed back into the front and she heard the engine turn over. She crept to the very edge of the roof, balancing on the balls of her feet, tensed, and sprang.

She landed silently on the ambulance roof. Immediately she went prone, flattening herself and holding her body a scant inch from the metal as the ambulance swung out the drive and onto the main road. A mile farther on, the ambulance drove beneath an overpass, darkness momentarily swallowing it. When the vehicle emerged, Catwoman was gone.

TWENTY-FIVE

The night sky was fading from black to gray to periwinkle blue as Patience Phillips rushed breathlessly through the downtown streets. She ducked into an alley, pulling on a pink hooded sweatshirt, the last of the clothes she'd stolen from Laurel Hedare, then leaned against the brick wall, eyes squeezed tightly closed. In the street just a few yards away police cars screamed past, sirens wailing.

They're looking for me, she thought desperately. She opened her eyes and stared down at her feet, clad in Laurel's shoes; at Laurel's expensive linen trousers, Laurel's shirt . . .

No! She shoved the thought away, shoving her leather pants and high-heeled boots into the canvas bag. *They're looking for Catwoman*.

She hurried back onto the sidewalk, running a hand through her disheveled hair. She walked briskly, trying to blend in with the first wave of early-morning commuters. Only, none of the office drones she passed was looking anxiously over her shoulder every three seconds.

And none of them was the object of a citywide police manhunt.

She wandered, distraught, into the heart of the downtown commercial district. The high-end shops and restaurants were still closed, but a huge plasma TV screen hung in front of a high-rise hotel. Pedestrians hurried past it without a glance, but Patience slowed her steps as she approached.

CATWOMAN KILLS AGAIN scrolled across the bottom of the screen. Above the words, taped footage ran, showing George Hedare's body being removed from the Hedare mansion. The footage ended and a recent glossy photo of George filled the screen, followed by a number for the police department.

Patience stopped, staring at the image. Her fear turned into anger, rage not just at Laurel Hedare but at herself—

No! she thought again fiercely. *Not me—Catwoman.*

She turned and ran across the street, turned again and went down another alley, a shortcut to her apartment. As she walked, she looked back furtively to see if anyone was observing her. Then, without pausing, she hurled the canvas bag holding all that remained of Catwoman toward a dumpster.

The bag landed with a thump. Patience kept going, fighting tears. She didn't see the bag slide open, dislodging a leather mask with feline eyes.

And she didn't see a small, leopard-spotted cat emerge from the near-darkness to sit on its haunches, watching as Patience Phillips ran home.

I can start over, she thought, as she ran up the stairs. *It's not too late. It was only a few days, that's all . . . just a few days out of an entire life.*

Her hand clenched into a fist, denying what came next.

Maybe the best days of my entire life.

She stood in front of the door to her apartment and pulled it open.

"Patience."

Tom Lone stood inside, his gun pointed at her.

"I'm sorry," he said. He wouldn't meet her eyes. He took a step backward, raised his gun, and pointed it at her. Patience flinched, then looked back wildly into the apartment. Blue lights flashed from the street below.

"Just business," said Tom sadly. He inclined his head toward his weapon. "I guess you could take this right out of my hands if you wanted."

Patience met his gaze. This time she didn't flinch.

"If I wanted," she said softly.

Tom holstered his gun and quickly withdrew a set of handcuffs. Dropping her head, Patience turned, offering no resistance as he cuffed her.

"Patience Phillips, also known as Catwoman, you are under arrest. You have the right to remain silent. . . ."

She remained silent through the ride in the back of the squad car to the station; through the fingerprinting; through the strip search in the station anteroom that ended with her being dressed in a standard-issue orange jail jumpsuit; through the first thirty minutes of interrogation by Detective Tom Lone in a small, windowless room where she was handcuffed to a chair, hands behind her back. After that she answered his questions—without changing her answers.

"I'm telling you," she said, with tears in her eyes. "Slavicky had evidence that proved Beau-line was toxic. That's why Laurel killed him! George found out and she killed him, too. She was covering it up!"

"Ballistics show the same weapon killed both men," Tom said wearily as he paced in front of the table. "The gun that was in *your* hands."

"Catwoman's hand."

"What's the difference?"

"Does it matter? You think we're both guilty." Patience lifted her eyes to meet his. "Catwoman didn't kill anybody, either."

Tom sighed and sank into the chair opposite her. When he spoke, his voice was pained. "You think I *wanted* to believe all this about you?"

"Detective?" Patience suddenly straightened, the cuffs chafing her wrists. "How long have I been a suspect?"

"Patience—"

"Did you *wait* to arrest me? Until you got what you wanted? Until we'd—"

"Stop playing the wronged woman here!" Tom's voice rose angrily. "I'*m* the one who should feel betrayed."

He leaned back in his chair and ran a hand across his face. "Jesus. I used to think I was a pretty fair judge of people. But I guess I got you wrong."

Patience lowered her eyes. Her shoulders moved in the tiniest shrug.

"I know I did," she whispered. Her entire body began to tremble.

"The evidence, Patience . . ."

"Is a lie," Patience finished for him. "But then, so am I."

Tom shook his head. His ravaged eyes betrayed how disturbed he was by all this. "Don't you understand? All the evidence, every piece—it all points to *you*. There's nothing that shows me anything different."

"Just me," pleaded Patience. "You could trust *me*."

But as she looked up into his eyes, she saw that he could not. Tears ran down her face as she asked, "Do you remember the first time you saw me?"

"Yeah."

"What did you see?"

"A girl." Tom's voice broke as the memory overwhelmed him. "Rescuing a cat . . ."

Patience shook her head. "No, you didn't. You saw a crazy person about to jump off a ledge. *All the evidence pointed to it.*"

Tom looked at her. Patience gazed back at him, putting her heart on the line.

"I need you to believe me, Tom."

He continued to stare at her, but said nothing. At last he shook his head. "How can I? I don't know what you are."

"I'm the same girl you were with last night," Patience whispered.

Tom stared at her, a young woman in a jail suit, her face streaked with tears. He rose and crossed to the door, and knocked.

A policeman unlocked it and let him out. For one last moment Tom stood outside, staring at Patience. Then he turned to the cop.

"Take her back," he said, and left.

* * *

Hoots and shouted obscenities followed Patience as the jail guard led her past rows of prisoners to a holding cell. She began by weeping uncontrollably; but as the catcalls and whispered suggestions continued, her despair hardened into something else, something that might be used as a weapon: raw rage.

"Here you are," the guard announced. He unlocked the door to her holding cell and pushed her inside. His expression grew salacious, and he added, "You be a good kitty, now."

Patience hissed at him, her face contorted by a snarl. Spooked, the guard hastily locked the door and retreated.

Pale moonlight washed over the tiny space, the cell's only light. Patience sank onto the floor in a corner. She didn't sleep, but fell into a gray twilight state between waking and anguish.

The full moon shone directly through the window in Patience's cell, but she didn't see it where she sat crouched in the same corner, head down and arms tightly wrapped around her knees. Only after the guard passed down the corridor shouting "LIGHTS OUT!" did she look up hopelessly.

Now there was not even a thread of light from the hallway; only the moon. Patience stared dully at the floor, where a lozenge of moonlight gleamed, a teasing outline of a trapdoor. A shadow moved across the moon, occluding the bright pool on the floor.

"Hello, Midnight," said Patience without looking up.

The moonlight vanished. Slowly Patience raised her head. In the center of the small barred window was the silhouette of a cat. As Patience watched, the shadow resolved into the leopard-spotted figure of the Mau. Silently it squeezed through the bars, leaped to the floor of the cell, and walked over to her.

The faintest smile flickered across Patience's face. She knelt, put her hands on the cold ground in front of her, and stared into the cat's gold-green eyes.

"I love you, baby, but Lassie would have brought me a key."

She stroked Midnight's thick fur, idly staring up at the barred window. Suddenly she cocked her head. She turned, gazing fixedly at the steel bars on the door confining her.

"I take it back," she said softly, glancing down at the cat. Then Patience stood, stretching. She sashayed over to the door and began to rub against the bars, eyes half-closed.

"I *accept*," she murmured, then licked her hand and slid it between the bars. Her arm followed, as she arched her back and her head twisted at an impossibly feline angle, edging between the bars as though her limbs had turned to silk. A minute later Catwoman stood in the corridor, looking back at the cat still sitting inside her cell.

"Funny thing about cages," she said to Midnight. "Sometimes the hardest part about getting out is making the decision to leave."

She stiffened at the sound of footsteps coming down the hallway. A guard turned the corner, angling his flashlight into each cell as he passed on his rounds. A shadow moved in the dimness and he swung around, instantly on alert.

There was no one there.

He took a few more steps, more slowly now. Another shadow passed across his face. He spun again.

Nothing.

The guard hesitated. He heard nothing, saw nothing, and continued on his rounds.

At the end of the corridor, Catwoman found a utility closet and slipped inside. She dug her nails beneath the window and jimmied it open, then peered out.

It was a ten-story drop to the ground. Catwoman looked up and down the darkened road. A car was approaching at a good clip—a late-model Jaguar.

Catwoman smiled. She clambered onto the windowsill, then jumped, arms and legs splayed as she plummeted to the street.

Brakes screeched. Catwoman landed on all fours, staring up at a steaming car grill surmounted by the sleek, chromium effigy of a charging cat.

"Jesus, are you okay?" cried the car's driver.

Catwoman sauntered toward him as he hurried from the car.

"A girl's got to know how to land on her feet," she said. "And a guy's got to know when to give it up—'scuse me!"

She pushed him aside and leaped into the driver's seat. "But I think my ride's here."

"Hey! That's my car! My car!" the driver shouted helplessly as the Jaguar peeled off into the night.

Tom Lone sat in his office, exhausted. In front of him photographs and police artists' sketches of Catwoman covered the wall, along with scrawled notes and newspaper clippings. He stared bleakly at the detritus of his most recent cast—of his life—scarcely glancing up when Bob, his detective colleague, dropped some more files on his desk.

"Look at it this way, Lone," he said. "You may have lost your woman, but at least you got your man."

"Did I?" said Tom, his voice deadened.

"Sure. Along with everything a hungry DA needs to convict. Why? Something bothering you?"

"Yeah." Tom leaned forward, gazing at a brief article headlined Daring Carnival Rescue. "Her . . ."

Bob glanced at him, then shrugged and walked off. Tom remained, brooding.

I'm the same girl you were with last night.

And the same girl who rescued the cat, and a frightened child; the same woman whose hands grabbed Tom before he could fall to his death in a darkened theater.

Slavicky had evidence that proved Beau-line was toxic. . . .

Tom slammed his hand onto his desk. He stood, checking to make sure his holster was where it should be, then hurried from the station house.

TWENTY-SIX

The city morgue's chill seeped through Tom's jacket. He pulled it more tightly around him as he listened to the coroner read from his report.

". . . most of the scratch marks occurred some hours after the actual time of death—"

"What?" Tom looked up sharply. In the chilly room behind him, a plastic-sheathed body lay on a stainless steel gurney. No amount of Botox or tanning was going to improve George Hedare's appearance now.

"The actual time?" The coroner glanced farther down his clipboard. "Between two and three A.M."

Tom stared at him, then stumbled to his feet.

"Thanks!" he called as he raced for the door.

The sky had deepened from blue to pale violet when the opening ceremonies of Hedare's annual sales conference began late that afternoon. Hedare employees and sales reps from all over the world sat at long tables in an enclosed patio. Waiters hurried back and forth, bearing trays of food and bottles of wine. A string quartet played softly in one corner.

At the front of the room, video cameras were trained on a podium with a huge video screen behind it. The excited murmurs of those assembled died suddenly as a tall, regally erect figure entered the hall and strode toward the podium—Laurel Hedare, elegantly clad in black, and seemingly oblivious to her own monolithic figure projected high above her head.

Slowly, in twos and threes at first, and then by entire rows, the Hedare employees got to their feet and began applauding. Laurel continued to walk with great dignity until she reached the podium. She climbed it gracefully: the grieving widow, beauty's martyr. Only when she turned and found herself facing the entire Hedare Corporation family did her composure break; dabbing her eyes, she inclined her head slightly, acknowledging the standing ovation.

"Thank you," she said. "Thank you for coming. A terrible tragedy has visited all of us here in the Hedare family—"

She swept her arm out, indicating all those in the room: sales representatives, secretaries, researchers, executives.

"Words cannot adequately pay tribute to my late husband," Laurel went on. "So I would like to request a moment of silence, in memory of our founder—George Hedare."

Behind her, the image on the video screen dissolved to a mediocre stock photo of George Hedare, posed as a generic Captain of Industry. Silence descended everywhere throughout the room.

At the podium, Laurel lifted her head once more

and stared out into the room. Her expression was carefully balanced between determination and sorrow; the caption would have read "Noble Grieving Widow Carries On With Grace." When she spoke, her voice rang out strong, unwavering; the voice of a survivor; the voice of one who has triumphed.

"My husband dreamed of a world in which every woman was as beautiful as she wanted to be. He dedicated his entire life to the pursuit of that dream. How can I do less?

"I realize that during this difficult period I owe it to George—and to every one of you—to stay on.

"To serve as chairwoman of this great company."

The room erupted into cheers and applause. Laurel remain standing, smiling bravely as the string quartet began to play once more and waiters rushed out with dinner plates. After a minute, she turned and quickly left the room, nodding efficiently to the assembled diners as she hurried to her next performance.

A press conference was awaiting her upstairs in the Hedare boardroom. A throng of reporters surged toward Laurel as she entered. Wesley nodded as she passed. A host of security guards pushed the journalists back as she made her way to the center of the room, commanding attention, and silence, by her hauteur.

"My husband dreamed of a world in which every woman was as beautiful as she wanted to be," she began, and continued with the same speech she had given minutes earlier. The reporters were riveted, though they didn't applaud. Flashbulbs went off like

miniature novas and hands shot up, but Laurel's dig-
nified voice retained command of the room. "As
Hedare's new chief executive, I intend to make that
dream a reality, by proceeding with tomorrow's launch
of Beau-line."

She paused, smiling, then made a slight gesture
with her hand. Wesley turned and opened the door.
Two assistants entered, carrying open cartons, and
began passing out sample jars of Beau-line to the
women in the room.

"I've been *dying* to get my hands on this stuff!" en-
thused a young television reporter.

Laurel watched approvingly as she, and most of
the other women, immediately began applying the
lotion to their faces.

"Well, my husband would have wanted you all to
have it," she said, nodding. "He wanted it for everyone."

The reporter slathered more Beau-line onto her
unblemished, flawless face. Laurel stepped away from
her, and almost walked into Tom Lone.

"Detective Lone?" One perfect eyebrow lifted in
mild surprise. "What a pleasure."

She turned to the reporters excitedly examining
their jars of Beau-line. "Ladies and gentlemen. I'd like
you to meet the man responsible for bringing my
husband's killer to justice."

More flashbulbs went off. Tom Lone looked around
uneasily, unaccustomed to being the center of attention. He cleared his throat, then spoke to Laurel in a
low voice.

"Mrs. Hedare—I was wondering if I could have a
word."

A twinge of unease disturbed Laurel's composure. Tom noted it but said nothing. Laurel nodded.

"Of course," she said graciously. She turned back to the reporters. "Well, ladies and gentlemen, I think we were just about finished. If you'll excuse me—"

She motioned for Tom to follow her into the corridor. As she passed Wesley, she shot him a look. The bodyguard nodded back at her, almost imperceptibly.

Laurel looked over her shoulder at Tom. "We'll have more privacy here, in my office."

Only days before, it had been George's office. But her husband's presence had been erased from it as smoothly and efficiently as Beau-line had removed the lines from Laurel's face. George's massive oaken desk was gone. In its place stood a streamlined platform of chrome and translucent pink resin. Gone too were the production photos of Drina, though her billboard-sized image could still be glimpsed atop a neighboring high-rise, gazing with sultry intent through the night as floodlights played upon her perfect face. Propped against the walls were numerous bright-colored placards displaying the Beau-line motto.

BEAU-LINE: BE MORE

"Please, sit," said Laurel, leaning against her desk.

"Thanks, I'd rather stand." Tom took out a notepad and looked at her measuringly. "I know this may be painful for you, Mrs. Hedare, but I'd like to go over the details of how you discovered your husband's body, and when you first saw Catwoman."

"Well, I was coming down to check on George—he's been working so hard on this campaign; we both have," replied Laurel. Her voice caught, as at a painful memory. "And when I went into his office I saw her standing over him. There were clawmarks all over his body."

Tom glanced at her, troubled. "But none were found on Slavicky."

Laurel shrugged. "She didn't have time."

"She also didn't have a motive."

Tom stopped. He stood there for a moment, thinking.

Slavicky had evidence that proved Beau-line was toxic. She was covering it up.

Abruptly he closed his notebook. When he spoke again, his voice was more assured and aggressive. His doubts were gone.

"What if I told you that I know the truth? That I know who really killed your husband? That I know about Beau-line?"

Laurel stared at him calmly. "Why, Detective. You make it sound like I'm a suspect."

"What if I told you I had evidence?"

Laurel turned brusquely and walked behind her desk, her heels tapping softly on the marble floor. "If you have evidence," she said in a smooth voice, "how come I'm not in cuffs?"

Tom met her challenging gaze. "You're a smart woman, Laurel. Beautiful. Rich . . ."

His voice now held a hint of menace, and suggestiveness. "I thought maybe we could . . . work something out . . ."

Laurel stood behind her desk. She paused. Then she drew herself up, her icy blue gaze controlled. "Seems like you have me over a barrel, Detective.

This evidence . . . you'll make it disappear? You'll pin everything on the girl?"

Tom's level gaze met hers. "If that's what you want."

"And you? How much do you want?"

"You just gave me what I want," said Tom coolly. "You just told me it was you."

Laurel looked at him in disbelief. She hesitated, then walked out slowly from behind her desk.

"How could you believe I did it?"

"How? I finally trusted a friend."

Laurel listened. Her ice-pale eyes darkened. "Well, your friend just got you killed."

She raised her arms, clutching a pistol. Without hesitation Tom reached for his gun—

BAM!

Too late. Tom staggered against the wall, his shoulder absorbing the blast. His gun fell from his hand. He looked up to see Laurel bearing down on him, pistol aimed at his head. Before he could move, she kicked his gun away.

"Don't be stupid, Laurel." Tom grimaced as he tried to staunch the wound. "You don't want to kill a cop."

"I'm a woman, Lone," she said with chilly resignation. "I'm used to doing things I don't want to do."

He heard her gun click as she took another step toward him. Desperately, he swung at her with his good hand.

And connected; and immediately fell back, crying out in pain and shock. He stared dumbfounded at his hand. It was already swelling, the fingers numb and bloodied as though he'd bashed a granite outcropping. He lifted his face to stare with revulsion and fear at Laurel Hedare.

"What the hell are you?" he gasped.

Laurel straightened, smiling; then backhanded him so he went reeling across the room, striking his head against one of the Beau-line advertising placards. Laurel stared mirthlessly at the slogan: BE MORE.

"I'm 'More'" She leveled the gun, aiming at his head. "Send my regards to my husband."

Tom shut his eyes. He felt the gun's cold barrel against his temple, like a stony finger boring into his skull, then heard the muted *click* of its chambers turning . . .

FFFWAAAAP!

Tom looked up, stunned, in time to see a black leather whip lashing the air like a striking cobra. With a crack, it snapped around Laurel's gun hand and yanked her backward. The pistol flew from her grasp, smashing onto the marble floor. Laurel looked up and saw a slender, leather-clad figure framed in the doorway.

"Surprised?" announced Catwoman as she strutted into the room. She stopped and ran her hand across her leather belt. "I would've been here sooner, but I had to pick up my clothes from the cleaners. Fortunately, that back-alley location is open all night."

Her face twisted into a snarl. "You really thought I was gonna let you kill again? Think again. A few bars and a little bit of concrete weren't gonna stop me from showing you for what you really are."

She snapped her whip; it uncoiled, freeing Laurel,

then seemed to hover restlessly beside Catwoman as she ran to Tom Lone's side.

"No—" He gestured to where Laurel was stooping to retrieve his sidearm. "Forget about me . . ."

"I can't," said Catwoman.

She helped him to his feet and rushed him through the door into the corridor.

"How sweet," Laurel called after them disdainfully. "But trust me, it won't last. Thanks anyway," she added to herself. "Now I can kill you both."

She hurried behind her desk and grabbed the phone.

"Get up here," she barked into the receiver. "Now."

Catwoman half-carried, half-dragged Tom down the hall until they reached a stairwell.

"I can walk," he said weakly. He staggered down the steps at her side, clinging to her for support.

"You knew," Catwoman said.

"I should have trusted you all along," Tom replied. Speaking was an effort, and he paused for breath.

Catwoman smiled. "I think you have me confused with someone else."

"Come on, Patience . . . ," he said.

"This Patience is a lucky girl," she said, and put an arm around him, hefting him to her side. "C'mon—think you can make it?"

Tom winced. "Depends where we're going."

The stairwell twisted around a corner. There, charging toward them, was Armando.

"Wrong turn," said Catwoman. She yanked Tom after her and they began running back upstairs.

BLAM!

Shattered concrete rained down on them as Armando fired, striking the wall just above their heads. They raced upstairs. Behind them, a door slammed, and another pair of footsteps joined Armando's in pursuit.

"That'll be Laurel," Tom said.

"Keep going," snapped Catwoman. "'Hell hath no fury . . .'"

They reached the next landing. She pulled at the door.

"Damn! It's locked, too."

They kept climbing. Above them the stairwell ended. Tom looked back and saw two dark figures clambering up the steps.

"Last chance," said Catwoman. She grabbed the door.

It opened.

"Quick!" She caught Tom as he nearly fell and pulled him inside.

"By my count, you have about three lives left," he murmured.

"Let's hope that's a few more than Laurel has," said Catwoman grimly. "God, look at this place."

They were at the very top of the Hedare Building, a vast industrial space that occupied the entire floor.

"I guess this is where Beauty goes to die," said Tom.

Catwoman nodded in silent agreement. Bluish moonlight streamed through a wall of floor-to-ceiling windows at the back of the huge room, casting an eerie mortuary gleam on decades of accumulated advertising materials. Immense billboard panels, life-sized posters and cardboard cutouts, Plexiglas kiosks and cartons and cartons of publicity stills—

All, all, were of Laurel Hedare.

"It's like the end of *Citizen Kane*, Tom said wonderingly. "I always wondered what they did with stuff like this. . . ."

"C'mon," urged Catwoman. "We can play Hedare Beauty Trivia later." She grabbed his hand and led him into the maze of oversized photographs. Seconds later, the door banged open and Laurel and Armando entered, followed by Wesley.

"Looks like the Two Stooges are back," whispered Catwoman. She and Tom slipped between massive billboard panels, Laurel's perfect features neatly divided into sections: nose, mouth, two huge and perpetually staring blue eyes.

"I feel like we're surrounded," murmured Tom.

"That's okay. I didn't come all the way here just to play hide-and-seek."

Tom halted. He slumped against one of the panels and turned woozily. A long streak of blood followed him, like a lipstick gash drawn across a portion of Laurel's cheek.

"Hang on there," said Catwoman. She listened for signs of pursuit, heard footsteps and muffled talk from the far end of the room. She turned back to Tom and steadied him, then helped him to a dark corner behind another billboard panel. His strength fading, he sank to the floor. Catwoman stared at him in concern, then stooped and touched his shirt.

It was soaked with blood. For the first time, a flicker of genuine fear passed over her face.

"Listen," said Tom. "If anything happens, I want

you to know—I'm sorry. I should have trusted you all along."

Catwoman fought to control her emotions. Then she smiled. "I think you have me confused with someone else."

"Come on, Patience—"

Tom reached for her leather mask. A gloved hand stopped him, diamond-clawed fingers entwining with his.

"This Patience is a lucky girl," she murmured. Her face was so close to his that, for an instant, their lips touched. Then Catwoman slowly pulled away.

"Stay here," she said. "I'll be back when it's safe."

"Wait—"

Tom stopped her. "Why did you come here tonight? To stop her—or for revenge?"

Catwoman stared down at him. Behind the mask, her emerald eyes glittered. "I came for both," she said, and slipped into the shadows.

In the center of the room, Wesley and Armando walked cautiously, separated by rows of billboards. A dark figure crouched atop a smiling image of Laurel Hedare in happier days. Wesley turned and began heading toward the corner where Tom Lone was hidden. Silently, like his own unmoored shadow, Catwoman stalked him, hanging on to a ceiling gantry as she tiptoed along the top of the panel.

Wesley turned again, edging between two of the panels, his gun at his side. Suddenly, a shadow blotted out the moonlight. He looked up and saw a black figure poised above him. With a cry, he raised his gun to fire—

But not fast enough. Soundlessly, Catwoman dropped onto him, grabbing his gun hand and flipping him to the floor. She gave his hand a final wrench; there was the crackle of small bones breaking, and his hand went limp. The gun fell. Before Wesley could groan in pain, Catwoman kneed him in the face and he collapsed, unconscious.

"Trust me, it's better this way," she murmured, and kicked the gun into the darkness. "You won't feel a thing. Not until you wake up, anyway."

At the sound of approaching footsteps, she darted into the shadows once more.

Laurel and Armando stepped warily to where Wesley lay prone beneath a man-sized pair of crimson lips. They looked at each other; then Laurel motioned for Armando to double back the way they'd come. She waited, then walked on slowly, a gun held at her side—Tom's sidearm, Catwoman noted.

She must've grabbed it when we left. Laurel doesn't miss a trick, I'll give her that, Catwoman thought, with grudging admiration.

She began to stalk her.

And so did not see where Armando paused, staring at something dark on the ground; then bent to touch it and turned, following a trail of blood.

The droplets grew larger, blooming black in the moonlight. Armando crept on, his gun nestled against him as he made his way through the labyrinth of billboards. The blood became a thin black line streaking the floor. Armando looked up and could dimly make out where the streak ended: in a corner beneath a panel showing Laurel's eyes. Armando straightened, then ran forward, gun poised to fire.

But no one was there. Armando looked around, perplexed; found himself staring into Tom Lone's ravaged face.

"Lose your way?" the detective said softly. Before Armando could react, his fist smashed into the bodyguard's jaw. Armando reeled backward, his gun tumbling from his grasp. Tom turned, lowering his good shoulder, and slammed Armando so that he went flying through the billboard panel. Before Armando could stagger back to his feet, Tom caught him again on the chin.

Armando dropped, sprawling on the floor. Tom swayed above him, savoring his triumph. Then he slowly sank to his knees, exhausted, and fell alongside the other man.

Catwoman saw none of this. She had eyes only for Laurel, the blond woman's deceptively vulnerable figure moving carefully among the billboards and posters below. Catwoman stood atop a panel of a gigantic ice blue eye, like an icon upon a temple's heights. She watched, her mouth tight, as Laurel moved forward, step by wary step, until she was standing directly beneath her.

Catwoman looked up, tensed, then sprang, grabbing a pipe suspended from the ceiling. As she did, her stiletto heels kicked out, connecting with the billboard so that it began to fall.

Laurel whirled and looked up. She dove out of the way, just as the huge eye slammed into the ground inches away, rolled and got to her feet again, gun leveled to where Catwoman hung above her.

"I've got my eye on you!" shouted Catwoman. "Or is that *your* eye?"

She leaped into the darkness, as Laurel sent a round of bullets flying toward her. They echoed uselessly through the great space. Laurel began firing everywhere, mowing down cardboard cutouts of her own graciously smiling self, blasting holes through her own perfect forehead, her own eyes, her mouth. Paper and cardboard sprayed everywhere as she ran, trying vainly to get a bead on that fleet, black-clad form forever springing just out of sight.

"At night all cats are gray," a mocking voice called from overhead. "Maybe you should have your eyes examined."

Laurel looked up and saw Catwoman balanced on a sprinkler pipe. As she raised her weapon, Catwoman leaped, claws extended. Gunfire echoed around her as she twisted and somersaulted in midair, performing a deadly gavotte with bullets as her partners. Then she struck the floor, feetfirst; lost her balance and bashed into Laurel.

The two women crashed to the ground. Catwoman whirled, landed on all fours, and prepared to leap—

Too late.

Laurel's gun pressed cold against her cheek. Catwoman stiffened. Laurel smiled, and pulled the trigger.

Click.

The chamber was empty.

With a hiss, Catwoman reared back and bared her claws. Laurel threw the gun aside. As Catwoman sprang at her she grabbed her arms and they tumbled, rolling across the floor toward the bank of windows. Laurel struck at Catwoman, over and over;

Catwoman retaliated but her claws only tore through Laurel's clothes, leaving no mark upon her skin.

"So you're not just another pretty face," Catwoman hissed.

"I was never *just* anything," retorted Laurel. "I was a model for fifteen years. Thick-skinned. And now I can't be hurt."

The windows loomed above them, and a cluster of retired factory components, ranks of rusted metal and steel. Catwoman clawed uselessly at Laurel's face.

"Beau-line," she snarled.

"That's right," said Laurel. She drew herself up in front of the machinery, pulling Catwoman with her. "Sure, if you *stop* taking it, your face disintegrates. But if you *keep* taking it, you become like me—perfect. Skin like living marble, and you can't feel a thing."

She punctuated this with a blow that sent Catwoman sailing into the broken machinery. A jagged steel blade sliced her leg and Catwoman yowled in pain. She moaned and tried to pull her leg up, like an animal caught in the jaws of a steel trap. Blood streamed from the open wound; a thin trickle pulsed from the corner of her mouth as she stared at Laurel with revulsion.

"I can't believe women ever looked up to you," she said through gritted teeth. "You're a facade. A lie—"

Laurel grabbed her by the head and tore her free of the machinery. Catwoman gave a low moan, then staggered toward the window.

"And what are you?" Laurel smiled as she advanced on her. "A heroine?"

Her fist shot out again, and Catwoman fell, rolling on the floor in agony. "A thief?" taunted Laurel. "A freak? If you don't have an identity of your own, why keep it a secret?"

Catwoman stared up at her. When she spoke, her voice was low and restrained, almost calm.

"Because that night, you killed me. You killed me, and then you flushed me down the pipe . . . I'm Patience Phillips."

"Phillips?" Laurel's face creased in disbelief. "It was you? That mousy girl from the art department?" She flicked at Catwoman's leather mask. "*That's* who's under there?"

Her hand swung back and delivered a blinding blow to Catwoman's temple. Catwoman crumpled and fell back against the window.

"I get it," said Laurel. "You're just a scared little girl who likes to play dress up." She kicked her. "A nobody. A nothing."

Beaten, Catwoman rolled and fell, her face pressed against the glass. "Lucky for me everyone thinks you're a psychokiller," Laurel breathed. "No surprise when they find out you killed a cop."

Catwoman turned. Her hands clenched.

"Aww," sneered Laurel. "You wanna save him? Honey, you can't even save yourself—"

With all her strength, Laurel smashed her fist against the window. The glass shattered and the metal mullions gave way, falling to the street thirty stories below.

"Game over," said Laurel, as Catwoman began to fall. Her emerald eyes widened, terror giving way to rage as she suddenly sprang into the air, her boots sending sprays of glass everywhere behind her.

"We're going into overtime," she shouted. One arm shot up to grab on to a metal joist. "One thing you'll never get, Laurel. . . . Real beauty *isn't* only skin deep. It goes all the way down, to the *soul*—"

She stared at Laurel, then leaped. She struck Laurel feetfirst and sent her flying. Laurel crashed into the wall, turned, and began to run for the door. As she did, Catwoman's whip snaked out and caught her by the ankle, drawing her back toward her.

For the first time, Laurel looked truly afraid.

"Beauty and the Beast," hissed Catwoman. "Care to guess which is which?"

Her clenched fist battered at Laurel's face, diamond-tipped claws raking across that perfect flesh but leaving no mark. Again and again, Catwoman struck, and with each blow Laurel recoiled, driven backward toward the broken window.

"You should have thought twice before you killed me, Laurel. And you should have thought more than that before you killed your husband, no matter how much of a bastard he was—"

One clawed hand hovered above Laurel's face. Then Catwoman slammed her hand against her cheek. Diamond claws embedded in marble skin, like a pickax striking into the ruins of a buried statue. There was a sharp, high-pitched sound; a crackling as of an unimaginably huge egg cracking.

Laurel began to scream.

"No!"

She staggered backward as Catwoman stared in horror at her face.

From the bottom of Laurel's jaw, a jagged fissure rippled, moving like spikes of lightning across her chin to her cheeks and eyes. A web of cracks radiated across her entire face, shedding flecks of skin like plaster flaking from a wall. Laurel flailed helplessly, then plunged through the broken window.

Crack!

Desperately, Catwoman raised her arm and snapped her whip. The leather uncoiled and snaked around Laurel's wrist. Her fingers closed around it and she clung with all her strength, her body dangling in the empty air as Catwoman raced to the sill.

"Please," whispered Laurel. Pale blue eyes gazed from a monstrous face, shattered skin peeling back to reveal clots of veins and capillaries beneath. "Help me. Don't let me fall."

Catwoman knelt and began to pull at the whip, dragging Laurel toward her. "I may not be a heroine, but I'm not a killer—and I want everyone to see you for what you really are. . . ."

She hauled her to the sill. Then suddenly Laurel gasped.

"My face!"

A shard of glass still clung to a twisted mullion. In it moved a reflected image, like the shattered remains of an ancient sarcophagus or death mask, pathetic and all the more horrifying because one could glimpse a remnant of something human there; something that had once been beautiful.

"No," whispered Laurel. Her free hand flashed across her face, dislodging bits of stony flesh. "I'm not perfect anymore."

"Laurel!" cried Catwoman. "Laurel, be careful, hang on—"

Laurel's grasp on the whip tightened. The leather cord went taut, catching on a jagged bit of broken glass. As Catwoman stared in horror, the whip began to fray.

"*Laurel!*"

Laurel scrabbled frantically to gain purchase on something, anything, as the broken glass sliced through the whip like a knife.

"No!" she screamed, as the leather gave way. "Help me, *nooooo*—"

Catwoman lunged to grab her—but her hand closed on empty air. Laurel Hedare's anguished face gazed up at her as she plummeted to her death. Catwoman stared after her in despair, the whip's remaining coils slithering uselessly from the window.

Someone walked softly up behind her. "At least now they know the truth," Catwoman said in a low voice.

"I saw what you did," said Tom. "You tried to save her."

Catwoman turned to him. "Surprised?"

"No," he said. "Not at all."

They stared at each other without speaking. Finally Tom said, "You know, if we could figure out some way that Patience could get back into her cell by the time they do morning rounds, it would be awfully hard to prove that she was Catwoman."

"Could happen. Like I said . . . I'm a lucky girl."

Tom smiled faintly. "No. You said *Patience* was a lucky girl."

"Exactly."

She leaned forward and kissed him; then slipped from his arms and began to walk away.

"Wait!" Tom called after her. "How're you going to work this?"

She stopped and looked back. "Ever have a cat that ran away?"

Tom shrugged. "Sure."

"And did it come back home?"

"Yeah."

"Any clue as to where it was while it was gone?" Catwoman asked.

"No."

"Any clue as to how it got back?"

Tom shook his head and smiled ruefully in defeat. "Nope."

Catwoman grinned. "Some mysteries just never get solved. Even everyday ones, like that. . . ."

And Tom watched as Catwoman turned, and made her way to freedom.

TWENTY-SEVEN

It was Artists in Action Week at the Rainbow Community Center. A small mob of kids and grown-ups scurried around, carrying buckets and brooms, gallons of paint, and drop cloths. Several artists had set themselves up along the sides of the building, where they'd blocked out sections to paint their own work on the brick. Abstract versions of the surrounding cityscape; realistic images of children playing, reading, dreaming; intense expressionistic blurs of color that made one think of exploded prisms. In some places, children worked side by side with adult artists, adding their own visions to those of their elders. Reporters and members of the local art establishment wandered around as well, talking quietly among themselves and stopping now and then to interview a painter.

An older woman carrying a leopard-spotted cat walked among the busy crowd of painters and onlookers, smiling and occasionally stopping to admire a child's handiwork.

"Very nice," she said. She paused so that a small

boy could stroke the Mau's soft fur. "Who helped you get all these art supplies?"

The boy pointed to where scaffolding had been set up against one side of the expansive brick building. Above the platform the outlines of a gorgeous leaping black panther had been painted on the wall as part of an immense mural. Beneath the giant cat a smaller figure worked, carefully daubing paint onto what would soon be one of the panther's claws. Another woman sat beside Patience, feet dangling over the side as she read a tabloid magazine.

"It says here that Elvis and Michael Jackson are actually the same person," announced Sally without looking up. "Did you know that?"

Patience stared at her friend. "I thought you were supposed to be helping me."

"I am."

"What exactly are you doing?"

Sally leaned back, pressed a finger to her cheek, and batted her eyes. "I'm your muse."

Patience shook her head and went back to her painting. Sally held her pose, fastidiously turning the pages of her tabloid.

"Pretty," someone called from below.

Patience looked down to see Tom Lone making his way among the kids adding their own artistic talents to the base of the wall. She raised her paintbrush and stepped aside so he could get a better look at the panther.

"Thanks," she called back.

"I was talking about *you*," said Tom, grinning. "Got a minute?"

Sally dropped her magazine and began to wave. "Hi, Tom Lone! I do, I do!"

"Well, if you got a minute, then *paint*." Patience shoved her brush into Sally's hand and clambered down the ladder. Sally made a kissy face and exaggerated smacking noises, then picked up her magazine again.

"Hey," said Tom as Patience stepped onto the ground. He gently wiped a smear of paint from her cheek.

"You know," he said, looking at the mural above them. "I spotted this artist a long time ago. Before she got famous." Patience smiled as he went on.

"Congratulations, Patience. I'm really proud of you."

They wandered off toward the parking lot, holding hands. With a smile, Ophelia Powers watched them go, absently stroking the Mau perched on her shoulder.

"Thanks," said Patience. "That means a lot, coming from you."

"I wanted to tell you," Tom said, when he and Patience were out of sight of curious eyes. "About what we were talking about a while ago—I didn't admit the whole truth?"

Patience looked at him, bemused. "Oh?"

"About Catwoman. The truth is, I was attracted to her, a bit. I was conflicted. Sort of."

Patience smiled. "I can understand that."

"Something else, too. I thought you might like to know—Wesley copped the plea. He told us everything. The files on both murders are officially closed."

Patience nodded thoughtfully. "What about the rest of it?"

"I'll just have to live with the fact that you can't catch them all."

"That's good."

Tom stopped and turned to her. "You once told me there had to be a place between good and bad. I didn't believe you. I guess I do now."

"I told you I was . . . complicated."

He drew her closer to him. "I like complicated."

Patience shook her head, drawing away slightly. "I'm sorry about—"

Tom cut her off. "Look, I know you think it could never work with us—"

"I'm not saying 'never,' Tom. But I've just figured out who or what I am. And I'm not sure I can be her with you . . . or if it would be fair to you to even try."

Tom gazed at her yearningly. Something glittered at the corner of his eye, a miniature starburst of prismatic red and indigo and violet and emerald. He reached gently to touch the pair of perfect diamond studs adorning Patience's ears, then took her hand in his.

"If you change your mind, you know where to find me," he said. He leaned toward her and kissed her, his mouth lingering on hers before he drew away, staring pointedly at the earrings.

"Don't do anything I wouldn't do," he said, and winked. Then he turned and walked off into the crowd. Patience watched him go, a wistful smile tugging at her mouth.

"Your work is remarkable!"

Patience looked up. A middle-aged man stood gazing at her mural rapturously. He wore an Armani suit and sunglasses with expensive frames sharp enough to cut glass. A name tag identified him as the art critic for the *City Herald*.

"I see such animalistic power in your painting," he went on, gushing. "Such strength in the brushstrokes! Such confidence in the color palette."

He handed Patience his card. "You have a bright future ahead of you."

Patience glanced at the card, then shoved it into a pocket. Her gaze returned to her own painting high above them.

"Thanks," she said after a moment. "I think I agree."

With a smile, she turned and strode confidently back to where her work awaited her.